MAIDEN LEAP

MAIDEN LEAP

CM Harris

Author of
The Children of Mother Glory

BInk

Bink Books
Bedazzled Ink Publishing Company • Fairfield, California

978-1-949290-43-1 paperback

Cover Design
by
CM Harris

Bink Books
a division of
Bedazzled Ink Publishing Company
Fairfield, California
http://www.bedazzledink.com

This novel is dedicated to the memory of William Elliot Gonzalez who was a compassionate advocate, conservationist, animal lover, and beekeeper.

Acknowledgments

A big shout of thanks to all the folks at Bedazzled Ink who helped bring this book into the world.

A boatload of gratitude also goes to early readers: Pamela Malpas, Mary Logue, Philip Elliot, Amy Dawson Robertson, Miriam Queensen, Mary Gardner, Cathy Rowlands, Laura Lively, Tracey Laibson, Rebecca Dickens, and Jo Haugen. Your suggestions and encouragement kept me motivated along the way.

And of course, much appreciation goes to my wife, Cheryl Gordon, who not only puts up with, but actually indulges this writing stuff.

"Now I understood that the same road was to bring us together again. Whatever we had missed, we possessed together the precious, the incommunicable past."

My Ántonia, Willa Cather

CHAPTER ONE

2007
Kate

A GHOST TURNS the corner in a flash of black, her overcoat lapping at the legs of passersby. Those touched, slow in her wake, alerted to something gone askew in their world. Some turn to catch a glimpse, but the flow of Black Friday shoppers engulfs her, and the briefly molested carry on with their errands, their revelry.

Watching this dark whirlwind from the safety of her minivan, Kate Larson gently nibbles the inside of her cheek. If it was merely a ghost, she could drive on without another thought, blaming imagination, holiday enchantment, Thanksgiving leftovers. But there's something about that woman—her determined gait, dark whipping strands of hair, strong jaw—which sets Kate's heart thumping, her skin tingling. This is no phantom.

"No way," Kate whispers. She hangs a right at the corner without signaling, only to earn a quick toot from the car behind. "Oh, fuck the fuck off."

Kate winces. Not because she dropped the f-bomb for the first time in years, but because the oncoming driver has read her lips and raises his hands in outrage.

She smiles meekly, waving him off. In a town the size of Wicasa Bluffs, it will surely come back to bite her.

To maintain a visual on the woman in black, Kate eases the minivan to a crawl. Her chest seizes up as if it might collapse in upon itself if she doesn't remember to breathe. Meanwhile, the specter on the sidewalk storms along, as oblivious to the swath she is clearing as she had been stalking the halls of Wicasa Bluffs High School nineteen years ago. Kate flicks on her right-turn signal. Cars zoom past, engines revving with annoyance. But she needs to make sure. *Could it really be Lucy?* Kate hunches down, shielding half her face behind the passenger headrest. The woman glances at the street and darts into the Gonzo Fox antique store. It is, without question, Lucy.

HALF AN HOUR later, Mark Fox catches Kate at Risdahl's Supermarket. His tight orange curls and matching beard, usually a friendly beacon, are today a warning. The two lock eyes, ending any thought Kate might have had of swinging a U-turn out of the pasta aisle.

Mark rushes at her in a blur of cream cable knit and corduroy, accompanied by the slightest whiff of leather from his lace-up packer boots. "There you are," he says with a snap, "You know a cell phone only works if you have it on. Had to call your house. The deer hunter said you'd be shopping." In his hands, he balances a leaning tower of deli containers filled with salads, olives, mozzarella balls.

"Something wrong?" Kate says airily. Her gaze drifts up and down the shelves, while her perspiration gathers under his delving glare.

"You tell me. Guess who's back in town and as *what*." He croaks the last word like a bullfrog.

"Who?"

"Lucy. Van. Buren."

"Oh yeah?" Kate tries to focus on her tour of duty. *Whole-wheat penne for Erik's irregularity. A value pack of Mac 'n Cheese for Brace. This obscurely branded, organic, multi-colored ravioli for Samantha—*

Mark's gaze stays on her. "Came into the shop this morning."

Kate rakes cans of SpaghettiOs into her cart, though she hasn't craved them since her sophomore year. She shivers. "Is it cold in here? Risdahl always has those freezers so high."

"Hello?" Mark stops in front of Kate's cart, eyeing her bounty with confused distaste. "Don't you even want to know what Lucy's up to?"

Kate stares through Mark. "Sure. Is she well?"

"*Well?* Yeah, she's well." Mark scratches thoughtfully at his beard. "Maybe a little saggy. But no more than the rest of us."

"Yikes." *Good. She's old and ugly.*

"What did you think, she'd gone off to drink from the fountain of youth? Gin and cigarettes more like. Anyway"—Mark pokes Kate's arm and murmurs—"she's one of *you people* now."

"Whopeople?"

Mark snickers, slightly crouched, waiting for her to figure it out.

"Wait a second. What?" Kate frowned. "She's married?"

"No, not yet." Mark rolls his eyes. "Can you imagine the poor guy who tries to rope Lucy Veebee?"

Actually, Kate could. Lucy had won plenty of admirers in high school. They always seemed to transform from cocky young bucks to bumbling, glassy-eyed zombies.

Sorta like I did.

"She's been through Sojourn Reclaimers," Mark says.

Kate's lip curls as she pushes the cart forward. "That sounds familiar." Too familiar. Mommy-in-law-dearest familiar.

"It's an ex-gay ministry."

"Okay, yeah, they're one of Claudia's campaign contributors. She's showed us one of their recruitment videos. She has no idea it looks just like an SNL sketch."

"Lucy said they 'reversed her polarity,'" he says with a smirk. "She's still got a sense of humor at least."

Kate pictures high school Lucy lying on a slab in Frankenstein's laboratory, gas blue lightning bolts arcing at her temples and curling her dark hair. And for a moment the corner of her mouth turns up because that's just what young Lucy would have pictured too. But the smile quickly fades.

"Are you sure? Last I heard her band was coming out with another album."

"Yeah, well, apparently she hit bottom, went through detox, and the whole thing imploded. Checked into Sojourn Reclaimers to *change her ways*, she said. Bought the old Gainsborough place up on the Leap. It's way too big for her. She'll just rattle around in that mausoleum. Guess her mom's going to help decorate it." He sniffs. "I give it six months."

Kate's blinking gaze drifts upward as if the puzzle might be solved there amongst the fluorescent lighting. "Not possible, Mark. It just isn't."

He shrugs. "Some people change. Or think they do."

As Kate rolls her cart slowly on, they watch the throng gathering at the registers.

"Jeez," he shakes his head, "what on earth are you going to say to her?"

"Gawd, I don't know." Kate's mental shopping list grows hazier. "What did you say to her?"

"Well, I was going to tell her she'd been brainwashed, but I sorta chickened out."

"Ha! Some activist you are."

"Speaking of," he says, "we still on for the rally?"

"Can't this time."

Mark's jaw juts to the side. "What? Oh, come on."

"The Senator needs us for a photoshoot—before you get angry, think about it. If Claudia is at a soup kitchen serving leftover turkey, she's got no time to hassle you at the capitol."

Mark looks at her with a disgusted incredulity that always burns, always reminds Kate that she supports his causes only when convenient. She'll never live it like he does. But Mark will also never walk the line she walks, the shades of grey she must paint with while married to the son of a conservative state senator.

"Gotta go clean the house." Mark looks defeated at his deli fare. "The *Scrooge* cast is coming over for dinner."

"Mark," Kate calls as he slouches toward the *10 Items or Less* line. "I'll drop off the signs Samantha painted for the protest tomorrow."

He shrugs a shoulder and shuffles away from her.

Great.

THE MINIVAN IDLES at the front of a long line of cars along Portage Avenue. Inside, Kate hums, adjusts the side mirrors, checks the state of her face in the sun visor.

"Least I'm not saggy."

Deception, she knows. The tiny marquee lights bathe parched winter skin in warm glamour and produce a twinkle in the mossiest shade of green eyes. And, because she is looking upward, the fine lines flatten. She catches the eye of the driver behind her and flips the visor closed.

The iron spine of the Wicasa Bluffs lift bridge stretches to the eastern shore of the St. Croix River, where bare trees form a gray-brown mist. The Larsons' split-level ranch waits in a cul-de-sac less than a mile away, but it might as well be twenty. The bridge's midsection is climbing with a slow rumble to allow an icebreaking barge to continue along the purgatorial artery between the craggy banks of Minnesota and Wisconsin. Above the rising exhaust of fellow bridge strandees, an iridescent sundog lights the morning sky. Dry air roars through the minivan. Samantha's banana popsicles will soon turn to yellow slush, but it's too cold to roll down the windows. Kate settles for turning off the blower.

Lucy was your first. And your last.

This Sojourn Reclaimers bullshit is one hell of a leap on the crooked path of enlightenment Lucy had sung about in her songs. Kate had counted on the woman to be true to at least herself, even if no one else could be true to her. Knowing Lucy was out there living large was how Kate made peace with the past, why she didn't feel as guilty about how it fell apart, why she'd started supporting Mark's pro-gay marriage battles so readily. This is more than Lucy betraying herself; it is a whitewash of their shared memory as if it could all be erased with a little God therapy.

Kate glances back at the bluffs, where the old Gainsborough estate sits tucked behind the clearing of Maiden Leap, the highest cliff in town. She can only see the home's gray-shingled turret cone from here. Mark's right. It's the last place Lucy would settle down in.

What will Lucy be like after all this time? Will she consider Kate too bourgeois? Too fat? Too married? Too *mom*? Kate was going to let the summer sun lighten her dark blonde curls. Should she hasten the effect with a cut and color at *Trés Jolie*?

"Oh fer goshsakes. Just. Don't." Her breath comes hard and quick. She presses her lower back into the heated lumbar support, commanding her shoulders to loosen. The lift bridge finally lowers, but the minivan does not budge. Kate is lost at age fifteen, remembering the day she ran across the bridge as it split in two—ran for her life, ran in shame from being publicly serenaded by another girl. Cars honk impatiently behind her.

She slips her foot on the gas and the minivan lurches forward.

Throughout the years, Kate had always averted her eyes when anyone mentioned Lucy Van Buren, though her ears remained alert.

"Lucy is homeless."

"Lucy is a bazillionaire."

"Lucy won a surfing contest in Malibu."

"Lucy was arrested on drug trafficking charges in Barcelona."

"Lucy climbed the Matterhorn."

"Lucy went schizo."

All right, sure, Lucy a Scientologist, maybe. But an evangelical? Never. The Van Burens were not that religious. Kate has no recollection of young Lucy suffering fire and brimstone propaganda, just the unceremonious slap of her father's open palm. Compared to Kate's zealous in-laws, the Van Burens were downright pagan—a sensual people with strong hearts and a bit too friendly with the liquor.

Lucy's mother Bridget has only recently shown up for Sunday services since Lucy's father died. She is more often seen in a kimono and flip-flops, walking her cats down the sidewalk, coffee mug in hand, her breath smelling like coconut tanning oil—Malibu Rum, according to Mark. Not such a bad way to retire, Kate supposes, save for the fact that if your name isn't something like Nordquist or Svengard you're supposed to be taking your last meander in a gated community outside Tucson. To this, Lucy "Veebee" of the indie band Cake for Horses has returned to pay penance? As Kate's daughter Samantha likes to say in a cockney accent: *not bloody likely*.

AS THE FLAKES begin to fall, Kate arrives home, welcomed back into the Larson habitat by a crackling fireplace, Badger hockey on the flat screen, and her husband extruding bruisy deer meat through the sausage grinder. The scent of fennel and sage and a gamey tang rolls down from the kitchen.

"Hey, babe," Erik says, sleeves pushed up over his ropey forearms, hands glossy with venison fat.

Kate kisses his scratchy cheek, which glitters with graying stubble. He always waits to shave and shower until after dressing a deer. She likes her husband like this, thoroughly smelling like himself and the woods. Same as the day they met.

"Took you a while," he says.

"Oh. Sorry. Yeah, bridge was up." She first rescues the sagging box of banana pops from the bag and rams it into the freezer.

"Uh, don't fill that up, got meat needs to go in there."

"Can't you put it in the basement freezer?"

"Nope, the new buck's in there."

She cannot decide if seeing Erik's hands on those thick phallic casings is sexy or disturbing. Maybe both. By spring, she'll have run out of exciting deer sausage recipes. And Samantha is already one bite away from becoming a vegan.

The front door huffs open. Brace lumbers up the stairs and into the kitchen. His blond hair is still wet from the locker room and more the color of butterscotch than when it's dry. Kate smiles her adoring smile, which has embarrassed Brace since he was eleven. Now at seventeen, he barely meets her eyes anymore.

His hockey bag hits the foyer linoleum and a sweaty funk wafts up to the kitchen. "Hey, peeps." He pokes around in the groceries.

Erik grumbles. "We are not your peeps."

"Well, whose are you?"

"We are your parents."

"So you say, so you say. Where's Samster the goth hamster?"

"At Jamie's," Kate says.

Their silvery Weimaraner, Chuck Norris, clicks around the kitchen, his snout denting the bags and leaving a snail trail. Kate plucks a Post-it note and jots down *nail trimming*.

"Good." Brace pulls a Gatorade off the plastic six-pack device that Samantha has dubbed the duck-strangler. "The guys'r comin' over for the rest of the game. Zev will only half pay attention to it if she's spooking around all moody and stuff."

Kate punches her hands onto her hips. "Please remind Zev Cohen that Sam is two years too young for him."

Brace sniffs out the bag of rotisserie chicken. "Um, you're *ten* years younger than Dad." He cracks the drink and tucks the bag of chicken under his arm like a football.

Kate eyes her husband.

Erik shrugs. "I like that he didn't say I'm ten years *older*."

Brace saunters down to the rec room, Chuck invisibly tethered by the scent of hen.

Kate calls after him, "Two years is a lot in school. It's like dog years."

"Yeah, it's practically cradle-robbing." Erik grins.

"It's not funny. Sometimes I can still smell the baby powder on Sam."

He wrinkles his nose. "Too bad it's not Brace."

Kate nods and grabs Brace's hockey bag. She holds it at arm's length and starts downstairs toward the laundry room. She slows at the foyer, her eyes not fully seeing the present. *Two years was indeed like ten in the old days.* Lucy Van Buren was a senior, Katie Andern a sophomore. Their parents called it perverted.

Kate and Lucy called it forever.

CHAPTER TWO

1985
Wicasa Bluffs High School

SOPHOMORE KATIE ANDERN rounded the corner on a mission to retrieve books for the librarian. Shadows of autumn leaves flickered along the quiet hallway.

"Crap," she said under her breath.

Lucy Van Buren stood in front of an open locker further down the passageway, decked out in tight black pants with an over-abundance of straps and a big torn blouse with Japanese lettering swashed across it. Staring into a mirror glued onto her locker door, Lucy shaped her hair into a Flock of Seagulls affair by combing her bangs down and the sides up like wings.

Katie weighed slowing versus speeding up. She glanced down at herself to see if her own clothes were in order and brushed the hair from her eyes.

Everyone knew Lucy Veebee. Strikingly pretty, with dark hair and dark eyes, the senior girl stalked the halls whenever she liked, pulling pranks on the cheerleaders, performing dubious magic tricks for the middle-schoolers, teaching the senior boys how to moonwalk. She often sported various colored kilts and talked in different accents. And if the popular girls made fun of this oddity spooking about, chances were a football jock would rise up to defend her. The rumor was that her brother had died in a shipwreck and her father had become a drunken tyrant. Up until that year, when Principal Hamm retired, Lucy was quite possibly WBHS's first poster child for tolerance.

Katie opted to slow her pace, gulping, and kept her head down. Her shoes betrayed her with a squeak.

Lucy turned, her heavily-kohled eyes flashing with recognition. Katie knew what that look was; she'd seen it from boys lately. It made the hairs of her arms stand up and heat rise in her cheeks.

"Ooh, it's wee Katie Andirons," Lucy said in a dodgy Scottish brogue and cocked her head.

"Andern," Katie mumbled.

"Hold on. You gotta hall pass?"

Katie halted in her tracks with a sigh.

After nearly a decade of mostly going unnoticed by anyone other than her classmates, Katie had begun earning attention from boys like fellow farm nerd Gary Lindstrom, and for some strange reason this odd girl. During P.E., Lucy would remove her softball glove and set it on Katie's head, leaving it there until she had to play outfield. After a few weeks of this, Katie felt an odd sensation in her chest, a perceptible thrill at being the victim of such a unique form of hazing. You just couldn't be sure about upperclassmen. It was never good to be too defensive, nor was it a good idea to kiss ass. But the fact that all this newfound attention coincided with Katie's parents letting her switch from eyeglasses to contact lenses, and from training bras to B cups? Annoyingly predictable.

Newly emboldened, Katie asked, "Why do you always call me that?"

"I dunno." Lucy peered back into the mirror and cocked her head left, then right. "Suits you I guess."

"Aren't they just those stupid poles that hold wood in the fireplace?"

"I wouldn't call them stupid. But yeah, they keep the fire in." Lucy's reflection wiggled eyebrows and she turned back around. "Alright, cough it up, Andirons." She twiddled fingers.

Katie presented the small square sheet the librarian had written on. Could Lucy see it fluttering in her hands?

"Lemme take a look."

Katie let go, immediately regretting it.

Lucy chuckled. "Thanks, I'll just switch the name here."

"Hey. Give it."

Lucy turned, placing her body between the slip of paper and its owner. She cackled dramatically wicked, her spiky mullet flicking strands left and right.

Katie's heart galloped. The librarian was not to be trifled with, but that didn't stop the laugh from slipping out. She grabbed Lucy's shoulder, felt the warmth underneath, and they stood there, eyes locked, for an infinite second. "Seriously, please."

"Eeeeee!" A screech from down the hall interrupted her pathetic attempt at outrage.

One of the seventh graders tore out of the girls' restroom, lips peeled back to reveal a mouthful of braces.

"Oh my god, somebody tortured a mouse in there," the girl said. She clutched at Lucy and pleaded, "I think it's still alive. The tail is moooving."

What kind of heinous cretin would torture a mouse, Katie wondered. Although she knew very well that there were girls in WBHS that would rip the ears off a bunny rabbit—smokers, loose girls, tanning bed girls.

Lucy raised an eyebrow at Katie, a Sherlock Holmesian scowl that instantly made Katie feel like Lucy's sidekick in front of this middle-schooler. Surely, this school-wide emergency would provide a proper excuse for the librarian.

Whatever has happened to this mouse, we shall attend to it.

To the bathroom they went, the seventh-grader hiding behind Lucy and Katie.

The girl pointed at one of the toilet stalls. Lucy slowly pushed the door open with a creak. She looked down at the toilet and motioned over her shoulder at Katie. Katie eased forward, imagining enough blood and guts to fill a large marsupial. She peered wincing into the stall, past the black horseshoe toilet seat and into the bowl, the sickeningly sweet air freshener stinging her eyes. Lodged in the basin was a spent tampon, the water's ambient current waving its string like a tail.

Lucy slowly turned to Katie then, with searching eyes—eyes that said, *whatever you do, do not laugh.*

Katie's mouth twitched, but she blinked calmly back.

"Poor little guy," the seventh-grader said from over their shoulders. "Shouldn't we tell someone?"

Lucy seemed to consider this.

What the kid needed was a real heart-to-heart. A couple of older girls who would take her out to the baseball diamond, sit her down and give it to her like an *After School Special.* That's what Katie would have liked when she was twelve. Back then, a lot of parents left it to the school to do the work and health class was far too clinical.

Lucy raised her buckled boot, stamped the handle and the toilet flushed with a thunderous *whoosh.* It kept on flushing well after the fact, the tampon halfway to Iowa by the time it finished. Then she threw an arm around the kid and walked her out the door.

"He's in mouse heaven now," Lucy said with a low, official voice.

"But—"

"We'll report it. You should get back to class."

The girl nodded and sniffled and they watched her go.

Then they burst out in snickers.

"Mouse heaven?"

Lucy shrugged, leaned against the tiled wall. "You going to homecoming?"

Was a fake-out coming? Katie weighed her choices. "I don't—"

"Yeah, lame."

"I mean, I might."

"Yeah, me too. Maybe we could hang out."

"Okaaay?" *Was this a joke? Was an insult coming?* "Oh man," Katie yelped, realizing she had wasted nine minutes of a ten-minute task and took off in a panic.

"Don't forget your pass."

"Thanks." She sprinted back, snatched it from Lucy, and ran down the hall.

"No problem, Andirons. No problem."

"Andern," Katie said unable to hide her grin.

BLOGGING MY SOJOURN

One Woman's Journey from Gay to Straight

They say you should never start a blog at night because that's when you're prone to hyperbole. They say you should compose at night then correct and post in the clear light of morning. But I never do what I'm told.

Since this is my first post, a little background, which will be found on the About page after tonight. I'm an ex-riot grrrl, recovering lesbian, and the new owner of a bed and breakfast. This blog will reflect on my time in a reparative therapy program and my life now as I navigate my hometown, which I arrived in last week. It is two towns actually; two sisters estranged by a river and by the cordial rivalry that wages between two great Midwestern states.

So how did my teenage quest for understanding land me right back in the place where I was once so sure there was nothing left to know? Though I wandered the world for many years, I guess home never left me. I finally heard it calling through all the noise. More about that in coming posts. And I'm using a pseudonym to protect the innocent, as well as the guilty.

The Sojourn Reclaimers™ Three Simple Steps® program:
1. Admit the past
2. Acknowledge the present
3. Turn to face heaven

All for now. Got my work cut out. The wallpaper in this drawing room is red flock and no one consulted the furniture, which is Herman Miller.

Praise Jesus

Posted by Liesl ~ 10:00 PM ~ 2 comments

Patrice commented:
Just found you on the Bloggin4God feed. I'm so proud of what
you are doing. It is very brave. May the Lord be with you through
your soul journey.

Rolf68 commented:
Liesl, you are probably more confused than when you entered
Sojourn. As a gay man, I am offended that you would think your
sexuality is something that you need to recover from. Wake up.

CHAPTER THREE

Samantha

SHE RAN INTO her room, shut the door and threw herself onto the bed. As she dialed her best friend Jamie's cellphone, she kicked off Mom's borrowed high heels and one landed high on the bookshelf.

"You gotta watch the news tonight."

"Um, hello," Jamie said in her soft, sleepy voice. "And why?"

Samantha pulled the hairclip from her straight, dark locks and they fell around her shoulders. "You will never in a gazillion years believe what happened at the rally," she spat rapid fire into the phone.

"I thought you were going to the soup kitchen?"

Samantha switched to speaker and rolled the cornflower blue dress up her torso. "We were, but Grandma launched a sneak attack on Civil Diss instead. She guilted Dad into taking us and, boy, is Mom piiissed." She yanked the dress over her shoulders and tossed it onto her desk chair.

"You're shitting me."

"Yeah, I had no choice. I swear, Jame."

"Dude, I believe you."

"Okay, but that's not all. Apes happened."

"W-w-what?"

Samantha crawled across her bed and located last night's pajama bottoms in a heap on the floor. "Grandma got attacked by apes in the middle of her speech." She pulled them on.

"What the heck?" Jamie tittered. It was contagious. "Like, real apes?"

Samantha burst out with a laugh. This was a long-overdue release. Going from outright terror to shame, to everyone screaming at each other in the car, hilarity seemed the next logical step. "Hold on." She tugged on her favorite old sweatshirt with a curlicue treble clef that read: *Here Comes Treble*. "There were a ton of protesters at the rally, *way* more than Mark's Civil Diss contingent. A bunch of people in gorilla suits piling out of vans."

"That's the Simian Avengers, Sam. Yes-yes-*yes*!"

"I know, right?"

"Oh, man, what channel should I check?"

"Try *Nine at Nine* first."

This was a dream come true for the two of them. Last spring, Jamie had written a social studies paper about the Simian Avengers and Samantha had contributed research notes. The SA were a rag-tag troupe of protesters taking on all the marriage amendments, which had sprouted up in red states across the country. Inspired by British protestors in monkey suits that had once invaded Parliament to demand equal rights, the SA formed in San Francisco during the mayor's marriage battle with the courts. Their motto? *EQUALITY THROUGH GORILLA WARFARE!* They challenged religion's "against nature" argument on their website by quoting evolutionary psychologists and displaying photos of same-sex bonobos getting it on.

Perfectly dorky. Just the girls' style. Apes were Samantha's "spirit animal" after all. She hoped to study them someday and minor in astronomy. *Or major in astronomy and minor in anthropology? Or major in music theory and minor in—*

"Ugh. It's not on yet," Jamie said. "So what else? Did they get to speak?"

"No, no, no. It was a mess," Samantha said reaching for a glass of water on the bedside table. "This one ape tried to hump Grandma—"

Jamie's guffaws overloaded the phone speaker.

Water lurched up Samantha's nose and she coughed.

"—S-so she started quoting scripture. Something about man's dominion over the beasts of the kingdom. That really got them all hooting."

"Wow. Just wow. Can't believe I missed it. So unfair."

Samantha recounted how one of the apes had run up to her at the protest and she fought hard not to retreat behind her brother. The eyes inside the mask blinked at her, all dark and piercing. The ape had reached out, ruffled Samantha's hair, and did a little boogie. Samantha couldn't help but chuckle nervously. Who wouldn't? Brace even high-fived it. That was enough for Mom. She dragged her children away as the police, their number unprepared for a jungle ambush, moved in.

As they pushed through the police scrum, Samantha had glanced over her shoulder to watch her grandma, *a Senator from this great state of Minnesota*, take a few steps back from the podium with that look on her face, the toothy smile that always stays afloat, even though at that moment she was drowning in a wave of ratty gorilla costumes. Grandpa had batted at some of them, fumbling to pull them away from Grandma without throwing a punch. With his white hair and red face, he himself resembled a very angry Japanese snow monkey.

Samantha hadn't been entirely sure just how this protest was going to help the Simian Avengers. It seemed more to prove Grandma's point. Maybe she was missing something. "That is not something you want to see though, Jame. Yunno? Apes sexing on your gram? Dad grabbed the ape that was still trying to get at her and the mask came off." It had been some blonde lady with cropped hair and an angry sneer. "Then everything just went—"

"Apeshit? Bananas?"

"Um, yeah," Samantha said, fully realizing the gravity of the situation. "But Dad and Grampa got her out safe. It was mostly apes vs. cops after that."

"Gah, I'm so jealous."

"Seriously, though? I am *so* not looking forward to the holidays now. It's going to be all stabby around the Christmas tree. Mom and Dad are in their room right now. It ain't pretty."

Jamie sighed. "Sure wish I'd been there. Coulda got a selfie."

"Just a few more months, Jame, then we can drive ourselves to this stuff and you can write a follow-up paper."

"Woot!"

CHAPTER FOUR

Kate

ALL OF CLAUDIA Larson's campaigns for public office, from school board to state senator, tended to kick off with a holy war of some sort. Why Kate thought that her mother-in-law's second senatorial run would be any different was, in hindsight, a matter of extreme denial for the sake of family unity. But this latest foray was likely to earn national attention. A feature on TMZ at the very least.

The morning of the gorilla attack, three generations of Larsons had driven to a St. Paul soup kitchen to help Claudia serve lunch to the homeless in front of a video camera. Not exactly news, but it would make charming footage for the campaign website. Senator Larson swanned about like a sixty-something Mary Poppins, hair dyed a monochrome auburn, gorgeous in her cream dress suit and white apron, wielding a silver ladle as a wand of sorts, while Samantha, Brace, and Kate filled trays with turkey dinner under the near solar glare of tungsten lighting. Meanwhile, Erik and his father Bert rolled up their sleeves and carted stainless trays of food from the kitchen.

The campaign manager whooshed in from the cold, wearing a suit and long navy coat. He stamped the slush from his boots. "Things are hotting up nicely at the capitol, Claudia. Time to deploy the troops."

"Troops?" Kate's smile dropped. "Whoa. What? She just got here. Don't you think she should finish this? We *just* started."

"Oh, well they don't mind, do they?" Claudia said. "They serve themselves all the time I'm sure."

"Actually, I don't think they do—" Kate forced a smile as she handed a meal to the next man in line. She picked up another tray as if continuing to work would keep Claudia still.

"Kate, don't belittle them," Claudia said, shrugging into her camelhair coat. "These people don't want your pity. Kids get your coats. History is in the making."

Claudia's spry husband Bert, who matched her in age, came around the counter and peered at the video camera as if he could see into it. "We got plenty of footage, don't you think?"

The videographer bit his lip. "Well . . ."

"Shall we?" Claudia was aglow. She draped her arms over Samantha and Brace as if she were taking them to the State Fair.

"Erik, do something," Kate said, nearly hissing.

Erik gulped and looked from his wife to his mother. "Mommm," he intoned sternly and yet not the slightest bit convincingly, "we're not really comfortable with this. It's not our—"

"Oh, Erik," Claudia said. "This is the perfect time for the children to see their First Amendment rights in action. Why would you deny them that?" She cocked her head at him in cordial seriousness and then she shot him "The Look" that says, *Sweetheart, we bailed ya out a number of times when your granite business was, well, on the rocks, now it's time to do a little something for us.* Judiciously deployed, it was ten times more powerful than anything Kate could aim at him.

Still, Kate didn't lower her stare on him either. "Erik?"

The kids joined in, choosing sides.

"Dad?"

"Mom?"

"Kate?" Erik's jaw set.

The videographer nervously documented the volley until Claudia laid a hand on his shoulder and he lowered the camera. She walked to the entrance where Bert held the door for her. And after she passed, he continued to hold it open.

"Let's just get this over with," Erik said. "Please?"

Kate opened her mouth.

"Please, Kate. Please don't embarrass me."

"That's the least of your worries," she said and stormed past him, kids in tow.

When the Larson bus arrived at the foot of the capitol building and parked by a barrier of squad cars, there was already a podium set up beneath a red, white, and blue Marrisota banner ("Marrisota" being Claudia's think tank/ prayer group for traditional marriage). It was cold out and cloudy and beginning to sleet. Bright video-camera lights and flashbulbs illuminated her and glared unforgivingly into the Larson family's stunned faces, briefly obliterating their view of the crowd gathered before them. The campaign manager maneuvered them into a line beside Claudia, like bullet points in Claudia's family values brochure.

"Well, folks," Claudia said into the microphone, "in fairness, and I know you're all for fairness, don't you think both sides should be heard?"

No!

Go back to Stepford!

Let her talk!

"Thank you." Claudia pulled the mic from its gooseneck and stepped beside the podium. "How blessed are we? To have this glorious building behind us, protecting our voices, protecting our families?" She gracefully gestured her manicured hand at the dome as if it were the grand prize on a game show. She lowered her gaze. "Lord God, we pray . . ."

The woman truly was a mesmerizing sight to behold, but Kate forced herself to squint out into the crowd, where she quickly found her oldest friend, Mark Fox, and his Civil Diss contingent. They were all carrying the signs Samantha and Jamie had helped make for them the week before, the ones Kate had driven over to Mark's house and had to leave on the lawn when no one came to the door. The ones that said things like MARRIAGE4ALL and LOVE WINS.

Mark stood solid, sign drooping in the sleet, staring at the Larsons in shock. Kate shook her head and mouthed *I'm Sorry*. Samantha had tried to shrink into the smallest form a fifteen-year-old girl could take and inched halfway behind her brother. Brace simply yawned.

The inexplicable hooting and chest thumping of a horde of fake apes came next, facilitating a hasty exit, but the damage had been done.

How on earth was she going to serve this woman a holiday dinner without tearing out patches of her own hair?

"THAT'S A MIGHTY wicked clipper moving in." Bert Larson stamps the snow from his galoshes onto his son's welcome mat.

Claudia shivers in agreement. "Abominable."

Their wintry draft smells of damp metal and cologne. Kate can't help being glad to see them safe inside her home, although their disappearance in a blizzard would have also been convenient. The elder Larsons straighten her spine whenever they enter her house. Today they're still in their Sunday best, he in a dark wool suit and she in a doe brown, drape-neck cashmere sweater and chocolate-colored skirt.

Kate yelps, "Well, get in here and get yourselves warm," so boisterously that Erik balks at her.

He takes their coats and escorts them up to the living room where Kate had long done away with furniture to make room for what he called her OCQ (obsessive compulsive quilting).

"Sorry about the mess," he says, "once we finish the kitchen reno, we'll have lots more space."

Brace saunters upstairs from the rec room in his favorite green tracksuit. The kids threw off their church clothes the moment they got home. He gives his grandmother a big hug and grandfather a rough handshake. Samantha hugs them both. Claudia raises an eyebrow at Samantha's strategically torn black jeans and black, cropped sweater, which appears to be constructed from decorative Halloween cobwebs.

Why couldn't she have waited until later tonight to dye her hair jet black?

"The new table is on backorder." Kate digs her thumbnail into the scrollwork on the old oak dining room table. "This is such a pain to keep clean. When the kids were younger, I'd find all sorts of sticky stuff in it."

Claudia delivers a lukewarm smile and rubs Kate's arm. "All you have to do is apply a little elbow grease, kiddo."

"So busy these days."

"Well, you've got to *make* time. Put Samantha on it." Claudia's gaze travels to the chandelier, over the china cabinet and halts at the bookshelf, where Kate forgot to dust the family photos. "If you need a Swiffer, I have scads of them."

"Thanks." Kate downs half her glass of chardonnay.

The serving begins, without discussion, amid the clack of silverware, Handel's *Messiah* on public radio and the distant whine-whistle of Chuck Norris protesting his exile to the garage. Erik leans back to the sideboard and taps the volume a little higher.

"Surely. Surely. He hath borne our griefs and carried our sorrows."

Kate raises the platter of venison tenderloins. "Bert, would you like seconds? Claudia?"

Bert smiles. "Sure would."

"No, thank you." Claudia straightens her sweater down over her narrow hips. "I'm putting on too much this season. The camera bloats me."

"It's all the cookies and pies that get to me," Kate says. Claudia raises her eyebrows, and Kate sips her wine, which seems to be the only Larson antidote these days. "I work at this, you know. Mildly plump doesn't come easy."

"Yeah, she works out pretty hard," Erik says. "Her butt used to be really flat. Ow, what?"

Brace shudders across the table. Samantha slaps a hand to her mouth.

"Samantha," Claudia says, "Why aren't you eating?"

Samantha swallows and looks down at her plate, which is covered in yams, stuffing, cranberries, green beans. "Um. I am."

"You didn't become a vegetarian, did you?"

"She did," Kate says. "And we're very proud of her."

"Why would you be proud of your child starving? She looks anemic."

Brace is full-on grinning now. At least Samantha's blush is adding color to her pale-against-the-black complexion.

"Did you know Sam has a solo in the concert at Grace Lutheran?" Kate takes another sip of wine.

"I did know." Claudia smiles at her granddaughter, all bright and shining and forgiving of Samantha's over-abundance of vegetables. "She's got the best voice on either side of the river."

"Can't wait, Samantha," Bert says, beaming at her. "Did you also know Mr. Sandvik is retiring, and one of the graduates from Sojourn Reclaimers is taking over?"

Kate sprays wine into her palm. "You can't mean Lucy."

Erik nudges the wine glass away from Kate.

"Mmm, I believe that's her name," Bert says. "Another success story, right dear?"

Claudia nods, glints at Kate. "Did you catch yourself on TV? It was on again last night."

Kate blinks. "Hmm?"

"The rally, remember? They zoomed in on you pretty close."

"Oh, yeah," Kate says with a sigh. "I looked terrible. What was I thinking with that plaid dress? Looked like I was wearing a Christmas tree skirt."

Claudia's eyelashes flutter. "You need to be less self-deprecating, dear."

Just beating you to the punch, Kate mouths under her breath.

"What?"

The table shakes and Erik says *ow* again.

"Mom," he turns to Claudia and rubs his eyes, "we got an interview request from the *Pioneer Press* last week. Gotta tell you, we're a little uncomfortable talking about the marriage amendment. You know, Kate's best friend is gay."

"He's your friend too," Kate says with a glare.

Erik rolls his eyes. "Of course, Kate. Come on."

The kids look on with trepidation.

"Well, you've got to choose your own path," Bert says. "I just wish it was a little closer to your mother's. You know we have nothing against Mark and that pal of his."

Claudia dabs her mouth with a napkin and clasps the table. "Listen, folks, the homosexualists can live their lives any way they see fit, this is a free country. But there is no way on earth they can turn back thousands of years of nature and tradition. And I'm here to make sure of it. I don't care how many monkey suits they throw at me."

Samantha perks up. "I saw this really interesting video on bonobo apes the other day. Um, I guess homosexuality is pretty common in the animal kingdom.

Holds the social structure intact. The females do the deed multiple times per day."

"Monkeys are so gay," Brace says.

Erik sniggers.

"Sam," Kate says, "close your mouth when you talk."

Samantha's forehead wrinkles. "Huh? How can I talk—?"

"I meant eat." *Eat*, Kate mouths at her.

"Well, I'm just saying. A spectrum of sexuality *is* natural."

"But we are not Borneo monkeys, are we?" Claudia asks.

"They're not monkeys. They're apes. There's a difference. And uh, it's bonobo."

"Ape, monkey, Borneo, bon bon—what*ever*. We are human beings, the only animal that Our Lord instilled with a sense of decency. And if you please, after all I went through with those monkey-people, I'd rather not discuss it."

"Well, I just think if you start talking about what's natural," Samantha continues as Claudia's unblinking stare settles on her, "we should embrace the gays," she finishes quietly. "They add something."

"Can't wait to see you in that t-shirt," her brother says, "Embrace the Gays! They add something!"

Samantha looks desperately to her mother, likely preparing to bolt from the table as she has started doing at the drop of a hat.

Kate considers the truce arranged by Erik earlier that week so that the family could exchange gifts. There have been vast silences on the phone lines following any lengthy discussion of Iraq or gay marriage or race or immigration or stem cells or birth control or "intelligent design." She and Claudia should be arguing over lefse recipes, not politics. But here is a table spread with the best she and Erik have to offer, their dog shivering in the garage, their house clean as it will ever get. If not now, when?

"Mark and Ray want to adopt," she says and everyone turns to her. "Out of wedlock, obviously. But they'll make great dads, married or not."

Claudia straightens further. "Well, two fathers is not—"

"And I've agreed to meet with a social worker on their behalf. To testify to their fitness as parents."

Bert sits back.

Claudia blinks. "Do you understand the ramifications for the child? For society?"

"I do."

Claudia looks to her son.

Erik cannot meet his mother's ice blue eyes. "I'm with Kate on this, Mom. They'll make a great family."

"Mmm. Well, *this* is the family I'm worried about." Claudia's gaze visits each of them. "You will be in my prayers tonight."

BLOGGING MY SOJOURN

One Woman's Journey from Gay to Straight

I'm sure not looking forward to this Christmas concert. It's going to be a true test. Not of faith or sexuality, but sanity. I'm probably going to see people I haven't laid eyes on in nineteen years. Some of whom I made a complete fool of myself with and in front of.

Two decades may sound like a very long time but somehow it flew by—with each year passing faster than the last. Of course, a wild life does tend to throw lighter fluid on the candle's flame.

It's difficult to put into words exactly how I leapt from rocker to repentant. And just when I think I've landed on the epiphany date, I have to go back another year.

Anyway, the first set of business is the duty of reacquainting. I'm not going to spend the holidays sitting up on the hill, in this reanimated corpse of a home, like some cranky spinster. Too soon for that. Besides, I can't very well run a B&B or conduct a church choir without making nice.

Need to see what I'm dealing with here.

Praise Jesus

Posted by Liesl ~ 5:PM ~ 4 comments

Patrice commented:
I am praying for you Liesl.

Rolf68 commented:
This could be a train wreck. <munches popcorn>

InChrist *commented:*

Rolf you need to show a little respect.

Rolf68 *commented:*

Dear Jeebus, please vacuum up your followers already so we can fix this planet.

CHAPTER FIVE

Samantha

"I'M ON THE phone. *God!*"

"You don't have that much time," Mom said from the other side of the door.

"Thank you for adding to my anxiety!"

"Please don't talk to me like that," Mom's voice lowered. "You need to get ready."

"*Seriously?* Like I don't know that." Samantha uncovered the mic on her phone. "Ugh. Anyway, attending one little holiday performance doesn't make you a Christian."

"Sorry, Sam," Jamie said on the other end, "you know churches make me six kinds of ill. It's not the place—"

"—It's the people. Well, it was worth a try. Oh, great, I'm getting a bump. Thanks, Mom." Samantha sneered into her makeup mirror, dabbing on a spot of makeup. She didn't get normally incapacitated over performing like other kids did; this should be nothing like the vertigo she felt before a pre-calculus exam. However, she had sprouted an itchy pink spot, near her lip. "It's like all my anxiety is stacking up on one nerve ending." And she sensed that after the performance, she could run to the powder room mirror and the spot would be completely gone. "Is it a temporary zit, what the hell?"

"I wish I could trade all my zits for one ginormous zit," Jamie said, "like on my thigh or something, where I could hack at it in private."

Samantha sketched on her eyeliner, lighter than she did for school. "Did you know we're the only primate with acne? The price we pay for dropping our fur too fast."

"Wow, fascinating," Jamie said dryly. "How about Zev, isn't he coming?"

At the mention of Samantha's latest crush, the pink spot stung. "Are you kidding? Half our congregation still think the Jews killed Jesus. Who needs that baggage?"

"Good point."

"Besides, Brace forbids all his friends from coming within a mile of Grace Lutheran."

"Aw, I bet he looks cute in his choral gown."

"I'll let the puckhead know you said that."

"Do it and you're dead."

"Five minutes!" Mom called from upstairs.

"I'm coming! Jesus, that woman's killing me." A chill ran down Samantha's back and her teeth chattered. "I'm kinda glad Zev isn't coming actually. It's entirely possible that I am indeed scared shitless."

"You're going to do fine, Sam. You always do."

"But the new choir director is going to be in the audience tonight." Mr. Sandvik, the old clueless choir director was retiring and the new one would be out there, watching, judging. "How many rehearsals before she nails me as a fraud?"

"You're not a fraud, Sam. You don't know the meaning of the word."

Samantha twisted her hair into an updo. "I can't even figure out notes without singing Do-Re-Mi in my head. That's like doing math on your fingers."

"Neither can I."

"Well, you're not going up in front of your family and half the town." She smudged one last dab of makeup on the bump, covering the red, but the relief of it remained.

Jamie made a shuddering sound on the other line. "And that's a good thing, trust me."

CHAPTER SIX

Kate

GRACE LUTHERAN'S ANNUAL Christmas Concert comes to a bumpy end with a frenetically-paced *Joy to the World* and the cellist's sheet music fluttering to the floor like a downed pigeon.

Kate glances from her son to her daughter in the white-frocked choir. While Brace's tenor blends with the other men, Samantha's high-powered soprano blasts the congregation in unfocused bursts. Much like her moods lately, it oscillates between timid and shattering. At least Brace managed to keep a straight face while Samantha sang, "How Beautiful are the Feet," even though it had provided no end of hilarity when she tried to practice the solo at home, and ended with a screaming match.

The lights come up and the congregation stirs. Kate can now get a better look at Wicasa Bluff's newest resident sitting two rows in front of the Larson pew. With shiny dark hair layered like a morning show host, Lucy Van Buren resembles her mother, Bridget, thirty years younger. But it can't be of course. Bridget is grey-haired, shorter now, and she sits hunched up next to her only living kin.

Kate bites back the sweet satisfaction of knowing that Lucy has returned in defeat, cocky tail retracted, to verify that Kate might have made better choices. But the delight soon descends into a queasy sadness for Lucy that hasn't fully subsided since Kate first saw her on the sidewalk.

After the director bows and presents the choir for applause, the crowd departs their pews. Kate watches as Lucy turns and says something in her mother's ear, to which the older woman nods and taps her own cheek. Lucy kisses it, stands, and smooths down the folds of her black velvet dress. She walks to the now-retired choir director to shake his hand. The regality with which she once carried herself is less flippant, a chin-up groove Lucy's worn into a style so genteel she could be any of the PTA moms in this church. According to the articles Kate had read about ex-gay programs, the graduates emerged like hermetically-sealed produce, irradiated of sin by God's holy light. They were sexless looking, tone-deaf animatrons in buttoned-up oxfords, not fashion plates wearing a string of pearls and a Clinique counter makeup job. But then, Lucy had always been a master of disguise.

Kate stands and clambers out of the pew, nailing Erik's foot in the process. She weaves upstream, past the congregants pushing toward the greeting hall with its punch bowls and cookie trays. Each time she thinks she's caught Lucy's eye, Lucy turns away, greeting an acquaintance from the past with a dentist-whitened smile and kind words.

And then Kate hears that voice and it is the same, if a little throatier, a bit less Midwestern.

> *Please tell them I was with you, Katie.*
> *You told them it wasn't me that set the fire, right?*
> *Katie, you'll back me up, won't you?*

Kate halts, letting the crowd slowly push her back toward the snack tables. She retreats toward Erik, who stands munching away with Brace.

Samantha rushes past them and out the door.

"Good job, honey," Kate says to the breeze. Erik and Brace shrug, mouths full.

AFTER SUNSET, DIAMOND-bright halogens pierce the crowded greeting hall. Kate percolates with restlessness. It's as if she's in the high school auditorium again after graduation—hoping to escape her family, looking for her classmates, wondering what trouble they could get into on the main drag or atop the bluffs. She tucked her husband into a chat with Mark and his partner Ray to keep them away from Senator Larson, though she's not entirely sure which party she meant to protect. However, she is confident that her chat with Claudia and Bert lasted long enough to at least release her for the rest of the evening. Too bad her yoga partner Anita gave up church for Netflix, what with all the gossip desperately in need of sharing.

As she passes the south atrium, Kate senses a lone silhouette from the corner of her eye and stops. There, at the glass panels that rise from the floor and curve upward to form a roof, a woman gazes outside into the knit of maple and conifer, her long black coat folded over one arm. Tonight, the clouds have abandoned the moon, and the proudest of snowflakes sparkle along the church's south lawn like constellations.

Despite the woman's sophisticated attire, Kate recognizes that thoughtful stance and two decades simply fall away. Young Katie was never sure if Lucy meant to pose like that. Mom had always said, "that girl's just starved for attention." And Katie had always wondered why adults were so miserly with said attention. If anyone had earned it, it was Lucy. So, whether it was for show—a silent plea or proposition—or not, it worked. And still does.

Kate's heart flutters, but she takes a calming breath and ventures into the dimly lit atrium, past rows of red, white, and chartreuse poinsettia. It's cool in here, and she hugs herself, smoothing her biceps. The disconcerting burble of trickling water rises from plug-in Zen fountains like a leaky tap.

"Okay, Lucy." She taps her foot and offers up a conspiratorial squint. "What are you up to?"

"Ah. Mrs. Larson." Lucy side-eyes her, betrays only a slight smile. "Getting reacquainted with the weather. Beautiful, isn't it?"

"Yes. I'm familiar with snow." Kate supposed a hug was off the table. "Actually, I meant with Sojourn Reclaimers. That's a joke, right?"

Lucy fully turns to her, eyebrow raised. "Excuse me?" The close-up sight of that same crooked smirk and those mischievous black irises that were always searching, reading, deciding, nearly overwhelms Kate.

"What happened?" she asks, gesturing at Lucy's dress.

"Consider it a rebranding."

As Mark had said, time and gravity have begun to conspire against Lucy, same as everyone else. When her smirk wavers, the lines remain. It's still a wonderful face though, one of a kind, with high cheekbones and that same sculpted upturn of nose. Underneath the makeup, there glows the same warm blush. That face still reminds Kate of the pretty teenager she once hung out with on the Leap, but also foretells the handsome matron Lucy will become when that cocoa hair gives way to encroaching silver filaments. Maybe it already has; it's difficult to tell in this light.

"This sure isn't the Lucy *I* remember," Kate says quietly. "The girl I knew didn't need to fit into their Barbie doll ensembles." She glances toward the main room. "She was beyond Barbie." *What the heck was in that punch?* "And Ken."

"Maybe I wanted a little security." Lucy nods as if considering this for the first time.

"Hello, silly, there's a lesbian couple in town with three kids, a house and plenty of security." But this isn't entirely true. The women live in an apartment, and foster children are always being ripped out of their home. And actually, one of them does dress like a Barbie. "Mark and Ray are very secure." *Probably.*

"Okay. Great. That's nice," Lucy says, a hand raised in capitulation.

Kate sighs. It's been forever, could she have remembered their relationship all wrong? "It's just that, well, high school, and what happened—"

"Yeah." Lucy clicks her tongue, "I've wanted to apologize about that for a long time."

Kate shakes her head, insistent. "There's no need. Really."

"I should go." Lucy pinches her smile in that god-awfully polite way people do when acknowledging someone across a gas pump. She begins to unfold her coat.

"Wow," Kate says. "You still do it."

After years of watching her children learn how to emotionally manipulate, how to protect their egos, Kate can see the mechanics.

Lucy halts. "Still do what?"

"Never mind. Tell me about this Sojourn thing. Is that like AA where you have to find every woman you've known and force your apology?" Kate doesn't mean for it to have an edge, but it does and her sarcasm echoes through the room.

"Um, *you* came in here."

A few people glance over into the atrium, their lips puckered. It could be from tart cranberry punch, or it could be from gossip. Do they still remember Lucy? The vandalism? The romantic pronouncements of a teenage lesbian? The old shame, a stale sadness, comes over Kate like an overcast sky.

Lucy lowers her voice, squinting. "Honestly Katie, I thought you, of all people, would understand what Sojourn's about."

"Why would I—?"

"Your mother-in-law? I saw you on TV. No, wait—it's okay. She's right about marriage. It's *biblical*." And whispers the last word like its magic.

Kate scoffs. "I can't believe I'm hearing this. You clearly have no idea what I think about gay marriage. I got dragged to that rally."

"So, you're still not in charge of your life?"

The mirth that once brightened young Lucy's eyes appears cruel now in the shadows, takes Kate aback. This person is a long-lost twin of Lucy, the one who let the Jehovah's Witnesses in the door.

"What has gotten into you?"

"The holy spirit?" Lucy's gaze drifts to the windows again.

Bridget Van Buren stands outdoors, where the end of the walk meets the parking lot. The woman's hands raise in frustration. Lucy extracts a key fob from her coat, points it out the window and car lights flash in the distance. Bridget walks off toward them.

Kate speaks faster. "I don't even—listen, I have no right to judge you after all this time, but this ex-gay thing masquerading as—I dunno—responsibility? It's totally irresponsible." She points at the ground. "There are gay kids growing up here. And they see you. Don't you remember what it was like for us?"

"Oh, yes. I do, Katie." Lucy's jaw hardens. "I remember. Very well."

Lucy twirls the long coat onto her shoulders and shrugs into it. The scent released from her jacket—earthy, pungent, intangible—brings a flood of memories, memories of longing. She heads for the atrium's glass door and is out into the night, the coat flowing behind her legs like a cape. The three-quarter moon blues the snow and the tall conifers absorb everything else into their pitched shadows. Including Lucy.

Kate swallows. Her mouth is dry, the zipper down her back biting, itching. She cried about this for too many years. She can't cry anymore.

CHAPTER SEVEN

1985
Wicasa Bluffs High School

"I GUESS WE won." Katie snickered.

She clasped the wooden plank above her, lifted her legs and swung back and forth, climbing the slats backward until it was too high risk a fall. Just a slip of a girl, her grandmother called her. She didn't really understand what that meant.

The homecoming of Katie's sophomore year had been a warm one. A few brave crickets still chirped in the chill of an October night. The bleachers above the two girls had emptied of football fans, the field lights all switched off. The second to last car in the high school parking lot pulled onto Second Street and its tires squealed away in revelry. The moon provided only a hazy cut of light. It would be a tricky walk to Lucy's escape pod (what she called her AMC Pacer because it did look as if it had been shot out the back end of a spaceship).

Katie dropped back down into the gravel.

"We probably should have watched the last quarter," Lucy said. "You sure you're not embarrassed to be seen with me?"

"Of course not. It's just that . . ." Katie blushed. Fortunately, it was too dark to see.

"Mmm. Oh, almost forgot," Lucy said quietly and dug the toe of her sneaker into the rocks. "I got the part."

"What, in *Sound of Music*?"

"Yeah."

"Why didn't you tell me sooner? Wow, that's so awesome."

Lucy chuckled. "It's no big deal. I'm sure it will be a disaster. Gotta wear a dress."

Back then WBHS performed Christmas plays of sketchy quality. Classes had barely started before kids began debating who would be the next group of stooges to be marched up on the auditorium stage. It was nearly as important as voting for the homecoming court. Except the school play was more of a vote for the anti-royalty.

"You will be fantastic, Luce. You know I'll be right there in the front row."

Lucy shuddered. "Yikes. Maybe you shouldn't. I'll flub my lines. You will be so—distracting." She betrayed a sly smile.

Katie pushed at her. "I wouldn't miss it." She wedged her flashlight under her chin and murmured, "I should get home before the ghost of Maiden Leap shows up."

"Hey, it's only six o'clock in the morning."

Katie flicked off the flashlight. "Huh?"

"In Paris." Lucy wore four Swatches up the same wrist, set to different time zones, all the places she wanted to go in life: New York, Hong Kong, Paris, L.A. She said it helped her picture what people were doing anywhere at any point in time, said it reminded her there was a world beyond Wicasa Bluffs. "Let's go to the diner, get some breakfast crepes, speak French, and drive the waitress nuts."

Katie groaned. "Oh, I wish I could. But my parents would kill me."

Lucy's teeth shone brighter than anything. "One more kiss then?"

"Two more." Katie wrapped her arms around Lucy's over-sized pea coat, the wool had already scratched her cheeks raw. She would tell her mother it was from Gary Lindstrom's attempt at a beard. "Okay, three, but seriously no more. Jeez."

BLOGGING MY SOJOURN

One Woman's Journey from Gay to Straight

My life spun off its axis the night I turned 35. The band had decamped in a stinky hotel just outside Paris. I turned on the bedside lamp, slipped the *Down Home Almanac* I'd bought in La Guardia out of its paper bag (the bag I was using to hide total lameness from my bandmates). The feature article showcased American bridgeworks, everything from the Golden Gate to those quaint Tennessee covered bridges. The article ended in the back of the magazine. And there it was: the bony lift bridge from my hometown looking like a giant erector set perched just above black floodwaters.

On the nightstand sat two empty bottles of Bordeaux and three roaches—the smoking kind. A long crack on the wall seemed to change position, like the second hand of a clock. Beside me slept a girl, fifteen years my junior. I didn't know French very well and she'd taken out her awkward fury on my body. Something about her nails in my back, her teeth in my neck and her sophisticated European desires at odds with my desire to wrap *POLICE LINE: DO NOT CROSS* around my butt inexplicably reminded me of Vicky, my high school crush. Actually, Vicky had a more timid intensity than this girl, but she had something powerful, not yet unleashed back when I knew her.

My lyrics were often about this Vicky. As if she might hear them. But that was as effective as sending a message in a bottle to someone who never visits the sea. *My God,* I thought, I am never going to see Vicky again. And then it came, that first existential swarm of regrets you get at that age. Vicky was alive in the world somewhere. Perhaps still in my hometown. But what if she'd been struck down by disease? What if she'd taken the switchbacks up on the bluff too fast? What if she got pregnant and bled out in childbirth or . . . I leapt from the bed, ran to the bath but not before the Bordeaux came back up and splashed across the floor planks. A couple pink pills I don't remember taking glared up at me.

After a shower and another clumsy session with nameless girl, I still could not sleep. Yes, Vicky probably was married. And why wouldn't she be? She'd dated guys before and after me. I had no reason, no right to invade her life and say "How are you, Vicky, who did you marry, do you remember me, do you still think of me, do you forgive me?" No, we would go to our graves as mere memory fragments to each other.

I lay on my belly, one eye closed into the pillow, the other staring at the nightstand. A small black and white ad spoke from the back of the magazine: *Make the Journey Home from Homosexuality*. It was for Sojourn Reclaimers.

Praise Jesus

Posted by Liesl ~ 9:45 PM ~ 24 comments

Patrice commented:
I am speechless. Why did you feel the need to fill this post with your filthy past? Move forward with Jesus.

Rolf68 commented:
Patrice, you're on the right track being speechless. Liesl, you came home for Vicky, not God. Be careful.

InChrist commented:
Blessed is the man that endureth temptation: for when he is tried, he shall receive the crown of life — James 1, 12

RugbyLVR commented:
LOL! I can't believe there are still people devoted to the scribblings of ancient sheepherders.

Patrice commented:

I second that scripture InChrist. Without temptation, there is no salvation. We're all praying for you Liesl.

RugbyLVR commented:

OMG. Places like Sojourn are making a killing off you people.

Comments truncated |

CHAPTER EIGHT

Samantha

BACON!

Like some sort of zombie vampire in a bad teen novel, she'd been waking up craving meat. Refusing to admit it to her family or even Jamie, Samantha missed the fat, the salt, and, well, the blood. For breakfast she rammed down a granola bar slathered with an extra coating of organic peanut butter in hopes the oil and protein would stifle her rabid taste for murdered creatures. Lunch was easy, however, the grey meatloaf having no such kryptonite effect. She could eat mashed potatoes until they were scloiching out her ears.

That afternoon, Samantha skipped over to Jamie. The school buses were rolling in to pick up the kids and take them home for holiday break.

"Happy-happy. Joy-joy."

"Tell me about it." Jamie fist-bumped her. "No physics for two weeks. Rah."

Her nose was pink and running from the cold, but other than that she looked good in her puffy blue parka and purple jeans. Since the braces had come off, it seemed to Samantha like all Jamie'd had to do was grow out her honey-blonde hair, poke it behind her ears and she looked like the average girl, albeit on the tall side. And being an average girl was more than enough for now.

Jamie had once been Samantha's boyfriend James in grade school (the one Brace's friend Maddox called Snowplow because before the braces his two front teeth poked forward and formed a perfect wedge) the boy who liked to come over and play dress up with all her princess gowns. When the two began their sophomore year as best girl friends, they expected their classmates to freak.

But something had happened in WBHS at some point. Maybe it was a punk or a trench coat that had gone before and who had inspired the guidance counselor, the principal, the teachers to take gender-questioning Jamie under their wing. And now Samantha can't remember what Jamie was like as that gawky, shorthaired, wedge-toothed guy in cargo pants, even though Jamie still uses the boys' restroom to keep the peace with some of the kids whose parents are not so pleased, even though she grows taller every month, even though her voice is cracking.

"Hey, I met the new choir director last night," Samantha said. "You'll never guess—"

"Lucy Veebee from Cake for Horses. I heard."

"Oh. Well, isn't it awesome?"

Lucy Veebee wasn't exactly a star in a grand sense, more like a red dwarf or maybe a large planet like Saturn. Okay, maybe a comet. Still, she was an icon to anyone who dug the riot grrrl movement of the nineties and she'd run with the supermassive stars who'd gone full-on supernova like Courtney Love and Gwen Stefani. Next season was going to be a blast. Granted, *Ms. Van Buren* had become a born-again of the Grandma Larson variety. But no one was perfect. Besides, no one could be as hard core as Grandma. And Grandma was still a good person deep down.

"I told her about you. And how your voice hasn't changed yet. She didn't even blink."

"You did *what?*"

"Sorry. Guess I was a little starstruck and babbling at that point. But listen, she said that castrato had sung soprano and falsetto for centuries and she would find a place for you this spring if you wanted. Course I told her that you wouldn't set foot in a church but it was a nice offer, don't you think?"

"Yeh. I guess so." Jamie glanced over Samantha's shoulder and her eyes widened.

Zev Cohen walked up to them, nodding at Jamie and smiling at Samantha. He opened with the ever-popular, "Hi."

"Hi," Samantha replied. The way his curly brown hair fell over his big chunky glasses made her feel all squirrelly inside. Maybe she'd eaten too many carbs.

"You guys want a ride home?" he asked, then under his breath. "I mean girls. Gals. Ladies. Oh, God."

Jamie chuckled.

"Sure," Samantha said and glared a plea at Jamie.

"Sure," she said. "Thanks."

Jamie climbed in the back of the old Ford sedan and Samantha got in the front.

This. Is. Huge. Samantha could feel the hugeness of the moment gathering in her belly. Brace's other puckhead friend Maddox wouldn't even talk to Samantha when she was around Jamie. Brace barely did either. But Zev talked to them both the whole ride. Asking stuff about their classes and laughing at the principal's lame send-off over the intercom.

At the usual lift bridge backup, Zev turned to Samantha. "You wanna go out over break? See a movie or something?" *Straight to it, a man of action.* "Jamie you could come too."

"Oh, thanks, I'll be busy." Jamie smirked at Samantha.

"I'll need to ask my parents, but, yeah, that sounds fun." Samantha turned away from them to grin cross-eyed out the window. *Bacon!*

CHAPTER NINE

Kate

AT EIGHTEEN DEGREES, the dry air begrudges only the ashen scent of car exhaust and the vanilla camphor of lip balm. As if they might counteract the loss of more humid aromas (the river's fishy tang, the woodsy summer breeze) retail stores pump out eye-watering doses of eucalyptus, pine, and cinnamon (via aerosols, scented candles, and potpourri) all in an attempt to sell a few last-minute Christmas presents. At the Gonzo Fox, Mark prefers an organic approach. His roasting cashews can transform a window-shopper into the dazed owner of a vintage bedroom set and a maxed-out credit card.

When Kate enters their store, dinging the brass bell above, Ray Gonzalez is already behind the glass counter, scooping nuts into a wax paper bag for her. The gallery and back halls are crowded with customers ogling furniture and knickknacks; estate odds and ends with origins obscured by a little spit and polish.

She whistles at the price tag on a gothic minister's throne that will probably end up heading the table of some dining room on St. Paul's Summit Avenue. "How do you sell so much used stuff to people who refused to buy a pre-owned car?"

"Nostalgia is a heady narcotic," Mark says, taking the bag of nuts from Ray. "It only needs," he passes the cashews beneath Kate's nose, "a trigger," and drops it in her hands. He always seems to know these things. He's even earned the moniker The Great Foxtradamus from the locals by predicting every divorce in town.

"Thanks." She gives him a shy smile and hug. His muscles feel tense. "Okay, listen." She warms her hands with the bag. "We were hog-tied into that situation. You know how the senator is. It will never happen again though. Trust me. Cut me some slack this time, okay?"

Ray raises a dark eyebrow. "Well, that depends. Will you be at our wedding?" He comes away from the glass counter with its pink heat lamp and mounds of sweet and savory nuts then wanders into the clutter of the back hall.

Kate has always found Ray quirkily appealing. His dark head of short-cropped hair with its patch of grey on one side looks as if he's had a mishap with a paint roller. His brown glass eye (the one he received after a beating in his teens for being a gay Puerto-Rican) is a near-perfect match for its natural twin and its slight cast inward gives him an innocent air.

"Of course I'll be there," she calls after him. "I want to be a bridesmaid or groomsperson or—something."

"Um," Mark says from across the store, "we were thinking best matron. But you may be demoted to flower girl if I'm still feeling oppressed by you."

"Can I wear eggplant? I look good in eggplant." She pops a roasted cashew; eyes close. *Ah, dinner and dessert in one bite.*

"Honey," Mark says, "you can wear palm fronds and a pineapple on your head for all we care. I just want to do this already. Ray isn't getting any younger." He huffs. "So you're really going to stop letting the MIL run all over you?"

Ray elbows him.

"New leaf," Kate says. "You guys would have been so proud of Sam last week. Really put the senator in her place." She drops three nuts onto her tongue.

"Good for her," Mark says. "She deserves everything that's coming her way."

Kate halts. "Claudia or Sam?"

"Both." Mark sidles up. "Now, don't breathe a word of this, but my sources tell me Sam's just about guaranteed the lead in the high school musical this spring."

Kate honks, slaps her chest, and coughs. She raises the bag and rattles it. "My baby."

Mark wags a finger. "You *can't* tell her."

Ray nods. "She's gonna tell."

Kate helps Mark and Ray haul out a scroll-armed park bench to the sidewalk by plopping down on it before they can lift it and tucking back into the cashews. Ray says nothing of the added hundred and forty pounds. Mark grunts, insists he's sprouting a hernia. Kate kicks heels, imagining all the costume shopping and altering she could do with Samantha. One of the cars passing on Main toots twice. Mark and Ray set Kate down with a thud and look up.

A hand in a black fingerless glove extends from the sunroof of a road-salted BMW Z coupe. The car, with its long front end and hearse-like hatchback, looks like the sort of hot rod Cruella DeVille would drive.

"Lucy," Mark says, faking a smile and waving back.

The roadster growls by in a blur of shabby black. Its wide sports tires grab onto twisty Bluff Road, which curves up to the Gainsborough house and dead ends at Maiden Leap lookout point. The car disappears around the wooded corner and hums up the hill.

Mark straightens his hand-lettered sign.

> *Too many relatives home for the holidays?*
> *Bench 'Em — $150*

"Miss Ex-Lez came in the other day to sell me some O'Keefe prints," he says.

Ray nods. "Can't handle all that vulva imagery around."

Kate struggles to contain her nuts.

"Boy, she's let herself go," Mark chatters on. "Setting foot outside of the house without makeup when you're twenty is precious. When you're forty it's just plain irresponsible."

"Brrr." Kate shivers, follows the two back inside. She silently disagrees. If Lucy took off her Clinique mask, it's a step in the right direction. *Letting go* conjures up images of abandoned barns leaning to one side, foreclosed farmhouses burnt darn near to the foundation, prairie grasses reclaiming a wheat field. All beautiful things in their own way. *So let them go in a blaze of glory. That's willfulness.*

"Neglect has nothing to do with it," she mumbles.

"What's that?" Ray says.

"Nothing." She eyes the bottom of the bag, shakes it, and raises it to her mouth. The last shreds of nuts and a dusting of sea salt scatter across her tongue. Lucy's been back for two seconds and is already a burr in the brain. "Let's get back to the top story. What's the play going to be?"

"Not supposed to tell." Mark peers into the cash register readout as he pecks the keys. "But I can promise you, it's going to be really wicked."

THAT EVENING, THE doorbell rings at the Larson split-level ranch.

Samantha ambles downstairs from the kitchen to the foyer as though she isn't thrilled to be going on her first date, as if this is some UPS delivery she needs to sign for.

Kate leans against the entryway to the kitchen, pressing her pruned hands to a dishtowel and savoring the moment. She'd been dying to share the good news about the play with her daughter but decided the kid could only handle one milestone at a time.

At the doorway, Zev Cohen smiles at Samantha and looks up the stairs through his Clark Kent glasses and shaggy, light brown coils of hair. "Hey, Mrs. Larson."

"Hi, Zev. C'mon in. Make yourself at home."

Samantha's shoulders sink. "Mom."

"Erik!" Kate yells, startling Zev. "Zev's here!"

Brace's size twelve footsteps rumble up from the rec room. He nods his chin at Zev. "S'up."

Zev nods back. "S'up."

Samantha strains toward the door as if leaning into a windstorm. She's in black as usual, but wearing a dress this time with a fuzzy raspberry-pink sweater on top. Her hair has some wave to it, meaning she finally unpackaged that hair-crimper Kate got her for her birthday in August.

"Have you got my perfume on again?" Kate asks the air.

Samantha turns and answers Kate with puckered mouth and bulging eyes.

Kate throws the dishtowel over her shoulder. "So, Zev, what's on this evening's schedule?"

Erik lumbers up from the rec room and grunts as he attempts to take the stairs as fast as his son. "Mr. Cohen." He shakes Zev's hand with a boisterous yank.

"Mr. Larson." Zev's face now matches Samantha's sweater. He looks at Kate again and pushes up his glasses at the bridge of his nose. It's a tic she used to have, nearly endearing enough to quiet her worry. "We're heading out to the mall. Dinner at Ruby Tuesdays, then see that comedy with Matthew McConaughey and Lindsay Lohan?"

"Oh, he's dreamy," Brace says.

"Shut up, bro," Zev mutters.

Samantha sneers at her brother. "Yeah, *bro*."

"And then they're going to Maiden Leap," Brace says with a coo.

Kate nods. "Oh no they're not."

"We weren't, Mrs. Larson, I swear."

"Well, then, you kids have fun." Kate waves them through the threshold.

She retreats to the kitchen and leans on the sink, hoping Erik will come upstairs to witness her tears, wondering why she's the only one stunned by this moment. But he doesn't come. He goes back downstairs to watch TV with Brace.

Kate stands, tears drying, eyes glazing.

Maiden Leap. *Damn that place.* Zev wouldn't take her there, would he? No, he didn't have the chutzpah. His own mother would murder him. But damn that place. The tallest bluff on the St. Croix (once known as Squaw Leap in the last century) was a landmark Kate could not fully ignore as long as she lived in the river valley. Just north of downtown Wicasa Bluffs, it loomed solid as an anvil and was not going anywhere any time soon.

CHAPTER TEN

1986
Maiden Leap

"COMFORTABLE?" LUCY ASKED.

She had spread out a plaid blanket atop the grassy clearing and they lay next to each other under a full dome of stars that seemed close enough to grab.

"Relatively speaking," Katie said, cuddling up next to her. "I can't believe we really did it."

After a few boastful letters of daring each other, the two had synchronized watches, snuck out of their homes, and rendezvoused at the lift bridge. From upriver, Maiden Leap jutted over the St. Croix like the bow of a haunted ocean freighter. In those days, the bluffs were less developed and the only home nearby was the Gainsborough estate, set back at the edge of the woods. As they hiked up the dark road, Katie had battled the urge to run back down.

"Are you scaaared?" Lucy asked with a giggle.

Tonight she wore a brass ear cuff on her right ear, replete with dangling feathers. She smelled of the citrusy cologne Katie had given her for Valentine's Day. Underneath that, burnt vegetable oil and possibly ketchup, because Lucy said tater tot hot dish had been on the Van Buren supper menu.

Katie looked around. "Not anymore."

Besides the night sky, Maiden Leap also provided a twinkling view of the new Riverton subdivision to the East, the onyx St. Croix winding around bends to the north and south and the ominous glow of the Twin Cities far out in the west. Below the bluff, Wicasa Falls flowed from a hidden spring in the cliff face. It created just enough condensation for steam to rise on a cool night.

"They do say the Gainsborough mansion is haunted by the ghost of Maiden Leap," Lucy said, her teeth shining in the dark.

"Nice try," Katie scoffed. "And which one?"

There were plenty of tales about the Leap, from legends to news reports.

"Wicasa, of course."

"Oh, well, she's probably just lonely."

"Maybe she's happy." Lucy rolled up on her side and pressed a palm to Katie's.

They shared a pulse, the tiny hammering at their fingertips, "two energies desperate to interact," she'd said. Lucy was always talking up the paranormal to kids; more than Katie would have preferred. She wanted Lucy all to herself. As the first of four children, Katie longed for an older, wiser sister. Lucy filled the role—and then some.

"Go ahead. Tell me the story." Katie had heard it many times but she knew this version would be totally better than her dad's.

"Okay, here's the deal," Lucy said, her voice quiet and conspiring. "So this Lakota boy named Chelee and his Ojibwe girlfriend, Wicasa, used to come here to make out. You know, 'cause their tribes were at war and they needed some privacy."

"Did they make out like paleface?" Katie giggled.

"I dunno. Maybe they rubbed noses. Lemme tell this."

"Well, I need to be able to picture it."

"Okay, here." Lucy clasped Katie's jaw and kissed her softly.

Yep, ketchup.

"Wow," Katie said. "Now, see, I totally get their attraction."

"Yeah, they were hot for each other. So anyway, Wicasa's father planned to marry her off to some bozo cousin. Which was totally gross, I know, but this cousin was half Lakota, half Ojibwe, good politics."

"Gosh, that is so typical."

"I know. But listen . . ." Lucy flicked an eyebrow. "During their next meeting, Chelee said to Wicasa, you must meet me here tomorrow on the Great Mother's breast and then we will fly off to Father Sky together. Forever. No, you will never see your family again, but you will never feel heartache again either. After *many* kisses, Wicasa said yes to Chelee. She told the wind spirits she had no choice but to follow the will of her soul. The next day, knowing it to be her last, Wicasa climbed this very bluff and waited for her boyfriend. But. Her cousin, who was totally obsessed with Wicasa, had followed her here too. When he saw Chelee reveal himself from those trees over there, he plucked an arrow." Lucy rose to her knees, pulled an invisible arrow from a quiver behind her back, gracefully drew back the bow, and pointed it at the cliff. Her silhouette blacked out the stars.

Katie sucked in a breath.

Lucy held the stance, her arm shuddering under the pressure of the phantom bowstring, and said into her shoulder, "Blinded by jealousy, the cousin pointed his arrow at *Wicasa* and said 'Run to her thief, run. If you can catch my arrow, you may take my bride. Otherwise she's dead to both of us.'

"Wicasa just nodded all calm-like to Chelee and spread her arms, prepared to take flight from the cliff. Chelee sprinted forward before the arrow was set loose, but he could never be fast enough." Lucy' splayed her fingers. "The cousin shot Wicasa through the heart. As the cousin cried out in shock at what he had done, Chelee reached the girl. He grabbed her in his arms and the two fell into the soul of the Great Mother together. Just—beyond—there." She eased back down onto the blanket. "And, sometimes, in that steam, you can see their souls entwined."

The clearing went silent save for the simmer of insects.

Though Katie lay prone, knowing the craggy edge was only ten feet away inspired dizziness, as if the Leap were rotating beneath her. She sat up and the feeling subsided.

Katie rose to her feet and crept toward the edge of the lookout point, to the short fence that only seemed capable of hampering toddlers. Stubborn tufts of brush grew upward from the cliff face and made the drop seem less abrupt. But that outgrowth would hardly break a fall. Could that be how the 1950s suicide had happened? A misjudgment?

Cars, toy-sized from here, sped along Main Street and out into the night.

Lucy rose from the blanket. "Actually, the Ojibwe say the whole thing was made up by some white councilman in the twenties to pull in tourists. They're trying to get people to change the name. Guess most river bluff towns have a suicidal Indian story. Pretty cheesy."

"Well, maybe so, but I like the way you tell it, Luce." Katie no longer felt dizzy, but still tingly. Maybe there *was* magic in the rising steams of Wicasa Falls. *Happy ghosts*.

Lucy chuckled softly behind her. "You know, I used to think Lake Superior fed the St. Croix. But I guess the river just starts up on some smaller lake."

"St. Croix Lake."

"Yeah, duh, right?" Lucy pocketed hands. "Anyway, I used to come up here and imagine my brother's spirit running downstream. Yunno, from where his ship wrecked? Like eventually the same water molecules would drift through here." She stared at the lift bridge, which was on the rise for a police boat. "Dumb, eh?"

"Must have been really awful to lose Daniel like that."

"I was pretty young, barely remember what he looked like. And Mom and Dad sure don't talk about it. It's against the law or something. Doesn't matter. Hell, all they do is sit and drink and smoke and watch PBS, who wants to talk to that? As if watching *Masterpiece The-a-tah* and drinking scotch is better than watching *Knots Landing* and drinking Schlitz." Lucy looked up to the stars. "I can't wait to leave this stupid place."

"Yeah, me too," Katie said quietly.

Lucy peered out over the edge. "My dad knew that last guy who jumped. Called him the n-word."

"I didn't know any black people lived here back then."

"Yeah, can you imagine how hard it must have been to grow up here in the fifties? At least kids like us can blend in."

At first, Katie didn't know what Lucy meant. *Like us.* When she realized, it turned her stomach just a bit. She shook it off. "Well, I don't see you blending into anything."

"True." Lucy chuckled. "Mark and I are starting a band, and if we pull it off, I'm outta here."

"Hmm." Katie frowned. She pressed her thighs against the railing, testing its strength. She teased herself with the idea of a somersault over the edge. "If I leaned over—if I slipped—do you think you could you pull me back up?"

"I would never let you go. Seriously, be careful, Katie. The Leap is magnetic. It's got an iron core, yunno. Attracts the iron in our blood. But if you go too close to the cliff, that's where the poles are reversed and it'll repel you—bam—right off the edge."

Katie knew this was utter bull, yet just convincing enough to suspend disbelief. After all, the Leap did seem to dare someone to jump every other generation.

Lucy hooked a finger through one of Katie's belt loops and gently pulled her close, breasts pressing Katie's back. "If you were too heavy for me, guess we'd both go down," she said softly into Katie's ear. "And I'm not okay with that."

Katie's heart thrummed. *No better time than now to give Luce the surprise for once.* She turned in Lucy's arms and plunged her tongue into her mouth. Lucy squeaked a bit, pulled away for a moment then returned the kiss. They found a rhythm, got lost in it, and pressed tight. For the first time, Katie had lowered defenses long enough to feel something stirring deep down and within.

"You're a very good kisser," Lucy whispered.

"Thanks. You too."

"You have to say that 'cause I said it."

"No I don't. You are so much better than Gary. He slobbers all over me."

"Yeah, why do they do that? It's like rubbing a sliced kiwi all over your face."

"It's foreplay. A promise. It's like 'I'm gonna do *that* to you—down there.' Of course, they never get around to that. They do anything to get you all hot, except that."

"Whoa." Lucy leaned back. "How do you know all this?"

"I—overheard Anita Funk in the locker room."

"Ah, a woman of the world."

"She's cool."

Lucy shrugged. "She's all right."

"Not my type actually." Katie bit her lip and wrinkled her nose.

Lucy made a little purring growl at the back of her throat. Her smile shown bright in the starlight, then it faded. "Wish I'd never suggested you date Gary. I can't stand to think of it."

"Aw, Luce." Katie hugged her, and they stood like that for a while. "I don't want you to leave town."

"Don't worry." Lucy kissed her neck, her tongue darting behind Katie's ear. "I'm not leaving without you."

Katie let out a small huff, anticipating a night filled with more surprises. The hard denim flap of Lucy's button-fly teased at her groin. Her ears rumbled with the sound of Lucy's warm breath but something else as well, something mechanical.

She sensed bright light beyond her closed eyelids.

"Katie!" her mom screeched with the slamming of car doors. "Oh my God! Brad*ford*!"

Katie pushed out of Lucy's arms a bit more furiously than she'd meant to and backed away.

"What are you girls doing?" her father said with a boom.

"Katherine Louise Andern, you get in this car—right now! You are supposed to be in bed."

The ground seemed to vibrate then, the Leap drawing Katie toward its edge. If she jumped, there would be no arguments, no punishments, no merciless shaming. If she jumped, would Lucy run to join her? She looked to Lucy who stared back with dark eyes and also began to back toward the edge.

If they jumped, would it be over quick? Would they stay connected until the end?

Her parents slowed their approach.

"Katie," her father yelped, hand outstretched.

Something desperate in his voice shook her loose and she obeyed its greater power. Still, she skirted his grasp and sulked toward the car. The dewy grass had soaked her Converse All-Stars halfway up the ankle and the rubber was slick as a seal. She tripped on a mole hole, slid down the gulley toward the road, and landed on her butt in the rocks.

From the VW Beetle's side window, she watched panting as her parents stomped up to Lucy and hovered nearly as close as Katie had been just moments before.

She pressed her fingertips to the window and her pulse pounded at the glass.

Her father thrust a piece of paper before Lucy's face. Katie realized it was one of their letters—they'd grown careless, talking about Maiden Leap as if they owned it.

Evidence, her mother cried out.

Lucy nodded intently, staring at the ground.

Her mom thrust a finger at Katie sitting huddled in the car and a wave of embarrassment rose up from Katie's stomach.

Lucy shook her head.

Then they left Lucy there in the red dark of the taillights, hand raised, fingertips reaching.

BLOGGING MY SOJOURN

One Woman's Journey from Gay to Straight

For our last tour, the band's contract involved gigging for a radio station contest at the Oregon State Fair. They had a load of losers riding the rollercoaster over and over until the last discombobulated contestant hit the road in a new car. Meanwhile, we played the cheesy-fun-time bandstand as the coaster roared by. The low-rent aroma of grease, cotton candy and chlorine from the lazy river crowded the already thick summer air. Teenagers formed a mosh pit while bemused adults stood on the perimeter. I flicked away on the Rickenbacker thinking, "Every day is just another ride on the same rickety coaster." The peaks and valleys were flattening out.

There was also the matter of the lump my girlfriend had just found in my left breast. I couldn't avoid getting it checked out any longer. I knew I had to make some changes in my life, I just didn't know where to start. So after the gig I walked aimlessly, beer in hand, through the crowds, amidst the smell of the animals and the clamor of the Midway.

Resting in the shade of the Sojourn Reclaimers tent, I recalled the advertisement I'd seen in the back of *Down Home Almanac*. The president, Henry S. Cleaver, caught me standing there between my third and fourth PBR. He gazed into my bloodshot eyes and said it didn't have to be this way. Actually, he merely confirmed it. Such an epiphany is like snuffing out the stump of a candle in the morning—there's little point because it's nearly a pool of wax. I wasn't sure if I liked what he was selling, but I've always been up for an adventure. Tell me more, Henry, I laughed. Tell me more.

Praise Jesus

Posted by Liesl ~ 10:00 AM ~ 3 comments

Rolf68 commented:
Okay, I get it now. You stunk as a musician and gave up. Do you think you were the first dreamer to fail? Adjust your concept of success.

InChrist commented:
Lay off Rolf. I think I know what Liesl is trying to say. She's still a little rough around the edges but she senses the futility in trying to find perfection on this earth.

Patrice commented:
Yes. Only the Lord Jesus can fulfill.

CHAPTER ELEVEN

Samantha

"JUST HOW AWKWARD?" Jamie asked as they walked briskly up the hill to Grace Lutheran. All around, the trees cast periwinkle shadows across the January snow.

Someone had forgot to tell Samantha one crucial thing. From the time she was thirteen, Mom had explained every possible dating scenario from how to maintain fresh breath to how to escape a rapist. The one thing the woman failed to mention was how to hold a conversation with a guy you have little in common with. But Samantha liked Zev, she honestly did. She found him gorgeous in a lanky, shy way. And he smelled like Hawaiian bread (thankfully not meat). And she liked that he was a Jewish hockey jock who wanted to date a Norwegian goth. They laughed at all the same jokes in the movie, and there was plenty of electricity just sitting next to him. If it hadn't been for the big clanging silence between it all, things would have been perfect.

"We have no musical common ground, Jame." Sure, having an older brother meant she could easily chat about famous hockey players and ironically recite OutKast raps, but, "Every time he asked about me I sounded insane." Samantha mimicked baby talk, "Oh, I listen to Goldfrapp and Scissor Sisters." And, "I'm not sure if I want to major in astronomy or primatology. Shut. Up."

"You should be happy he even bothered to ask about you," Jamie said. "A lot of guys don't give a crap. Why don't you play him some crossover music and, um, maybe even explain what's so cool about primate behavior? I love your randomness. Just be yourself. I think that's what he wants."

Jamie halted and stared up at the spire of Grace Lutheran, which thrust its fine point up to the heavens. Samantha nudged her forward. It wasn't like they were going to Church-church—as in Pastor Bob reading from scripture—but Grace Lutheran's basement, for the first choir practice of the New Year. Brace had quit to concentrate on hockey, but there was no way Samantha was missing this season.

The first Saturday afternoon in January, Ms. Van Buren introduced the choir to the music they'd be tackling, Brahms *Requiem*, handing them each a copied

CD and sheet music. Then she grouped the men and women by voice, had them do exercises, then some songs they'd mastered the year before. She even asked Jamie if she'd like to join the sopranos or the tenors, without any commitment of course, for something to do.

The throat clearing around the choir did not go unnoticed.

Jamie declined, her face going pink when everyone turned toward her chair in the corner. She'd only joined Samantha because one of her musical heroes had crash-landed in Wicasa Bluffs, live in the flesh. And through her squirming, it was apparent she now thought coming was a mistake. After all, they were singing about the resurrection of a man she didn't believe existed, let alone woke from the dead and floated up to the sky, a man whose followers occasionally liked to hurl Leviticus quotes at her. Plenty of them in this very room, Samantha reckoned. It also didn't help that Ms. Van Buren was merely dressed in grey slacks and a white button-down, a far cry from the leather stovepipes and tight tank top she wore in videos. Only the shadow of a chest tattoo peeked above her camisole.

At least she wasn't the hard case Samantha feared. Practice only lasted forty-five minutes. But as the others left, there came this, "Brian and Samantha, can you stay for a while?"

"Actually—" Samantha eyed Jamie for assistance, "I have a—a thing."

"Won't take long." Ms. Van Buren rifled through papers on her music stand. "Just want to try out a couple bits here. Everyone else, I'll see you next week."

"Can I go first," good old Brian asked. "I—I have to meet my wife for Lamaze class. Thanks, Sam."

Samantha glared at him. Why did adults constantly steamroll kids? If she'd been an adult man there's no way he would have pulled that. But Brian seemed unrepentant and joined Ms. Van Buren at her upright piano. She drove him up and down the scales and had him recite some German, first in speaking voice then singing from sheet music.

Even though the basement was cool and damp, sweat dripped down Samantha's scalp and into her turtleneck. The moment of truth was bearing down on her.

"Very nice," Ms. Van Buren told him. "Next time, we'll work on controlling those glottal stops. Are you keen on a solo then?"

Keen? That would undoubtedly be Jamie's new word.

"Yes. Absolutely." Maybe it was because he was happy to be done with it and get off to his pregnant wife, but Brian shook Ms. Van Buren's hand vigorously and made for the door.

"Oh, one more thing," she said.

Brian halted, his smile wavering.

"Next time, let Samantha go first."

He balked a little at her brazenness, then, "Sure thing."

After he'd gone Ms. Van Buren turned to Samantha and smiled warmly. Then she chuckled a low easy sound; the generous laughter of a woman who's dealt with all kinds.

Samantha died. Then she came back to life and died again. Like, five times.

"You're nervous."

Samantha gulped. "Yeah."

Ms. Van Buren turned to Jamie. "You girls sing together?"

Jamie laughed. "All the time."

"Well, come on up. Both of you. I don't bite."

They joined her and leaned on the back of the upright piano.

"What do you like to sing the most? When you're just hanging out?"

"Like when no one else can hear?" Jamie asked.

—Oh, please don't. Please don't—

"Cake for Horses."

Ms. Van Buren grinned and nodded. "Well, believe it or not, that emo stuff is not the most challenging. What else?"

"ABBA?"

"Oh my God, you are so embarrassing." Samantha covered her face with her hands.

Jamie nudged her. "Well, we do. Sam's mom listens to it when she cleans the house."

Ms. Van Buren smiled even broader and shook her head. "I'll bet she does. All right, let's give it a try." She leaned down to the piano and tinkled the first tiptoeing notes of "Mamma Mia." The three sang the first verse together then she let them finish. Next they tried "S.O.S."

Ms. Van Buren sat down on the piano bench for a moment, quiet, working the side of her mouth. "You two harmonize really well. And there might be something we can do with that in the future. But, Samantha, I'd like to try you out Movement Five. I know we've only just listened to it today. But would you be willing to take it home and think about it?"

"Um. Well . . ."

"Sam can't read music," Jamie blurted.

"Wow." Samantha glared at her. "Just put that out there for me why don't ya?"

Ms. Van Buren shrugged. "I couldn't at your age either." She reached in her knapsack and pulled out a recorder, like the kind the girls had learned to play

"Hot Cross Buns" on when they were in third grade. "This little guy is pitch perfect. I want you to pick a new note every night, close your eyes, picture it on the staff and sing it. The point is, keep it simple until you're comfortable with each note. It's the basics of language really."

Jamie elbowed Samantha. "Like when apes first learned to talk."

"Uh, sure, sort of," Ms. Van Buren said. "Now I don't want you running the full scale together yet though, that just encourages sliding around."

That couldn't be all there was to it, could it? "Sounds easy enough."

"It will be, for you. Your pitch is tight. Teenage vocal cords are usually flat and sharp like bagpipes. So, try that and if you have time, listen to Movement Five. Okay?"

"Okay. Wow. Thank you." Jamie and Samantha shuffled to the stairs.

"Oh, and Jamie?" Ms. Van Buren called after them. "You need to talk to the school choir director."

"Believe me," Samantha said. "I've tried."

"Yeh," Jamie leaned into the wall as they walked up, "I dunno . . ."

"Mrs. Reynolds is pretty cool," Ms. Van Buren said. "The glee club would welcome a voice like yours. Maybe she'd even arrange an ABBA duet for you two." Her low chuckles followed them up the stairs, reverberating like a panther somewhere deep in a forest.

The walk home was non-stop song and dance.

Unclear as to the date and exact circumstances of their big moment, they nevertheless were convinced it would be jam-packed awesomeness.

"Okay, okay." Jamie nodded. "Maybe I will talk to Miss Reynolds."

"Dude, forget that. Lame, lame, lame. You just get stuck doing cheesy songs and have to go to contests and sell candy bars and junk. Come to the play tryouts with me next week. Nothing's been decided yet. I guarantee, we will kick arse."

Jamie chewed her lip.

"Are you keen," Samantha asked in a muddled accent.

"I'm keen," Jamie returned, like over-stuffed royalty.

"You are so keen."

"We are both very keen, I've noticed."

On it went.

CHAPTER TWELVE

Kate

ON THE HIND side of winter, when the eastern sky blushes early in the morning and a few brave sparrows chirp in damp air, hope blooms in Kate's thoughts. The kids are chasing their dreams on the ice rink and the stage. Erik's business, Taken4Granite, is on the cusp. His formulation of a substrate that out-performs stone countertops and costs less than other man-made materials has won him a meeting with 3M Corporation.

By late morning, as she heads out the door, Kate inhales the promise of spring. And underneath that, the vaguely ominous scent of that which is defrosting in the snow after months of letting Chuck Norris outside unassisted. In her groin, sure as seasons, comes the tear and pinch of ovulation. She thinks little of it as her minivan crosses the bridge to Wicasa Bluffs. The town looks hung over and in need of a hot shower before the real crowds arrive. Christmas, New Years, and Valentine's Day have passed in a bloated procession of buying, selling, eating, drinking. Faded boughs of fir sag from the light posts. Snow lines the boulevards; mixed with sand from the plows, the resulting slush is the same color and consistency of spice cake batter. No driver has committed to a carwash yet and the newly exposed patches of grass need reminding of their addiction to chlorophyll.

Kate parks the minivan at the near-empty Portage Avenue parking lot, which will fill with out-of-town cars come summer. She slings a plastic-wrapped quilt over her shoulders and heads for the Gonzo Fox. It won't be long before she can strap a quilt or two onto the carrier of her old green Schwinn and accomplish exercise and commerce at the same time.

She's only walked a block before halting.

Lucy Van Buren stands in the middle of the sidewalk at Portage and Main wearing her long black coat and feathery dark hair with eyes closed to the porcelain skies of late February. Behind the veil of clouds, the sun hangs like an enormous pearl. And Lucy's like the cat that's picked out a sunny patch of carpeting by the door and purrs there, daring to be tripped over. It's too late for Kate to cross the street. If new Lucy is anything like old Lucy, she already knows she's being watched.

Kate slows her approach to take Lucy in, in all her moody glory. Lucy's worn around the edges, but still the most enigmatic person, besides Claudia Larson, that ever walked these streets. A half dozen openers offer themselves up, none quite fitting for small talk. *So, how's that Sojourn thing working out? Found a husband yet? How thrilling is conducting a small-town choir after Lollapalooza? You do realize there's no mosh pit, right?*

When Kate steps up alongside her, Lucy tilts her head. "Smell that?"

Kate' looks back and forth as she attempts to discern whether Lucy's talking about car exhaust or Northern Roast's burnt java.

"Don't get that smell in Paris." Lucy nods in agreement with herself. "Actually, I think I smelled it in Norway once. In the forest. It's like, I dunno, sap maybe. Sweet. It's really nice. Reminds me of home."

"You are home." The light changes, Kate starts for the crosswalk.

"Oh. Right. Well, there you go." Lucy wraps arms around herself and rocks back on her boots. "Hey, so congrats on Samantha."

"What?" Kate halts.

"The part in *Wicke*d. The play?"

"She got it?"

"Yeah, Elphaba. The lead." Lucy cringes. "Woops, thought you knew. I told her to text me as soon as she found out."

"She only texts me shopping lists." The light goes red again.

"Kid's got some lungs." Lucy licks her lips. "So, about that conversation we had at the church a while back."

"Yeah?"

"I'm sorry, I um, if I hurt your feelings, Katie."

"You didn't."

"Or disappointed you."

"It's none of my business, anymore."

"True."

The traffic light changes.

"Bye." Kate's crosses the street, and over her shoulder yells, "Also, I go by Kate now."

AT THE GONZO Fox, Kate fails to mention the brief encounter and can't concentrate on Ray's adoption discussion. Mark tells her about some complaint the last quilt recipient had and she nods complacently, promising to do better next time.

She'd certainly seen Lucy in town several times now. They'd smiled, waved, offered polite hellos. Mark and Ray were making generous furniture trades for Lucy's cache of art without trouble. Samantha was finally learning how to sing from her diaphragm, for gosh sakes. If they could befriend her, so could Kate. After all, in a small town, you don't have the luxury of protracted warfare. So there is no reason to skulk around all self-righteous and bitter. The woman shaped who she was. Who she is. What if Lucy decided to leave again? Kate would kick herself daily for not getting to know Lucy in whatever crazy form she wished to take.

Maybe Sojourn wasn't all bad. It isn't like Lucy goes around evangelizing. According to the owner of Risdahl's supermarket, she's a bit prickly, but certainly speaks without the usual condescension of the heaven-bound. She even showed up at Mark's production of *Guys & Dolls* where she endured the looks and the murmurs. But forty is still young enough to want and need, far too young to be alone without intimacy. Can there even be a cutoff for such a thing? Anyway, she's far too young to never give again, to never receive. And according to Mark, no men have ascended Bluff Road to volunteer for the Sojourn Reclaimers experiment. But they sure hear plenty of music descending it. Music rattles the panes of the Gainsborough three-story Queen Anne late into the night. Not hymns or opera as tumbles down the hills in the daytime, but rock 'n roll.

Maybe it's that awful Christian rock stuff.

Kate snorts. Nah.

IN THE LATE afternoon, Kate sits in the living room basking in the heat of a particularly sweet-smelling fire from the mulberry tree she ordered a hit on. A pile of mismatched quilt pieces lays at her right with nothing to do. Chuck sputters to her left, legs twitching as he dreams.

It's too hot in here. So hot she can't tell if she's bored, sad, or angry.

She doesn't hear the door open from the garage, yet she knows it has by the whooshing change in air pressure. The fire rises and falls back. Chuck's ear flutters.

"You baking a cake?" Erik asks as he takes the stairs.

"No," she says quietly, "a tree."

"Huh?" His keys hit the mottled tan countertop instead of sliding onto the key pegs she had him install at the top of the stairs the week before.

"How did it go with 3M?"

"All right. Not as well as we'd hoped . . ." And he goes on. Whatever it is that transpired in that windowless conference room, it always works out. Everything just happens, good, then bad, then average, then back again and there's nothing you can do about it but react or choose not to react, which is only another form of reacting, now isn't it?

Erik walks into the living room and looks up from the mail he's sorting through. "Where's dinner?"

"Oh, that."

"Kate, I'm starving."

"Pizza?"

He sighs.

"I'm sorry."

"What's wrong?"

"I feel sort of bad that I had you cut down that tree."

"The mulberry." Erik nods solemnly at Chuck. It was those purple dog turds that finally did it in.

"Yeah. You know?" Kate shakes her head slowly. "Once it burns—it's gone."

Erik squints at her. "Are you on your period already?"

Her words flood out at such a shrill pitch, Kate knows her husband has no idea what she is babbling about. "Life is so transitory, Erik. It just—it just wants to run amok. We're always trying to control it. When it gets too messy," she tosses a hand, "we just clear it all out."

"Have you been drinking?" Erik kneels beside the couch.

She stares at him for a moment.

"I saw Lucy."

His gaze arcs across the ceiling. "Oh, great. All that woman does is upset you."

Chuck's snout invades their embrace; he volunteers his head so that they can scratch it together.

Kate sniffles. "We were talking about Sam's musical. She got the part."

"That's fantastic!"

"I know. I know." Kate tries to smile. "But all I could think about was the promise of youth. How it can all go *so* wrong."

Erik stands and shuffles off to their bedroom to change into sweats. "Sam's gonna be all right. She's got a better noggin on her shoulders than that woman."

"Mmm." Kate stares into the fire. It warms her face, dries Chuck's kisses and the tears that don't want drying.

"Hey, why don't you invite Lucy over for dinner some night? I'd love to grill her on what you were like back then."

Kate glowers at Chuck. His ears flatten.

CHAPTER THIRTEEN

1986
Andern Residence

KATIE HUDDLED UNDER her covers, staring at her princess phone.

After the night her parents found the bed empty and nearly called the cops, the night they found Lucy's love letters and gifts, the night they found the girls together at Maiden Leap—everything changed in the Andern household. Suddenly, the oldest child wasn't someone to look up to. Suddenly, the oldest couldn't even be trusted to babysit her brothers. Everything had to be earned back. And even then, things might never be the same. She yearned for someone who understood.

Katie laid a hand on the receiver. Her ears rang in the silence as she tried to detect any movement from outside her closed door.

She slowly raised the receiver and dialed the Van Burens' number.

Lucy picked up after the first ring. "Hello," She sounded desperate. "Katie. *Katie?*" she whispered.

A distant click sounded on the other line. Katie hung up and sat staring at the now radioactive phone. It rang out and she jumped. She covered her face and the phone stopped in the middle of its second ring.

From downstairs, her father's stern voice insisted, "You are not to call here ever again."

Then came the groan of his weight on the stairs, and Katie steeled herself for another round of talks. There was never so dreary an age as when she could nearly grasp freedom, only to be sharply reminded of the chain still attached.

The final straw came the week Lucy just happened to ride by the Andern farm on her ten-speed every dang evening after supper, a valiant effort in which Katie both delighted and dreaded. She'd go out to water the roses by the driveway, and on the fifth night of drowning the plants her dad caught her laughing and shooting Lucy with the hose as she sped by screaming.

There was only one thing left to do.

"YOU'LL FIND PLAYTIME'S over Ms. Van Buren," Principal Juhl said. "I'm not Hamm and I don't go soft when girls cry."

At the Anderns' insistence, the new principal had arranged a "pow-wow" in his office. He sat the Katie and Lucy right next to each other, their parents flanking them.

Mr. Van Buren sat loose in his chair, a scrappy, curly-haired man who exuded the scent of motor oil and pine needles. Considerably more upright, Mrs. Van Buren appeared on the leathery side of beautiful with high cheekbones, big pouffy hair, and lipstick the color of clotted blood. From her large macramé bag, she pulled out what looked like an elongated change purse. Mrs. Van Buren snapped it open and tapped out a Virgina Slims cigarette, which under normal circumstances would have made Katie giggle because Mark Fox called them vagina slimes. But she couldn't even scare up a nervous titter. Instead, Katie glared at the cigarette case, praying the smoke would set off the sprinklers.

Principal Juhl slid an ashtray across his desk. He knitted his fingers and stared at Lucy as if she were a captured Russian spy.

"We're all very sorry about this." Mrs. Van Buren dragged on her cigarette and talked the smoke out. "Aren't we, Lucinda?"

Lucy sighed. "Not really."

Katie's mom huffed a little at that.

Katie slid down in her chair. Now was definitely not the time for pride or bravery. Things went sooo much easier for kids who acquiesced and then slipped out the back. Lucy was either missing some essential smarts or knew something about adults that Katie didn't.

Mr. Van Buren turned a puckered glare on his child.

"Yes. I'm sorry," Lucy said monotone. "I'm very sorry."

As if that would be enough.

"Now, Katie." Principal Juhl rose from his chair and came to sit on the edge of his desk. This splayed his plaid polyester crotch before Katie directly at eye level. He smelled spicy, like Swisher Sweets cigarillos. "Did a, Ms. Van Buren come on to you in this school?" His sausage-like finger landed on the desk and his fingertip turned purplish.

Katie stared intently at Mrs. Van Buren's cigarette case. It was leather patchwork, made of bright colors and jagged shapes with thick, jaunty stitching—masquerading as harmless quilt work.

"It's okay, honey," her mother said, "This is where it started, right?"

"We became friends here. Sure."

"And a, how far did she go?" Juhl asked lowly.

"Not far. I mean, she didn't—"

"Katie, you can say," her mother insisted. "No one blames you."

Katie shook her head. She would not. She could not.

"Did she—Did she touch you in a bad place?"

Lucy leaked a nearly imperceptible snicker, the same snicker Katie had heard turn into the most joyous laughter a dozen times.

There were boys in school this willful, but never a girl. Katie wanted them to know she wasn't like that. She was a good girl. She could be trusted. She could be serious.

"Katie," her father said with a rumble, "answer."

Katie opened her mouth, pleading silently for mercy, tears gathering in her eyes.

"If you don't answer right this minute, you are grounded for summer. No car. No allowance."

Her bottom lip quivered. Then, "I guess so. Yeah."

"Oh my Lord." Her mother moaned.

Katie chanced a look at Lucy, who closed her eyes, sighed, and then opened them again. From then on she betrayed nothing more than a bulging muscle along her jaw line.

There was no air left in the room. All seven of them had sucked it empty. There was nothing left to breathe but Mrs. Van Buren's smoky exhaust that smelled faintly of coffee. The sound had been sucked out too.

Inside Katie, a rift as wide as the St. Croix cracked and widened between her and Lucy. Was there still time to take it back? She could be brave; she had been brave before. She could prove to Lucy she was worth all of this. Now was the time to walk to the edge and make the leap.

Principal Juhl turned to Lucy. "What do you have to say for yourself young lady?"

Now. Do it. Say something. Lie to them. Save both your skins.

Lucy shrugged. "Whatever."

"You'll serve two weeks detention at lunch or after school, your choice," he said. "And you are not to have any contact with Ms. Andern. Not in school, in town, or on the phone. You're damn lucky you're not eighteen yet, my dear, or the Anderns here could have you arrested for molestation."

"Gary Lindstrom's eighteen," Lucy muttered.

"He's a man." Juhl's upper lip curled over his teeth.

She glared back at him and slid her middle finger up and down along the side of her nose.

"What do you think you're doing?"

"Got an itch." Lucy slowly pulled her hand away but her eyes remained fixed on Juhl, widening with the challenge. "You ever get an itch. Sir?"

"Shut it," Mr. Van Buren said.

"Changed my mind," Juhl said. "I think two week's *suspension* would serve us all best."

"What?" Lucy sat forward. "I should burn this fucking school to the ground," she said with a hiss.

Katie squinched her eyes so tightly shut, tears rolling down, that all she could see was a purple afterimage of the room.

"One more word and I'll ask the board for a full expulsion. One more word and you can forget prom. One—more—word, and you can forget walking graduation with your class." He stood up. "We're done."

"Come here." Mr. Van Buren gripped Lucy's arm, pulled her out of her chair, and out the door. "You're in loads of trouble," he growled from the hall.

"I don't care."

Then came the slap of skin on skin and the metal crunch of the lockers. "If you ever want to see a college campus, you'll shut your disrespectful little hole."

Mrs. Van Buren gathered her things and slipped out the door. "Not here, Ronny. Not here."

"Get to the car. Now!"

Katie gaped in horror at her mother. Her skin crawled. She wanted out of this body. She knew she hadn't pulled the only trigger that day, but she still felt a full member of the firing squad.

BLOGGING MY SOJOURN

One Woman's Journey from Gay to Straight

Cancer is a playground bully. You know, the kid who pulls the wings off flies? There you are, yukking it up with your friends, swinging too high, getting dizzy on the merry-go-round. Then cancer comes out of nowhere, grabs you by the hair, tosses you off the monkey bars and shoves you to the ground. It forces you to see the earth up close and then rolls you over to blind you with the sun.

YOU COUNTERFEIT PUNK. THINK YOU'RE IMMORTAL? WHAT'S THAT IN YOUR TITS? YEAH YOU FELT ME RIGHT. THAT LUMP? THAT'S ME. NOW TRY FLYING WITHOUT WINGS.

I fought back best a person can with a bilateral mastectomy and lymph node dissection. Then with daily pills and monthly capsules shot into my belly with a needle the width of a swizzle stick that tricked my pituitary, shut down my ovaries, and stole my mojo so I could no more rise from the back of the band bus than a woman without a backbone.

Instead of adorning myself in pink ribbons, gathering donations and hobbling around a track with hundreds of other survivors, I plotted a different route. When I rose from the back of that bus centuries later, I quit the band and signed up for Sojourn Reclaimers.

Posted by Liesl ~ 10:00 PM ~ 50 comments

Patrice commented:
You forgot to praise Him. You are still on this earth because of your maker has not finished with you.

Rolf68 commented:

Yeah, that's some god you got there, Patrice. Intelligent design made cancer? Please. Liesl, we are here for you. All you have to do is ask. All you have to do is forgive.

WildeRosemary commented:

My thoughts and prayers are with you today.

RugbyLVR:

Ah, yes. Thoughts and prayers. If only it were so simple. Liesl, please tell us you are doing better.

Comments truncated |

CHAPTER FOURTEEN

Samantha

"GIVE ME AN E!" Brace yelled from downstairs.

Samantha sang out an E flat. "Dang. Hold on." She tooted on the recorder then sang the note out perfectly.

"I'll allow it."

"Gee, thanks."

The dining room table was perfect for homework, with plenty of room to spread out. True, there was Dad and Mom and Chuck spooking around, but usually they were easier to ignore than the Internet glowing next to Samantha's bed. Unfortunately, she had asked all of them to quiz her on music notes and now Brace was more than happy to interrupt any and all activities.

Nearby Mom was tucked in her quilting nook, her sewing machine whirring and stopping, whirring and stopping. She'd been working on this Frankenstein of a quilt for an old friend. It would be made up of all the material she'd collected from past projects. Samantha was no judge of craftwork but sometimes Mom's quilting reminded her of those spiders that scientists feed caffeine to, to make their webs all wonky. This new quilt? Spiders on acid. It looked like Samantha's old calico giraffe threw up all over the place. She preferred Mom's pottery stage when the garage was stacked floor to ceiling with glazed vases and canisters and Samantha was allowed to handle the clay and use the wheel herself.

Mom liked to chew sugarless bubblegum when she concentrated, two and three pieces at a time until her jaw got sore. Something about the snapping and popping and energy dispersal helped her focus. It always made Dad chuckle to see her blowing such huge pink bubbles. Apparently, before the Internet, bubblegum was all kids had to do. On the way down to his den he kissed her head and called her a kid. Samantha wasn't seeing it. But midpoint through graphing her last parabola, something did occur to her.

"Mom."

"Hmm?" a voice said from behind a mountain of fabric.

"Remember telling me that you went to school with one of the musicians from Cake for Horses?"

"Yeah."

"That was Ms. Van Buren, right?"

The answer came muffled, passing for the affirmative.

"What was she like?"

Mom made a cluck through her bubblegum, not quite a laugh, not quite a mumble and the machine whirred again. One foot tapped the control pedal, while the other, out of its slipper, gently rested on Chuck's ribcage, occasionally stroking his fur.

Samantha figured out the "x" value in her quadratic equation and then realized she'd never actually received an answer.

"Well?

"Mmm?"

"What was Lucy Veebee like?"

Mom glanced up. "Well, you know, she was two years ahead of me."

"Oh." Samantha sighed, closed her textbook, and gathered her papers into a stack.

"I do remember the first time I saw her sing."

Samantha sat up. "In a band?"

"No. She was in musicals first. Like you. But she lacked guidance . . ." Mom's voice trailed off, taking her sweet time accessing the databanks.

"She seems so familiar. Like an aunt or something."

"I don't want you getting too close to her." Mom got back to work, slowly and evenly pushing cloth through the machine. She began her aggressive gum chewing again.

"Why?"

"She's your teacher, Sam. Not you girls' buddy. I'm not totally convinced you can trust Ms. Van Buren yet. She's been through that ex-gay program your Gramma's nuts about. What if she tried to get Jamie into it?"

"I told you, Jamie's not gay. She likes boys."

"You know what I mean."

"Not really. I mean, I think you should give Ms. Van Buren a chance. She's really helped my voice and she's cool with Jamie. She can't be all bad."

"I didn't say she was *bad*."

"Grandma believes in Sojourn; we haven't stopped talking to her."

"If she wasn't your grandma, we would." Mom blew a small bubble with a snap. Sometimes Mom's brow bunched in two vertical lines, in what Samantha thought of as the "angry elevens." They were often a harbinger of severe doom-age.

"But, Mom, are we really good people if we're only good to the people it's easy to be good to?"

Mom stopped and squinted into the air. Okay, it hadn't exactly come out perfect, but it had managed to soften those angry elevens. They had been fighting too much lately.

"Uh, how about book recommendations?" Samantha cringed. "Is that getting too close?"

The quilt stopped its progress through the machine and Mom looked up.

"Luc—Ms. Van Buren loaned me a novel," Samantha said. "I mean she did loan Jamie a guitar and all I got was this crusty old book, but it's not bad I guess. It's called *Song of the Lark*. About a girl with a great voice who becomes kind of an opera diva. She has to leave her family and loses a lot for fame. Pretty good so far."

"Hmm. Never heard of it."

"You should really read more books, Mom."

"All right, finish up. It's late."

Samantha headed downstairs. The machine went back to whirring and stopping, whirring and stopping. Then came a wet *pop* and a, "darn it."

But Samantha couldn't sleep.

She logged onto her computer. Jamie was offline. So was Zev.

She Googled: Sojourn Ex-gay

CHAPTER FIFTEEN

Kate

I READ BOOKS!

Kate watches the puck fly back and forth during Brace's hockey game. She crams a handful of popcorn in her mouth. *Plenty of books.* Smart ones too. Not just best sellers, but Mark's recommendations from the indie bookstore (even though they had no plot at all, contained words like *insouciance*, and all anyone ever did was mope around doing meth and/or get themselves molested by truck drivers). Still, the implication irks. From her own daughter. And who told the church choir directors they could pass out fiction? Lucy has some nerve.

The voice of her yoga instructor reminds her to appreciate the moment. This is the first time in a while she's been able to sit in the stands instead of work a fundraiser booth at the game. Now that sort of hassle the junior varsity moms' burden.

"Oh brother," Erik says with moan.

"What?"

Brace is waiting out a crosschecking call in the penalty box like a caged tiger. He presses his helmet against the plexiglas and watches his teammates skate up and down the rink then goes back to pacing. His lips are dry, chapped. Kate knows, up close, they look like the flaking sugar of a glazed donut. His cheeks flush from effort and expectation. His heart beats in the service of winning.

Once he is released, Kate jumps to her feet, bares her teeth, and bellows out across the arena, "Go, baby! *GOOO!*"

This startles Senator Claudia Larson, who has joined the family for the semi-finals. "Oh!" she cries out as the rest of the crowd leaps up and swallows her. "Go, darling!"

Brace sweeps across the rink, passes to Maddox, Maddox flicks the puck to Zev. Samantha's boyfriend meets it with a slapshot into the goal.

Erik growls low. "Yeah. That's my boy." He nods at other parents. "Team player."

Kate yowls even louder now, a Viking raider. She and Erik high-ten. The auditorium fills with a pounding roar. Kate grabs Claudia and shakes her.

Claudia laughs nervously, plumps her hair, looks to the videotron but this time she's not on it.

Samantha guffaws and screams too. Next to her, Jamie yelps then pulls out the stops with a hearty, "Yeah!" after everyone else is finished. A few of the closest spectators turn to gawk at Jamie and then whisper to one another. Jamie dips her forehead and her dark blonde hair falls across her eyes. She and Samantha quickly sit down.

On the rink, Brace scissors over to Maddox, tries to hug him. The boy pats his helmet and hugs Zev instead. It's a subtle maneuver, but clear enough to Kate. Something is going on between her son and his friends.

Between periods, Samantha and Jamie slink off to the concession stand and Erik gallops down to the locker room.

Claudia regards Kate's baggy, blue hockey jersey and matching baseball hat with more amusement than vitriol. She leans in. "You really need more women friends."

"I know some women." Kate shovels in another wad of popcorn.

"Women your own age. Not the quilting bee ladies."

Kate chomps away, swallows just enough to mumble, "I had a chat with the choir director the other day. Ms. Van Buren."

Claudia flicks a popcorn crumb from the number seven crossing Kate's bosom. "Normal women."

Oh, brother. Kate shakes her head. "What about Anita Funk-Abel?"

"Wasn't she a cheerleader when you were in school?"

"Yep. She and I take yoga classes together now."

"Oh, well I like her. That one's a real go-getter."

Kate snorts.

Having been a pompom girl at WBHS in the late fifties, Claudia considers all cheerleaders family. But Anita was by far the wildest girl in school and now the brand of feminist that would set Claudia's high-altitude hair further on end. Anita considers being submissive to one's husband a bedroom novelty act.

"Honestly," Claudia says breezily, "I'm much more concerned about my granddaughter."

"You and me both."

"So you're not happy with her hanging out with this"—Claudia twiddles fingers toward the seats Samantha and Jamie vacated—"this *he/she* either."

"Who, Jamie? Jamie's a doll. I thought you meant Zev."

"Oh, he's the least of our worries. We need his folks on our side."

"But he's two years—wait." Kate frowns. "I thought you didn't like her dating a Jewish boy."

"Ah, I said I had a problem with her marrying one. No, no, no. I love the Jews. Our savior was one. God *knows* I love the Jews. But what are you going to do if they want to get married?"

"They're not getting married. Why in the—?" Then Kate remembers the tender age Claudia had been when she'd become pregnant with Erik, their only child. She had only evolved into a prude over years of self-flagellation.

This discussion has overloaded Kate's debate circuitry. Her eyes glaze as they track the zamboni making its slow, determined way up and down and around the rink. It coats the scarred ice with a glistening sheet. Her eyebrow raises, making sure every cut, every potential trip-up for her son, is polished glass-smooth.

Claudia sighs. "I cannot believe Erik is fine with this Jamie character." *Back for more? Why don't you ask* Erik *for once?* "I've always told Erik a sensitive husband is a dangerous husband."

Kate faces Claudia, stares into frost-blue eyes. "Jamie needs a friend. He's— I'm sorry—*she's* got no one beside her parents."

Claudia matches Kate's defiant gaze. "So you're happy to sacrifice your daughter to this boy's gender experiment?"

"People make sacrifices daily for each other. Life's messy. I dunno. They have fun together. Sam gets as much as she gives. Claudia, I—"

"Well, it really doesn't look good for the campaign. All these perverted strays running around town." Claudia looks away and down at the departing zamboni.

Kate struggles to think of a way to explain the latest development to Claudia. But this isn't the time or place to fully lay it out and savor the response. She licks her lips. Her heart flutters.

Ya see, the thing is, Claudia, Samantha's co-star in Wicked *broke her ankle in gymnastics last week. Ya see. And her understudy—which was initially a pity vote— will be playing opposite Samantha. Yes, Claudia, five-foot-ten Jamie Heathrow will be the first boy to play Glinda the Goodwitch of the North. And hey, doncha know, Ms. Van Buren helped get her the part.*

The period buzzer howls and a massive cheer goes up as the Snow Dogs claim another victory. Brace is headed to the playoffs. As the Larsons exit their seats, Kate watches the rink, the crowd, the lights, all shift in opposite directions. She hasn't felt this discombobulated since she got pregnant with Samantha and feels for the seatbacks for balance. A stop by the twenty-four-hour pharmacy for a test kit seems a good idea.

Outside the locker room, waiting for Erik to emerge from his testosterone-rich haze of nostalgia, Kate leans against the blue-painted cinderblock and gently knocks the back of her skull against it. In the opposite direction of the departing crowd, a familiar head of light brown hair—striped with highlights as bright as banana peels—bounces her way. Anita Funk-Abel opens her mouth wide and waves two-handed at Kate in celebration for their sons.

Somewhere in that ridiculous diatribe, Claudia had stumbled into the truth: Kate lacks a dependable pack of girlfriends. She and Samantha have their little talks, but it's not healthy to lean on her daughter. Kate adores the ladies in the quilting guild, but it's true, they're all nearly two decades older; they provide wisdom but not real-time advice. Claudia herself is fairly worthless when it comes to emotional support. No, Kate had walled herself off from women her own age for some long-forgotten reason.

"Hey girl. Isn't it awesome?" Anita says. "They're gonna to slay the Redhawks."

"No doubt. Coffee tomorrow after Spazzin'?"

"Love to." Anita drums Kate's arm as she glides by and stomps brazenly toward the locker room.

The captain of the WBHS cheerleading squad had scarcely known Katie Andern existed in high school. Anita Funk and her friends had always regarded Katie as if the kid was blocking their view. During the drama with Lucy, Katie had risen a bit from the horde of underclassman but it was mostly for gossip. When Anita's son Maddox was born the same year as Brace, the two mothers became friends. Then Anita landed a real estate job in the cities and Kate dropped from her radar until the past year, when they reconnected at Spa Zen, which Anita couldn't help but dub Spazzin'.

Yoga with Anita is like winning a spot on the varsity squad—laying on mats, stretching this way and that, trying not to fart, giggling at those who do, flirting aimlessly with any unfortunate male passing by, cursing the evil of thong panties, scoffing at the latest impossible diet, and mimicking their sons' gangster slang.

"SO, WHAT ARE we going to do about Glinda the Manwich?" Anita asks the next day at Northern Roast. "That's what Maddox calls Jamie Heathrow now."

"We'll make way," Kate says. "Yes, I'm serious."

"I just don't understand that whole sex-change thing. Why would you get your penis lobbed off? They're so nice."

"It hasn't come to that."

"For that matter can you even imagine changing into a man?"

"Only for shorter bathroom lines."

"Honestly, why bother?" Anita asks. "We all end up looking like Clint Eastwood anyway."

"You have to admit, Jamie's always been a girl at heart."

"Yeah, I suppose so," Anita says. "A good kid too. But what if her voice drops?"

"That would be a disaster." Kate searches the air. "God, I hope Miss Reynolds planned for that. Lucy Veebee put in a good word. Hope it doesn't bite her in the ass."

"I bet mother-in-law dearest is thrilled, I can just imagine your family gatherings."

"Yeah, it's all running like a finely tuned hairball." Kate counts off on her fingers. "Sam expects me to let out Jamie's costume, the senator wants me to stuff envelopes for her campaign, Mark is gearing up for another protest at the capitol. Piece of cake."

Anita snickers.

"I swear, Erik and I are two steps behind. It's like when the kids were young and ripping up the house. Only now we walk on eggshells over Sam's moods and Brace gets more opaque each day. In mean, I'd rather deal with diapers right now actually."

"Oh, just have sex. Nothing holds the family together like satisfied parents."

"Trust me, that's the only thing I can count on. Had to pee on a stick last night to make sure I wasn't pregnant again."

"My God can you imagine? Our bodies are conspiring against us, I'm telling you." Anita shifts in her seat, straightens her back, loosens it again. "I'm hornier than I was in high school. Feel like one of those sex-starved women you see on soaps."

Kate glances over the back of the booth for any prying eyes or ears. "That's totally normal. Sometimes I—"

Anita screeches, "Really? You too?"

"Well—"

"My cousin Jessica says it's a last ditch effort by our uteruses."

"Great," Kate says. "That is so me, by the book and right on schedule."

"Well, enjoy it while you can cause it's all gonna dry up and blow away."

Kate tries not to picture any part of herself doing such a thing.

"No, no, no—not to worry. If ya use it, ya never lose it. Jessica showed me the light at the end of the tunnel. It's called the happy caterpillar. I'm wearing it right now."

Kate shrinks back. "Umm." Hopefully it won't metamorphize anytime soon.

"It's so awesome. It's tucked in there. Got GPS or Bluetooth or something. Rob can text me at any time to activate it. Devil. It's really disconcerting. I never know when he's going to buzz me. They're still working out the kinks on the guy model, but when they do, he's *so* going to get it." Anita goes hazy for a moment then her hand leaps out to grasp Kate's. "So, anyways, I'm hosting a Private Pleasures party. And I expect you to be there."

Kate's eyes widen. "I—"

"Yep, erotic products. Put extra spice in your bedroom."

Kate pulls away, waves hands. "We do not need spice. It's mild to medium."

The door to Northern Roast bangs open; Lucy Van Buren shuffles in wearing a pair of wayfarer sunglasses so black they look as if she lifted them from a blind man. The feathers have fallen; her hair has gone shag. She's wearing torn jeans and a yellow plaid, paint-stained shirt (two sizes too small and buttoned wrong). She shuffles up to the barista's counter and gapes at the menu. She rubs fingers up under her glasses, drags them down her face, her bottom lip.

" . . . Jessica is top sales gal in all of Ramsey and Hennepin County," Anita continues on. "Who knew St. Paul was randier than Minneapolis? I know, but it's true. Conservatives. Anyways, she's helping me start my own little division. I'm mailing invitations this week."

"Yeah, wow. Anita. I dunno."

"Don't worry. It's going to be a blast. I'll have buckets of sangria. You can bring those nummy peanut butter thingies. Remember Jenny Braden? She's totally in. See? Just regular girls. Nothing crazy. It's not like we're going to look at our vaginas with mirrors or anything!"

"Augh." Kate raises a hand to brow, shielding herself from the stares of other customers. They didn't make Anita captain of the cheer squad for nothing.

"Oh, Katie. Grow up. I thought you were down with all that stuff."

"All right, what the hell. But only on one condition."

"Name it."

"Come with me to Mark's next Civil Diss protest."

"Do we have to ride in that giant flower bush?"

Kate bursts out laughing. The Shakespeare Under The Bluffs bus, the one he painted with roses. "Yes. That's the fun part."

"Okay." Anita smirks, her lozenge-blue eyes twinkle as she considers it. She wiggles her eyebrows. "It'll be just like an away game." She herds her cellphone, lipstick, and pilfered Equal packets into her Coco Chanel purse. "Bring a gal pal to my party. You'll get a twenty percent discount." She rises. "Hey, bring the senator," and hoots as she flicks fingernails over her shoulder.

Kate discovers that iced coffee through the nose is not a pleasant experience.

"Hey, Lucinda," Anita says as she swishes out.

"Huh?" Lucy whirls around. "Oh, hi—" She spots Kate and pushes down her glasses.

Kate edges out of the booth and fires a finger pistol. "Got something for you in the car."

Lucy looks over her shoulder, as if Kate's talking to someone else. "Oh, yeh?" She slides her venti cup from the counter, drops some change in the tip jar and mumbles, "Thanks."

They walk to Kate's minivan.

"It's a crazy quilt," Kate says. *Damn*, she was never good at surprises.

Lucy's mouth twists to the side. "For crazy people. Very funny."

Kate stops walking as if shot through the heart.

"You serious?" Lucy asks. Her grin stretches wide. She sucks at her coffee cup. "Yow!" She blows in the hole and it sputters more hot coffee at her.

"You deserved that." Instead of using the key fob, Kate yanks hard on the minivan's side door and it rolls open with a bang. She reaches in, grabs a plastic wrapped bundle, and pushes it at Lucy. "Here, you ingrate."

Lucy sets her coffee on the roof of Kate's van and tears open the plastic. Her fingers wander over the quilt and her gaze drifts as if she's reading Braille. She traces the gold zigzags, decoratively large (the functional stitches lie underneath), then unfurls the quilt without letting it touch asphalt. She smooths her palm across the copper velour patch, the v-formation of Canada geese in embroidery floss, the ebony satin, the crimson, the eggplant-colored paisley, and the calico border. It's all scattered like a bird's eye view of European farmland. In fact, Lucy stares wistfully at the crooked landscape as if she once lived in this province.

"Wow. I can't take this."

"Why not?"

"It's." Lucy gulps. "It's too nice."

"Nah, it's just my remnants."

"Oh. So I get your leftovers."

"Listen. I thought you would like the eclecticism of it. I worked day and night on it. It's kind of a thank you for helping out Sam and Jamie so much."

"Mark said your quilts were something else, but, I had no idea."

"Erik says it's a compulsion. Instead of literally smothering my children, I make quilts."

"So that's all you do? Like, for a job?"

"Well, I handle the books for Erik's business. Sometimes I volunteer at the animal shelter."

"I remember you wanted to be a vet."

"Did I?"

"Yeah, you were so mad at your dad when your dog died. That if you had been there it wouldn't have happened or you could have at least saved her."

"Oh, I was so dramatic."

"You would have made a great animal doc. Whatever happened to the horse balls?"

Kate laughs. "The *what*?"

"Those animal cakes."

"Oh, yeah, I forgot we called them that. My parents insisted I call them Horse Nuggets. Actually that went really well. Erik sold the business to Purina to fund Taken4Granite."

"Your husband made you sell your business for his?"

"Well, he didn't make me. It just—it just made sense."

Lucy nods politely.

"Yeah, so let me know if you need new countertops. He'll do them for you at cost."

"Ah. Okay, awesome." Lucy looks back down. "But this . . ." She holds up the quilt. "Do you realize what you create will last longer, be more appreciated, and have more to say about our culture fifty years down the line than any song I ever wrote? No, really—I used to scoff at crafts." She stretches the blanket out and holds it up between them. "But now I understand."

Kate pokes her head around. "Yeah, Well, I just thought, you know, whenever you need to—you just wrap yourself up in it. You know and . . ."

"Ahhh." Lucy nods. "So that's how these work."

"Shut up. Anyway, see, I made the backing musical notes. Lame, I know but—"

"Thank you *so* much." Lucy starts forward then seizes up. "Oh, you." She rubs a hand on Kate's shoulder. It's completely pathetic.

"You're welcome. So about this book you loaned Sam." Kate opens the driver's door and slides in. "It's appropriate, right?"

"Of course. There's a death or two in it I think, but—"

"Nothing religious?"

"No, no. It's about the costs of stardom. I'd hate to see Samantha go the pop star route."

"She cares more about real stars, trust me. So what's on your calendar next week?"

Lucy taps her chin. "Well, there is that costume ball at the prince's castle on Saturday."

"You are almost funny," Kate says.

"Oh, and I got the new Burpee seed catalog this morning. It's like porn for gardeners." Lucy hugs her new quilt with one arm and grabs her coffee off the roof. "Honestly, besides choir practice, schedule's mostly about putting off redecorating."

"Good. Erik has plans for you."

"Wha—?"

"I'll give you a buzz." Kate closes the door and starts the car.

Lucy crosses the street in front of her and they wave at each other.

Kate turns the key again only to be rewarded with the indignant screech of the starter.

"Woops. *Shit*. Ha-ha. Bye!"

CHAPTER SIXTEEN

1986
Wicasa Bluffs High School

"YOU SMELL GREAT," Gary said, grinning down at Katie as they danced.

"Thanks." She smiled weakly. He smelled like a thrift shop, the scent of celebrations past cloying to his rented polyester tux.

Attending prom with a senior boy was every sophomore girl's dream, but Katie Andern had only agreed to go for her parents and because breaking up with Gary Lindstrom that spring would have only fueled the rumors. Talk was Lucy Van Buren had been suspended for two weeks for some mysterious stunt and everyone looked to Mark and Katie for answers. The two told lie after lie involving graffiti, truancy, illegal fireworks. The only truth Katie managed to offer was that her parents didn't want her around the miscreant—so, no, she did not know how Lucy was doing.

Mark knew, however. Lucy had been working days at her father's tractor supply and repair shop. Every night after the garage closed, Mark and Lucy's band practiced songs for prom. It was the only thing keeping her afloat, he'd said. In fact, she was pretty damn stoked. By prom, the bruise around her eye would be mostly gone. She'd asked Mark to be her date, to keep up appearances, and promised they didn't have to wear formal attire like the other "hosers and posers" because they were the entertainment. She was even going to sneak in a bottle of gin she'd lifted from her dad's liquor cabinet.

Sweet lilac drifted on the breeze that night and Katie wore a simple, sleeveless satin dress the color of spring leaves. Prom's theme was British royalty and all the couples posed for pictures on a wobbly Tower Bridge replica built by the shop class. Anita Funk won queen and a teacher placed a brass and red velvet facsimile of Queen Elizabeth's crown on her maxed out blond hair. The hired band played a slow dance for the court and then took a break to humor Mark and Lucy's little ensemble.

"What a joke," Gary said.

While he and his friends stood and sniggered, Katie wandered from them toward the stage.

Lucy Veebee shakily plugged her guitar into the other band's amp. It buzzed and squawked until she turned it down, but this had at least served to gain full attention. Natch, she looked amazing and fuck-all-yas in her black and white striped tank top and purple lamé trousers. Katie's heart fluttered in her chest and her breath came light and ragged. She glanced around the crowd to see if any of the other kids could tell what was happening to her. But all eyes were trained on the stage in various states of credulity.

Mark Fox, looking like a Miami Vice detective in his white suit and sunglasses, stumbled up to the keyboard nearly knocking it over. One of the marching band drummers, sporting a powder blue tux, settled into the hired band's kit and twirled his sticks.

Mark nervously punched buttons on his keyboard and the auditorium filled with cascading melody. In response, the drummer stabbed around to locate the beat. Then Lucy quickly strummed her guitar and the PA system screeched, so she rolled her volume knob down. After a few bars they seemed relatively in control of the noise they were making and lurched into Duran Duran's "Girls on Film." Mark sang leads. Lucy harmonized and played a little too fast, but the kids started dancing, and they kept dancing even after the synth-pop disco beat switched to thrashy punk for the Violent Femmes song "Blister in the Sun."

Katie's skin tingled. She couldn't be sure if the band had won the kids over with their talent or if their schoolmates had merely elevated Lucy to a new echelon of coolness because of all the recent vandalism she was supposedly inflicting upon the innocent citizens of Wicasa Bluffs. One thing was for sure Lucy and Mark were buzzed and getting even higher on gin-spiked punch.

What was the point in staying, stranded here on the periphery? Katie wondered. Gary refused to dance to New Wave music and only wanted to stand along the wall and make out. Lucy was never going to speak to her, even if she'd wanted to. And Katie herself was in no mood to watch the two tumble drunk off the stage and get themselves in further trouble.

She threaded back through the crowd and found Gary. "I'm not feeling well," she told him.

"Want me to take you home?" he said.

Though she expected disappointment, he wiggled his eyebrows at his buddies; the sooner he got her in his car the better.

"Yes, please," she said, "give me five minutes."

On her way out, Katie looked to the stage once more. Lucy stared blindly into the lights as she sang, her face shining from sweat and makeup sparkles.

I don't have a chance anymore. It's too late.

Now Katie really did feel queasy. But she had to try. Just one last shot. She snuck off down the hallway toward the classrooms. She pulled the note she'd folded into a triangle from her sequined purse and slipped it through the vent of Lucy's locker.

Welcome Back Lucy.

I am a million times sorry. I know you probably hate me. But I dream about you every night and even when I can't sleep I'm still dreaming of you. All I can see is your father hurting you. I wish I had stood up to them. I really do. But I am trapped here. You have to know that. I've got to stay in their good graces. I get my license in a few weeks. And they promised me the Beetle if I keep my grades up and stay out of trouble. I just need a few more weeks . . .

(Okay, I counted all the "I's" in this letter. As in "I am so selfish.")

Please, please, please tell me you forgive me. But don't write back. It's too dangerous. Tell Mark, okay? Tell him what I need to hear. Tell him nothing's changed in your heart.

I love you. I always will.

Katie

At school the following week, Lucy continued to ignore her. And though it was logical, it stung. But the week after that, Mark presented Katie with a manila folder labeled with strange lettering. The cardstock inside held a set of the English alphabet and a matching foreign alphabet that looked almost Asian. Katie would need to memorize these hieroglyphics and hand the language key back to Mark before Lucy would send her actual correspondence.

When it arrived the week before graduation, this is what the note translated to:

Meet me at Bikini Tree.
Saturday at 9pm.
Tell no one.
Not even Mark.

BLOGGING MY SOJOURN

One Woman's Journey from Gay to Straight

The Sojourn Reclaimers campus is a quadrangle of metal fabricated buildings in rural Texas that used to be a turkey conversion factory. How exactly a turkey is converted, I'm not sure, but hopefully it is a swift and merciful process. Above the office door a laser-printed sign meant to look like cross-stitch reads, MAY ALL WHO ENTER, LEAVE UNBURDENED. A great comfort to the turkeys I'm sure.

On Day One, the intake clergy ask you to turn in any sort of homosexual articles you are wearing. I mean, it's not like we're wearing cock rings and dildos, yunno? Anyway, by this time, you've signed five pages of forms and are trying not to look at women. You don't want them to get the wrong idea, after all. Nor do you want the men to, since you would look like an eager beaver. So you stare at the ceiling, then the floor, while your lips retreat into your mouth and you consider bolting. But it's 20 miles to the next dusty town and you've already changed into the Sojourn-issue denim jumper dress and croc sandals. This ensemble declares to roving bands of polygamists, "I'm feminine, yet sensible. And I'd like to be one of your eight wives."

Now, it may seem odd to you that I'd gone from hardcore rocker to cancer survivor to potential sisterwife just like that, but there was an odd kind of synergy to it. I was running on miniscule hormones, after all, like a chalkboard erased. If ever there was a time to rewrite my formula, this was it.

Praise Jesus

Posted by Liesl ~ 6:45 PM ~ 30 comments

Patrice commented:
You know, I distinctly detect a note of sarcasm in this post and I really think it's inappropriate. There is a time and place for humor but it has no place alongside Jesus. Jesus was not a funny man.

WildeRosemary commented:
He may have shared a few light-hearted, strictly g-rated jokes with his disciples???

Patrice commented:
JESUS WAS NOT A CLOWN!

RugbyLVR commented:
ROFLMAO. You people need to take this show on the road. Come on Liesl, your heart's not in this thing. Throw off the crocs and run!

Comments truncated |

CHAPTER SEVENTEEN

Samantha

MOM YELLED FROM upstairs, "Supper!"

The smell of pork roast was heavenly goodness, Samantha's stomach begging noisily with her to get off the phone and come out of the carnivore closet. She'd been gabbing with Jamie for a half hour, neither of them believing for a second *Blogging My Sojourn* was some amazing coincidence. It had to be Lucy Veebee and the town had to be Wicasa Bluffs.

As soon as Samantha sat down at the table, Brace grumbled, "Potatoes."

Mom picked up the serving bowl but held it back. "Potatoes, *please?*"

His jaw hardened. "Yeah, what you said."

"Brace?"

He dropped his fork, sat back. "Forget it, I don't want the stupid potatoes."

Dad glowered at him. "You just beat the pants off the Icemen not twenty-four hours ago, what's with the mood? Is this about what went down in the locker room?"

"No." Brace turned to Samantha. "Hey, little comet. Gimme a roll."

She squinted at him. "Have you been reading my journal?"

"Like I care." He laughed. "It was open on the counter."

Samantha hurled a Pillsbury biscuit at Brace, her fury heightened by the proximity of pork roast glistening with reduction. "Mom. Brace looked in my journal." She reminded herself how disgusting meat looked taken out of the context of its scent, chunks all brown and stringy, the horrid death required to put it on the table. Pigs, for all their bad press, were highly intelligent. Nobody knew, or apparently cared to know, that they were smarter than the family pet, their flesh the closest to primate flesh.

"Sam, do *not* throw food."

"But *Mah-um*, it's got poetry in it. Private poetry."

Brace's gaze went distant, his voice airy. "Poetry to the stars. You and Jamie write that on Maiden Leap?" He sniggered.

"Shut up."

Dad straightened. "What are you doing up on the Leap?"

"Watching the northern lights. Luce was out there too."

Mom's fork stopped mid-air.

Samantha nodded. "She helped us find Andromeda. Got this awesome pair of binoculars, nearly a foot long."

"*Luce?*" Mom asked, "She's Ms. Van Buren to you."

"Bet that's not the only thing she's got's a foot long," Brace said. "And she's probably looking in bedrooms with them."

"They're astro-binoculars, puckhead."

"Sam, don't call your brother that. You know we don't like it." Mom set down her fork and looked to Brace. "Stop teasing your sister. And stop changing the subject. I want to know what went down in the locker room."

Samantha leaned forward. "Yeah. Hmm?" She refrained from mentioning the zit coming out on the tip of her brother's nose. Not that it required any aid in drawing attention to itself. A disgusted look at the angry red dot halted his attack. He filled his mouth with more bread and a big stringy piece of pork.

Mom turned to Dad with raised eyebrows.

"Well, it wasn't physical," Dad said, "but Zev and Brace were arguing with Maddox about something when I got there."

Samantha glowered. Ah, Maddox Funk-Abel, the asshole who once poured a pot of coffee in his parent's fish tank to see if the blue tangs would swim faster. The one who still calls Jamie Snowplow even though her braces came off a year ago. The one who upskirts photos of the girls in the halls of WBHS.

"Oh, thanks, Dad," Brace mumbled.

Samantha sat back. "I think the problem with men is they bury too much stuff."

Brace swallowed. "The problem with women is they think too much and never get any smarter."

"Brace." Mom's green-eyed stare was insistent. That was *The Deal* you made when you sat down at the table, not that you had a choice. "I really want to know what happened."

He looked at her, his tongue rooting around, considering his non-existent options.

For over a decade, Samantha's family had come together at this oak table for a real meal and dessert. The dining room had hosted homework sessions, tax paperwork, epic Monopoly games, debates on God. But since Brace's senior year, he'd become less inquisitive, more private and the suppers ended whenever his cellphone hammered out Linkin Park.

"It started with Sam," Brace said. "Some of the guys were kidding Zev about her."

"Who?" Samantha's shoulders tightened, internal bells clanging. "Whatdtheysay?"

Brace squinched his face angrily. "It doesn't matter. Just riding him, y'know? About scoring and stuff."

Samantha turned to her mother. "He hasn't scored, Mom. Nowhere close to the goal."

Mom nodded. But her stare remained locked on Brace.

He looked at his plate. "Zev was just saying about how nice Sam looked and Maddox was like, 'yeah I'd hit that, but it would probably hit back.' Zev got real pissed. And even I'm like, 'Hey, dude, she's not even sixteen yet.' And get this, Maddox says, 'Zev's not getting any because Sam's just like her mom—a *vag*etarian.' Can you believe that?" Brace shook his head with an incredulous smile then shrugged. "Guess I shoved him. A little."

Mom and Dad looked at each other.

Brace's smile dropped.

Samantha flicked her hair out of her eyes. "I'm not a lesbian. Although I did sort of kiss Ashley Parks in fourth grade."

Dad grunted his approval of the meal through a full mouth. Mom stared through the table to some distant dimension.

"But that was just because we ran into each other with our lips."

"Mom?" Brace asked.

Dad flicked a look at Mom. "Guess a few people are talking about it now that Lucy's back." He drew his thumbnail down the cleft between his nose and upper lip a few times. "So their kids are probably over-hearing the stories."

HOLY FRAK.

Samantha whirled on Mom and yelped, "Lucy Veebee? No. Effing. Way."

Brace cringed at Mom. "You had an *affair*?"

"No," Mom said to the ceiling. "It was way back in high school. You know I haven't always been old. I had my own desires—"

He plugged his ears. "Lalalalalalala."

"Stop it," Dad said, trying not to laugh. "It was really traumatic for your mom. Their parents weren't very understanding."

Brace shuddered, his wavy locks tousling. "Can we forget I mentioned it?"

"Well, it's no different than your father having dated Jennifer Turnquist," Mom said. "We've had this discussion about gay people a million times. You know how I feel about Mark and Ray. Despite what your grandparents say—"

"Human sexuality is fluid and on a continuum." Samantha nodded once. *Wow.* For a moment she gazed upon her mother like she used to, when the woman was the primary person in charge of her enlightenment. The gaze quickly turned to a cringe as she pondered again the discordance of Lucy Veebee having anything to do with such a boring parental unit.

But Mom did not meet her eyes. She did not appear to be quite as contemplative. Not even that gleam of old people pride.

Dad turned back to Brace. "You better start getting your head around it, bud. Because we invited Lucy for dinner next week."

"Alright. Whatever."

After clearing the table and fighting with Brace over who would wash and who would dry, Samantha casually sauntered to the stairs.

Once around the corner, she ran down to the basement, into her room, quietly shut the door, and called Jamie.

CHAPTER EIGHTEEN

Kate

"BEHOLD, LADIES. THE Bluejay." Anita raises her wildest Private Pleasures offering so far—the grand finale.

This sex toy resembles a blue and white tie-dyed letter J and isn't as rigid as the other cutesy, animal-named contraptions. It wobbles slightly in the air, alluding to a surly personality.

"Now," Anita says, serious as a preacher, "there are certain times when a man likes his wife to drive stick."

The women pass the Bluejay around over skirts of Burberry tan, black and red plaid cashmere (that ready-made badge of taste), past conservative twin sets, and eyelids fluttering best they can under the weight of mascara and falsies, through moisturized hands and expensive manicures. As the Bluejay bounces from one giggler to the next, so begins a discussion about the prostate gland and the lengths the brave and the few have gone to ferret it out. As if truffle hunting.

Kate chortles along with the others. Erik would endure it if she asked, maybe even come to enjoy it. He'd asked her to use her finger before. So when Felice hands her the Bluejay, dangling it as if it were a dead rodent, Kate does not immediately fling it to the next woman in the game of hot potato some have played. She observes the double-ended dildo clinically. She runs a thumb over the split underneath of the head, the glans being the only realistic feature on the silicon sculpture. Past the wide middle (a sort of flange) is the smaller end, the curve of the J. As Anita has all too thoroughly explained, this is for the wearer's enjoyment.

Felice mutters to her left, "I think Keith would laugh me right out of the bedroom."

"Well, Jerry wouldn't," Brandy says to her right. "That's right up his alley." She clowns a face and her head wobbles. "So to speak."

The gals screech. *Jerry!*

"Kate," Anita says with a wicked simper, "you should have brought Lucy. She could have shown us how it works." The women titter again. Anita straightens. "I'm serious."

"Ha. Ha." Kate rolls her eyes, sighs. But the thought of Lucy doing the honors to her husband is tucked in a mental drawer for later consideration. "Here you go, stud." She sets The Bluejay on Brandy's lap and rises quickly for another sangria. She smacks her lips. *No. Coffee, black.* She's sinking in a quicksand of sugar, alcohol, and the scent of raspberry lube.

Anita jumps up and follows her to the kitchen pass through. "Guess what, kid. I'm in love all over again."

"Congratulations." Kate reaches for the coffee decanter. "I hope it takes rechargeables."

"Kate," Anita whispers with such force she spritzes Kate's cheek. "This is not about product. This is burning. A real want, need, shake-you-to-the-core-and-make-you-want-to-rip-your-hair-out kind of burning."

"Oh, I'm happy for you two." Kate nods and sips bitter over-cooked coffee. It scorches her tongue. *Great.* She's going to get one of those painful, little bumps she can't stop scraping across her teeth.

"Well, don't be." Anita looks out over her now fully eroticized customers. "He's only twenty-one."

"Wait. Who." Kate sets down the coffee. "Anita."

"Shhh."

"Oh my God. You are married."

"Wellll. Actually. Rob has a cuckold fetish. He's thinking about being okay with it. Christophe teaches grade school. He's very non-threatening."

I need to get out of this sex cult and start another quilt.

"I don't know how you do it," Kate says. "Without one of you getting mad."

Anita shrugs. "I dunno, we make each other laugh. Doesn't Erik make you laugh?"

Kate thinks of Erik's red belt in a local offshoot of Kung Fu that seems to mostly consist of clawing rapidly at the air.

"Not intentionally," Kate mumbles. "Listen, 'Nita, about our other boys."

Anita huddles in. "Yeah? What's up?"

"Apparently there's some friction between Maddox and Brace."

"No way."

"Yeah. I guess Maddox was trolling Brace in front of the UW hockey scout, throwing him off his game."

"Well, Maddox is an all-around better player."

"Ha, very funny. No, he was specifically joking about Jamie's transition and my past with Lucy right in front of the scout. Apparently even Zev turned three shades of pink."

"Oh, gawd. I'm sorry. I'll say something to him. That little shit. He's harder and harder to talk to these days. And Rob only eggs him on." Anita gazes through the pass through. "The school called the other day about a girl he's been hazing."

"Seriously?"

"Mmm." Anita looks again to her customers. "Oooch, the natives are restless. We still on for the riot?"

Kate lurches. "The what?"

"The Civil Diss protest. Hello." She backs out of the kitchen. "Already got my sign made." She marquees the air. "I'M THE BIGGEST THREAT TO MY MARRIAGE."

"Oh, yeh. 'Course."

Anita cha-chas back to the front room. "All right, ladies, let's see how we strap this baby on. Then we'll draw for the free Brazilian wax."

Kate flinches. She has no desire to have her hair ripped out from Virginia City to Astoria. Why is all of this so easy for Anita? It's like she hasn't a qualm about anything. *Qualms are a good thing. Do I have enough qualms? Or too many? What the hell kind of word is qualm, anyway? Sounds religious.* Some couples loved to test the elasticity of their marriage, had to create drama for it to work. And that sneaking voice in Kate, the same inference she heard during gossip about the Funk-Abels, had always said that the two didn't love one another enough, respect one another enough.

Tonight, the opposite possibility breezes through Kate like straight-line winds crossing the prairies and pouring down the cliffs.

What if they're doing it right?

CHAPTER NINETEEN

1986
Wilson Park

THE STREETS OF San Francisco had nothing on the streets of Wicasa Bluffs. It took the skill of a Grand Prix driver to master a stick shift on the small town's steep and winding roads. But Katie had practiced throughout the year with her father instructing from the passenger seat. The Beetle was underpowered but sturdy and he preferred her wings clipped these days.

When she pulled into the lot at Wilson Park, Lucy's escape pod was nowhere to be seen.

Suddenly the driver's side window darkened and Katie jumped. "Ohgosh."

Lucy knelt down and tapped on the glass.

Katie rolled down the window. "Hi." She was so petrified, the last thing on her mind was romance. Even though the scent of Lucy—the oil of her scalp, the Fruit Stripe gum on her breath—pressed at Katie like an exquisite memory.

"You're gonna have to park down the street. The cops sweep this lot every half hour."

"Okay. I'll be right back."

"I know." Lucy winked, first time at Katie in weeks. Under her stare it took three tries to start the car.

Katie traced the footpath into the park, shivering as if it were cold out. But it wasn't anymore. The air had grown thick and seductive with summer's promise. She walked deep into the thicket where Bikini Tree, an old growth sycamore stood like a giant woman upended and buried to the waist. Many a kid had carved their angst on the two trunks, which split close to the ground with an obscene rip in the bark at the middle. Every spring it got a new pair of spray-painted bikini bottoms. That year, the theme had been hot pink with white polka dots.

"Hey Andirons," came a deep voice from above. "You changed your hair."

Katie twirled around, the limbs above spinning in the violet sunset.

"What are you doing up there?"

"Arts and crafts." Lucy had straddled one of the trunks of Bikini Tree, high up, working hard with a long butterfly knife and blowing shavings out of the heart she'd carved. "There you go, Katherine Louise. Can you see it?"

$$LVB$$
$$+$$
$$KLA$$

"Wow, does that mean we're married?" Katie sat down, cross-legged in the grass.

"Sure. Sounds good to me."

"Hey, where's your middle initial?"

"Don't have one."

"What?"

"We couldn't afford it." Lucy folded up the knife, pocketed it. "Just call me Van."

She could hear the smile in Lucy's voice. But what new parent refused a middle name in the hospital?

"Oh, fark." Lucy looked around. "I can't get down."

"Yes, you can." Katie lay back, gazing at the newborn stars and giggling. "You got up there, silly."

"Yeah but it was lighter out then. Katie, oh man—" Lucy shifted this way and that, slipped a bit and then hugged the trunk. "Oh shit. I can't."

Katie got up and went to the maple as she had once done to get her cat down from the backyard apple tree. She cried tears of laughter as Lucy hummed nervously and inched down into her arms. In the remaining light, she glistened with perspiration.

"I've never seen you so scared," Katie said softly.

"Sorry."

"Why? You risked life and limb." Katie brushed the wood from Lucy's white t-shirt. Tonight Lucy's bangs fell straight across her forehead, a few strands stuck to her moist skin and Katie brushed them back too. "All five feet up. Okay, maybe just limb."

"You got funny." Lucy's smile dropped, her dark eyes darting. She gulped.

Katie lifted a hand to Lucy's cheek. Lucy closed her eyes and drew a breath. Was this where he had slapped her? How could you raise up a child only to knock them down? Katie's mother had chased her around the house once with a wooden serving spoon, but it had turned to laughter between them before she could strike a blow.

"I'm sorry, Luce. I'm so sorry." She kissed her once on that cheek and then turned Lucy's face to kiss the eyelid where Mark said her dad had punched her.

Lucy's brow gathered, she shook her head and whispered something. Then she kissed Katie deeply before Katie could ask what it was. They fell into each other like stepping off Maiden Leap, but instead of sharp rocks or frozen river, they met silky heat. The corded bark of Bikini Tree pressing into Katie's back seemed the only thing left anchoring her to the world and the responsibilities of a sixteen-year-old.

Lucy had not brought a blanket. Katie had left hers in the car for fear of looking desperate. But there was never so desperate a feeling as *right this very moment*. She cupped the warm curve of Lucy's breast and watched devoutly as Lucy's hand smoothed up her bare thigh and under her skirt. Katie had touched herself many times, known adult pleasure already, but was not prepared for the spike of urgency that came with the feathery stroke of her first lover. She cried out, despite her innate shyness, and came alive in Lucy's arms. Then she returned the favor.

LATER, THEY LAY in the gloaming light, holding hands on grass soft as rabbit's fur. Katie ignored the chiggers likely making inroads on her exposed legs and arms. She had just had real sex. Not the kind that ticked off the boxes, the kind you do with someone who loves you back. Now she knew what all the fuss was about.

"Oh. Check this out." Lucy pulled out a wrinkled business card. Katie peered at it by the light of Lucy's glow-in-the-dark Swatch.

Kurt Jones
The Surf Daddies
668-8094

"The guitarist in that band at prom," Lucy said. "Knows somebody in Minneapolis looking for a girl bass player."

"You know how to play bass?"

"Nope. I'll figure it out. You can figure out anything. You know that, right?"

"You can. Me? Not so sure."

"Of course you can. It's all about visualization. Ya just gotta jump, Katie, and worry about the landing later." Lucy drew up on her elbow. "You know what you want to do after you graduate?"

"Vet school at the U maybe. And I want pets. Lots of pets. And maybe a kid someday. I'm working the register at Don's Feed Supply on Saturdays. Help my mom clean houses on Sundays. Saving up." She could feel Lucy's judgment burn into her. "And I've been baking a lot too. I came up with this recipe for treats for the neighbor's broodmare? It's got oats, and molasses and apples in it. It's like cake. For horses. They're going to let me sell them at Don's front counter."

"Hey, that's really cool. Everyone deserves cake. Especially broodmares."

"Yeah. Totally. I tried making patties at first but the horses kept nipping my fingers. So now I just roll them." She rubbed her palms together.

"You should call them Horse Balls." Lucy giggled. "Sell two in a bag."

But Katie didn't feel like laughing. "Why do you want to leave so much, Luce?"

Lucy pulled at the grass. "I want to *see*. I want to *know*."

Katie looked away. "Well, you know what they say about curiosity."

"That it makes everything happen?"

"That it killed the cat."

"Plenty of cats running 'round my neighborhood."

Katie rolled her eyes. "No doubt." *Ouch. Why did I say that?*

Lucy lay back down, searching the sky.

They said nothing for a while and Katie hoped they'd been quiet long enough to move on from it.

"You know what they say about people led and fed by clichés, old wives tales, bible verses?" Lucy asked.

Katie didn't answer.

"Not a damn thing," Lucy said. "Those suckers are lost to the ages."

"Okay. So you just want to be talked about?"

"I want to matter."

Katie stiffened. "You matter to me."

"If you're too afraid to come out, Katie, what's the point in staying?"

"I never said I wouldn't someday, but—"

A siren sounded down the street.

Katie bolted upright. "Oh my God, it's the police."

Lucy turned her head. Red lights flickered through the woods; the sound faded as the truck's diesel engine growled up the hill toward WBHS.

"Nah, fire department."

BLOGGING MY SOJOURN

One Woman's Journey from Gay to Straight

At Sojourn it was off-putting to, yet again, be relegated to second class. You'd think we'd be elevated, re-anointed as the female ideal, prepped for male worship. We'd been neutralized with prayer certainly, but no one seemed to pay us much heed unless we were teens: marriage and baby-making material for the college-age men. There were few temptations; only a couple of moody teens and a handful of septuagenarians there for the seven-day long church social. A shame really because after coming down from the hormone suppressors for my cancer treatment, my mojo was returning, and I felt like a million bucks.

Meanwhile, there was plenty of excitement on the male side. Where we got beauty* consultants, they got hug-therapy. Stolen glances and more crying and yelling and touching than I've seen from men since living with a drunk father.

It was on one of these tumultuous days that president Henry Cleaver showed up with a guest speaker. After an argument with the accounting department that had us all gossiping, Cleaver gathered us in the chapel and introduced a folksy gray-haired man dressed in a blue and white-striped seer-sucker suit. In a familiar accent, he spoke of rebirth through Christ while a few of the boys sobbed and my mind drifted, torn between wondering what this was all doing to the kids long-term and how the hell I knew this guy.

And then he told us how Jesus had blessed him and his wife's life with grandchildren and a successful political career in my home state—in my hometown. That's when his last name clarified for me. It belonged to someone who helped drive me from that very town.

That name yanked me back two decades, and I nearly fell out of my chair to hurl Jello salad on the ground. I fought the urge to scream and channeled it into the sharpest glare I could muster, clutching the sides of my chair white knuckled. I willed my new buddy Jesus to strike the man down with a lightning bolt. But as usual, when it comes to all things heavenly, you really can't wait for God to do anything. You have to take matters your own hands. I think he prefers it that way actually.

Praise Jesus

*I could put together a better femme ensemble than these ladies, bless their hearts.

Posted by Liesl ~ 11:00 PM ~ 2 comments

Patrice commented:
I have days like this too. It's only a matter of prayer. We are flawed creatures who must stay vigilant against thoughts of evil and vengance.

Rolf68 commented:
Proceed with caution Liesl!

CHAPTER TWENTY

Samantha

SNOWDOGS 0
REDHAWKS 2

"GO, LARSON!" DAD'S voice thundered through the stands. "Let's bring out the Hellmann's!"

"Erik." Mom yanked on his jersey until he sat down.

"Yeah!" He threw one last fist pump.

Jamie leaned into Samantha. "Please tell me your dad did not just invoke a condiment."

Samantha slouched back into her seat. "It's better when Brace says it."

The zero throbbed on the scoreboard for an agony of time—enough time for Mom and Dad to turn away from one another in the arena seats, as if they were standing over their son's lifeless body and each blaming the other for his demise. Mom smiled sadly in league with Samantha, but Samantha turned away.

The problem with being the lowest on the family totem pole was that no one noticed when she was giving the silent treatment. She couldn't look at Mom after last week's revelation. Not because Mom was a lesbian, or a hasbian, or a wannabian, or whatever, but because she never said a word about it to a daughter who would have been thrilled to associate her mother with rock 'n roll greatness instead of the Reebok-sporting, quilt-obsessed, yoga klutz she appeared to be.

"I swear we talked about Cake for Horses a dozen times," Sam whispered to Jamie. "Do you think if Lucy had been a 'Luke' Mom wouldn't have bragged and bragged about it? What a hypocrite." Mom, for all her speeches about Grandma, was just as homophobic herself.

"Parents have a whole 'nother life, Sam, that doesn't involve us. I have no desire to find out who my parents were boinking when they were kids."

"Ew, I don't want to know the gross parts. But come on, what if your dad dated Madonna or something?"

Jamie burst out laughing. "I gotta go, dude. I have a ton of homework." She stood and patted Samantha's head and scooted out of the bleacher seats.

The crowd moaned and booed. Samantha felt guilty then, as though her anger was determining the outcome of the game. The more furiously Brace, Zev, and Maddox swept up and down the rink, the sloppier they got. Brace's face had never been so flushed with desperation. Well, not in a decade or so. Those pink blotches around his eyes and mouth once indicated the tears were ready to flow. Now his jaw simply drew down in resignation. And Zev just skated in circles, anxiously waiting for the pass that never came.

The Redhawks were just a better team. Tighter. Stronger. Their goalie was quick, on and off his knees, and broad as a bear. Maddox finally scored in the second period but the Redhawks eventually won the championship three to one.

AFTERWARD, AT MEZZA Luna Pizzeria (where you receive half a pie whether you want it or not), the entire Larson family filled a semi-circle booth. Samantha had assumed that, whether the Snowdogs won the tournament or not, Brace would hang out with his teammates. But here he sat with his embarrassing family.

"Hey," Brace gently elbowed Samantha, "thanks for cheering so hard tonight."

She shrugged. "Of course."

"Nervous?" he asked.

"About?"

"The play."

"Nah. Jamie's kinda taking the spotlight off me. Got room to mess up."

"You're not gonna mess up. Try skating with Maddox. Talk about spotlight hogs."

Samantha mumbled the affirmative through a mouthful of veggie slice. When she looked up, Mom was staring through her with a wan smile.

"See?" Grandma said. "Kate's clearly exhausted. Just look at those rings under her eyes."

"I'm sorry, what?" Mom asked.

"I said, have you thought about what you're going to do when the kids leave?" Grandma dabbed a napkin to her mouth. "For college."

"Oh. Well, yeah," Mom said. "Of course."

Grandpa wrapped an arm around Mom's shoulder and squeezed. "Remember, Claud? She sells pottery. This gal's got lotsa potential."

"Actually it's quilting now."

"Kate got fourth place at Quiltarama last winter, Mom," Dad said.

Woo!

"Just finished one for the choir director."

Grandma glowered. She looked to Grandpa who sighed and then to Dad. "Excuse me, when am I going to receive one of these masterpieces?"

"I'll try to make something soon but Gonzo Fox is keeping me pretty busy."

"That Mark and Ray need to get themselves into Sojourn." Grandma went at her thin crust pizza with knife and fork, cutting it into smaller pieces until there was only enough room for an olive to hang on. "I talked to Henry Cleaver the other day. Charming man. He's doing a great service. Just look how it helped that Van Buren woman." She raised her fork.

"You wouldn't be seen within ten feet of *that Van Buren woman*," Mom said with a sneer.

Whoa. Samantha stopped eating. Brace slowed down.

"Kate," Grandma said, "how can you say that? I help fund that choir of hers. I'm surprised at you." Wide-eyed, she tilted her head at Dad. "And quite frankly, one has to question her qualifications."

"Lucy *is* kinda stuck in purgatory, Mom." Dad's voice had gravel in it, as if he'd grown weary of being in the middle of this same argument in all its many forms. It did seem to Samantha that something more was going on between the alpha females. She would have to research it.

Grandpa snorted. "Ms. Van Buren's B&B will do just fine."

"With tourists of course, not locals," Mom said.

"Oh, she's just offish." Grandma fluttered a hand. "Mark and Ray are good with people, nobody avoids them."

Mom crossed her arms. "Well, then, why should they change?"

They stared at each other. Grandma's face went lavender and it seemed a little over-the-top, even for Grandma. Her jaw retracted into her neck and she slapped her breastbone.

Samantha bolted up. "Oh, God, Gramma's choking."

Dad jumped from the booth and yanked out Grandma, then turned her around and wrapped arms around her midsection. There were gasps around the restaurant. The family sat in shock, even Bert, as Dad jerked Grandma around in circles. She sensed even then it was an image never to be erased.

He gave one last firm jerk and an olive at fault popped out, flew through the air, and into the breadbasket.

Samantha folded over the red and white checked napkin.

"Oh my gosh." Mom refilled Grandma's water glass. "Are you okay?"

"I'm fine." Grandma rasped at the neighboring tables. "Fine." She waved, then sat down, straightened her napkin, and stared pleadingly at the ceiling. "Dear lord and savior, Lucy Van Buren has opened a fissure in this town and all the freaks have flown out."

"Actually," Grandpa said, "maybe more cameras would bring us some PR for the amendment. These people do themselves in every time, acting ridiculous."

"Hmm." Grandma' shifted her eyes left to right. A smile sprouted.

There was a boundless energy to Grandma that amazed Samantha. If she made it to Washington, anything was possible.

Clearly Mom had realized the same thing. "You've resurrected that marriage bill three times now," Mom said shrilly.

"Kate," Dad murmured, a low growl.

"Let the people vote." Claudia shrugged. "Two-thirds don't want gay marriage." She took a sip of water.

"Well, two thirds are wrong." Mom smacked the table and the glasses clinked. The other customers in Mezza Luna turned back to them.

Dad shot a glare at Mom that Samantha had not seen in a long time.

Samantha slipped an arm around her mother. "Ma, chill."

Grandma took Mom and Dad's hands. "Let us pray for an end to this battle. Let us pray for Ms. Van Buren. And Mark. And that dear, nearly blind Ray." She closed her eyes. Then she opened them again. "Now about this friend of yours, Samantha."

Dad sighed.

"Who?"

"This drag queen person."

"Jamie is not a drag queen," Samantha said. "She is genderqueer. Currently."

"Oh, dear lord, let's pray for him too."

CHAPTER TWENTY-ONE

Kate

EVER SINCE HER mother-in-law dubbed the new dining set "Contemporary Vague" Kate has not served a meal on it. The kids are busy nowadays and Erik is often late, finalizing Taken4Granite contracts. It's been down to her, Chuck, and a Lean Cuisine in front of *Law & Order* reruns and quilt patterns.

But tonight is a special occasion. Ever since Erik mentioned having Lucy over, Samantha hasn't let it go and now here they sit, uncomfortably upright in the walnut straight backs—which are vaguely Asian, vaguely Shaker-style— trying desperately to make Lucy feel more at home than they do.

Kate turns her shoulders to Lucy as if it is possible to shield the empty chair where Brace should be. "So how is that quilt working for you?" She immediately wants to ram her forehead down onto the two-inch thick trestle table. *Who, but a complete asshole would remind someone of a gift?*

"Well, you know it's been really warm out."

"I know. Isn't it weird?" Kate snaps her fingers. "Global warming."

Samantha nudges Kate's foot. As the first to talk about the weather, Kate's out twenty dollars.

"Hey, Erik," Lucy asks. "Do me a favor and tell your daughter to back off singing around the house, okay? She needs to save it for the play."

"Done." Erik fakes a stern look at Samantha.

"Seriously, all she needs to do is nail that solo. She could whisper the rest; we have too many sopranos as it is." She points at Samantha. "If I can so much as hear you over Barbara, I'm going to bust you in front of the whole congregation."

"What?" Samantha raises hands, giggling. "Me? I would never."

Erik stands with the wine carafe, his tie dragging through the salad greens and leans over to Lucy's setting. Chardonnay glub-glubs into the bowl of what Kate now realizes in horror is a noncommittally-shaped wine glass. To someone well-traveled it won't be broad enough for red nor narrow enough for white. *And does she even drink anymore? What. Have. I. Done?*

Lucy's gaze wanders up to the bronze, square-lamped chandelier and down to the bamboo-green rug. "I love mission style in a home. It's like church." She lifts her glass. "Cheers."

Sigh. Chuckle. Erik and Kate meet her glass with theirs. Samantha insists on offering her water glass for the clink.

"It's only box wine, I'm sorry," Kate admits. "I didn't have time—"

"Box wines are big in France right now."

"Really?"

Lucy takes a small sip and sets down her glass. "Oh, yeah, and screw tops too. You'd be surprised."

Thank God.

"Hon, the—uh?" Erik tilts his head to the kitchen. Little puffs of steam roll from the sides of the oven.

"Oh, yes. Excuse me." Kate jumps up to rescue the main course.

Lucy scoots out her chair. "Can I—?"

"Sit." Kate shoots a piercing glare at her. In the kitchen, she catches a glimpse of her own desperate face in the oven window and exhales. "Sam, you want to get the bread, honey?"

Halfway through the meal, Brace ambles in and flickers a look at Lucy. "Hey."

"Hey," she says and extends her graceful hand across the table. "I don't think we've formally met."

He moves to shake it without meeting her eyes. But she holds him there, across the table, long enough that he would normally consider it a challenge to thumb wrestle.

"Nicetameecha," he says in a softer voice. He finally meets her eyes, letting a smile slip and then lowly, "Sorry I'm late."

She lets him go. "I hear you nearly won the playoffs." If his family had mentioned that game again he would have left the table. But she actually makes it sound like the accomplishment it is.

He sits down. "Something like that."

"Missing your tenor in the choir this season."

"Brace is trying to make up his schoolwork. A geography report on the Great Lakes," Kate says with a solid stare at him.

Lucy nods slowly. "My entire senior year was make-up work."

He piles his plate with long grain and wild rice, then chicken, then more rice.

"Don't just print out the satellite photo," Erik says. "Draw it. Show some effort."

"Like I have time for effort."

Kate dabs her mouth with a napkin, so delicately, so snootily, Erik's eyebrows gather. "Sam will help you, won't you, Sam?"

"The lakes are mostly blobs," she responds. "You can draw Lake Superior as an angry sock puppet."

Erik sits back. "And you could ask Lucy about the Bonnie Saint wreck."

Kate nudges him.

"Oh, no, it's okay," Lucy says, "it's a fascinating story."

No one speaks.

"I guess the Bonnie was there one minute"—she stays silent until Brace looks up—"gone the next." She lays down her fork. "My brother was a ship watchman, the youngest crewmember. Wanted to be a sailor ever since I can remember. He could read the sky like an ancient mariner." She combs her fingers through her hair. "Wasted most of his summers wrestling a sunfish up and down the river. Left home soon as he turned eighteen, got work in Duluth."

"Oh, man," Brace says.

Erik sighs. "That freighter was way too full of taconite."

"Yep." Lucy sets her elbows on the table and laces her fingers, sets her chin on the bridge. "And hit the worst storm of the season."

"I was just reading that the lakes can get as rough as the ocean," Brace says. His knife and fork lower to the table in his loose fists. He sits back.

"Well, close enough." She raises a half-hearted smile, a grimace. "They say she probably rose up on the largest wave of the squall, a freak wave, maybe— three stories tall." She ramps her hand up, lets it hover for a moment. "Rode it like a rollercoaster—up, over, and down to the bottom of the lake." Then her hand dives to the table. "Engine going full steam? Augered in, just like that." Her fingertips bunch the tablecloth, like a hull into sand, until her short fingernails whiten. "What must it have been like when it parted the waters, for those eternal seconds, to see the lake bottom exposed? That's a grand way to go, don't you think?"

Kate stares from Samantha to Brace. Samantha's mint blue eyes have dilated; she seems to not be breathing. Brace slowly blinks, lips parted.

Dammit, Luce, don't drag my children down there with you.

"I shouldn't have mentioned it," Erik says.

"It's okay. It's very interesting to me now. I hope I haven't put you off the research, Brace."

"No way. Not at all." Brace scoops in more food. "Wow," he mumbles around it.

"But they don't really know what happened though, do they?" Kate asks. "Since no one survived."

Lucy keeps her eyes on Brace. "Nah, there's a half dozen theories. We've got the reports at our house if you want to read them. 'Course you can find some of that online now too. You got my number." She pulls her napkin out of her lap and sets it on the table. "Well, that was delicious." Only the hum of the refrigerator fills the room.

Chuck Norris ambles in, sits, and stares statue-like at Lucy. She places her hand on his skull and his ears go droopy, his tail swishes.

"You feed him from the table?" she asks.

"Never," Erik says. "Ignore him and he'll go away."

"Easy to say." She gazes down at the dog and cups his chin. "Not so easy to do. Right, loverboy?"

Chucks falls over onto his back and exposes himself, tail wagging.

Samantha cackles.

Kate stands. "Dessert."

IF KATE COULD find another mulberry tree somewhere, she would whack it down with an axe all by herself. Everyone and everything seems determined to piss her off. When she sees Lucy at Northern Roast that next week, she slaps the latest *Valley Dispatch* down in front of her. Senator Claudia Larson stares up from the front page, frozen in mid-speech. The headline reads: SENATOR THREATENED.

"Uh-oh," Lucy says, "that's not good."

"Well, she's done everything in her power to keep gays and lesbians second class citizens. People don't tend to take that very well." Kate sighs. "God knows, I love my mother-in-law—the Larsons have been good to me—but if it were up to her, Mark and Ray wouldn't be allowed to even adopt. Forget marriage."

"That doesn't mean she should get death threats."

"Well, of course it doesn't, but she's not the victim here. She brought this on herself. Gah. Can't believe I'm arguing this with you of all people." Kate turns toward the door.

"Hey, whoa. C'mere. Sit with me." Lucy pushes the paper aside. "I'm buying. Got a royalty check this morning." She pulls out a large, blue bank check and accordions it with a snap. "Twenty five dollars and six cents."

"Hoo-wee." Kate leans against the booth. How easy it would be to just slide in. Start this friendship over on better footing. But what if she just kept sliding?

A stitch pulls Lucy's cheek. "Yeah. That band thing really paid off."

"Come on, it must have been *so* cool up in front of thousands of people, rockin' out."

"That was the payment in the beginning. But it's all the sound of beige after a while." Lucy's smirk seems deeper today; light from the blue sky ices her cheeks. "I promise you, living well is not the best revenge. I've tried it."

"Guess it depends upon your definition of living well." Kate's voice breaks to a whisper. "Definitely not Sojourn. I picture toothless people speaking in tongues and dancing with snakes." She removes the lid of her coffee and takes a sip.

"No. Nothing like that," Lucy says. "They opened their arms to me."

"In exchange for what?"

"Ten grand."

"And your conversion statistic. Which is worth a lot." Kate straightens and clears her throat. Her face takes on parental sternness. She pokes a finger on the table. This induces a tightlipped grin from Lucy. But Kate digs in, emboldened by this flippancy. "Places like Sojourn make it harder to prove that Mark and Ray deserve the right to marry and have kids."

"I wasn't trying to take anything away from anyone. I just wanted peace."

"Mmm, well, guess what, your peace has repercussions."

"Everything we do has repercussions." Lucy gazes out the window toward the bluffs. Two eagles circle, black against the blue, like ashes rising from a bonfire. "I've lost plenty of sleep over my actions. I just want to call it even."

"No such thing as even," Kate says quietly. "I can't help but wonder if I hadn't let you down in high school, maybe things wouldn't have been so bad. Maybe you wouldn't have ended up in Sojourn."

"Yeah, that's a funny thing about control freaks. They even want to take blame for the horrible stuff." Lucy shakes her head, belligerence returning. "You had a healthy dose of self-preservation, pure and simple. You actually think I've spent this whole time worrying about all that stupid high school drama? Skkk."

Kate raises an eyebrow. *Ah, there's the girl I remember.* "We were my kids' age. We were real people with difficult choices. How nice would it have been to have the adults' support?"

Lucy manages to shrug and nod at the same time. "Why are you standing? Just sit with me. Or are you still afraid to be seen with me?"

Kate rolls her eyes. "Please don't with that. I have ice cream in the car. Luce, why don't you come with us to St. Paul for the counter-demonstration? It's the first time I've gone against Claudia and I need backup."

Lucy's eyes widen. "I can't do that. You know I can't do that, Katie."

Kate grumbles, turns toward the door. *Again with the name.* She turns back. "You're at least coming to the play, right?"

Lucy brightens. "Oh, yeah! Of course."

"Um, Sam was . . . mentioning the other day that you girls were looking at the stars."

Lucy sits up. "Yep. She knows a ton more about astronomy than I did at her age."

"Erik and I really don't want her up on the Leap."

"Not to worry. It's actually too bright up there anyway. They installed so many streetlamps you can't see anything but Venus and the Moon." Lucy slowly cringes. "So, um, we walked back—to my yard."

"Oh. Well. That's okay then."

Lucy glowers at the table. "I'd never hurt Sam or Jamie, you know. I'd never touch them. Or even think about them that way."

Kate slaps her chest. "I know that. Oh, Luce. Did you think—? Ah, jeez. I wasn't even going there. Honestly." She laughs, sticks out her tongue a little, and clamps her teeth on it. She hopes Lucy will laugh too but she has that defensive mask she gets around the older folks, the ones that for all their talk of religious rebirth don't honestly believe she's been *fixed*. "So, what do you think of Jamie?"

"She needs help," Lucy says.

"Please tell me you're not suggesting she go through Sojourn."

"Of course not. We're talking gender here, not sexuality. And not for me to judge."

"See that's your problem. You've stopped judging. She could really use some guidance."

"Hey, I'm there as much as I can be. They showed me their poetry after all. That's an honor at my age." Lucy blinks. "What—you haven't seen it?"

"No. She hasn't volunteered and I would never invade Sam's privacy like my parents did."

Lucy shrugs. "Well, it's kinda good. Short stuff. I still remember one."

"Enlighten me." Kate's stomach burns. After only a couple months of being home, Lucy's already brandishing insider information.

Lucy recites slowly, halting between each line,

> *Little comet*
> *Off course*
> *Sun-bound*
> *Of course*

"That's it?"

"That's it."

"Say it again."

Lucy does, looking deeply into Kate. The cruelty in her eyes softens.

"Hmm. Guess it is kinda good." Kate stares into the last of her coffee, full of sugar granules and grounds. "Do you think Jamie is off course?"

"I dunno. I'm no gender dysphoria expert," Lucy says. "Women are frontiers. And Jamie's got a lot of traveling to do."

"Yeah. We are, aren't we? You know, as much as Claudia drives me nuts, there's something about her I really admire. Sometimes I wish I could look at things as directly as she does. To just pick up a book and live by it. She's so sure about everything. I wish I could be that sure."

"You are. Have you listened to yourself in the past five minutes?"

Kate scrunches her nose a bit. "I am so happy you came back, Luce. It feels like, like I found a part of me that I'd forgot was missing."

Lucy smiles softly and the smirk, the weariness, dissipates. "Me too. You're all through my songs." And then she cringes.

"I know." Kate keeps peering into her empty cup. "We had you for dinner because you do mean that much. Sam thinks the world of you. And I'm sorry I've been so intense, but you don't know what it's been like here." She looks up. "Mark and Ray—and Jamie? You've seen the world, Lucy. They could use your help."

Through this speech, Lucy returns to a smirk. Her lips redden and her stare does not waver.

"Oh, you think I'm playing activist mom," Kate says. Her shoulder is getting a bit sore leaning on the booth like this.

"I wasn't thinking anything like that. I'm just surprised by how you've turned out. I really didn't expect you to be so . . . open-minded."

"You sound disappointed."

"No, it's good to see you, so"—Lucy balls her hand into a fist and lays it on her heart—"so conscious and aware. You're not a robot like the rest."

"I'm nobody, Lucy. I was never as brave as you."

Lucy looks wounded by this. "You're ten times braver," she whispers. "You walked out into the dark with me. I was all talk. Still am. Choke in the clinch. I was a little shit."

"Are you kidding?" Kate asks full of good humor. "I *loved* knowing you in high school. Samantha is so much like you. So much more philosophical than I was at that age. Heck, she was even born the day before your birthday, Luce." She lays a hand to her heart too; it feels so good to finally have the chance to say it. "Everything you taught me, I taught Sam. Even the stuff you didn't mean to teach. Even stuff I didn't know I learned. Without what happened between us, I don't know what kind of mother I'd be."

"Really?" Lucy's cheek twitches and her eyebrows gather.

"Really." Kate reaches out for Lucy's hand. Lucy draws back. Kate tries to ignore it, but it stings. "Yeah, I never once hit my kids. Or let Erik either."

"Well, that's a nice thing to say. Still, the fact is, I—I tried to recruit you."

"Pfff. Then everyone recruits, everybody wants to be loved. Hey, this Sojourn place recruits, doesn't it?" Kate crosses her arms, glows proudly. Who knew she could be this brave?

"You know, she isn't really like me, Katie. She's much more sincere. Like you."

"Well, she's smart like you were."

"You were smart."

"I meant wise. You were wise."

"Okay. Yeah, that's true."

"Then again," Kate chuckles, "'member that last time on the Leap? When you played your guitar?"

Lucy sinks into the booth. "Isn't your ice cream melted by now?"

"I never got a chance to tell you I was there." Kate looks around and says quietly, "That I heard it."

Lucy's forehead gathers. "I wasn't even sure you knew about that."

"Um, hello. That graffiti didn't come off for ten years."

Lucy begins to say something but then closes her mouth. No safe words left. She turns to the eagles again, which a smaller bird is harrying; perhaps it's the owner of the nest the eagles are circling. The blue of the sky has deepened. It's so sapphire Kate can sense the night behind it. Time to start dinner. At least she said what needed to be said without screwing it up too badly. She could get run over by the big yellow Schwann's truck tomorrow and at least Lucy would finally know the score.

CHAPTER TWENTY-TWO

1986
Under the Bluff

ON A COOL summer Saturday, hard driving guitar strums echoed down from the bluffs and out over the water. River rats later said you could hear that racket all the way out to the party boats. Katie Andern was on her lunch break at Don's Feed Supply and heading down to Wilson Park to watch the gulls bob along the river. A crowd had gathered at the corner of Portage and Main in the open lot next to the train depot. They all looked to be waiting for aliens to land.

"Somebody's up on the Leap playing guitar," John Risdahl said from behind a set of camouflage binoculars.

"Gimmie those," his wife said. "Whoa, that's the Van Buren kid."

"The one who got expelled?"

"No the one who drowned on the Bonnie Saint, meathead. Yes, the girl. Go in, call the cops. She's gonna chase away all my customers."

"No way. Look at these people. She's bringing them *in*."

It would later be determined that the girl had loaded her AMC Pacer with a guitar, rental generator, a Marshall amp head, 4x12 speaker cabinet and hauled it all up to Maiden Leap.

Katie skipped backward from the crowd until she could make out the slight figure jamming away. Lucy was in full regalia: blue kilt, black turtleneck, engineer boots, and had shaved her Flock of Seagulls into a floppy Mohawk. Unlike the tame version of the original folk song (which she had earlier in the year recorded on a cassette and dropped in Katie's locker), this electrified version was a monstrous, jangling, minor-chorded dirge loud enough to rock the plaster off the Gainsborough estate ceilings.

"*OH, I—YI-YI-YI—I ACHE FOR YOU-U-U!*"

Katie swooned and goose bumps climbed her arms. She beamed up at the girl. Her girl.

Lucy stopped playing, raised the body of the guitar to her face—as if to take a bite out of the pick-ups. A dodgy Scottish voice buzzed out, "I love you, Katie Andirons!"

Laughter echoed throughout the parking lot. The Risdahls looked to Katie. Then everyone else looked to Katie, incredulous, and she realized she only had an hour before it all got back to her parents. In a lurch, she whirled around and sprinted down Portage Avenue, past slow moving cars aimed for the lift bridge.

From downriver came a low, musical honk like the largest pipe of a calliope organ. The Wicasa Queen paddlewheel boat was egg-beating her way up the St. Croix. It hadn't rained much that year and the water behind the old girl had stirred up all brown like Willy Wonka's chocolate river. Her tall, gold-crowned smokestacks, combined with the hiss of water falling from her paddles, filled Katie with dread. The Queen was right on schedule for her noon rendezvous with the lift bridge.

The bridge alarm, essentially a railroad crossing, began its insistent clanging, its red and white striped gates descending.

Do you hear me? I love you, Katie Andirons!

Katie's legs pumped faster. How could any basketball player think Converse all-stars contained proper arch support? She grimaced as she raced down the footpath and onto the lift section. The bridge tender was busy waving at the captain of the Wicasa Queen and chatting into his CB radio. Cars honked behind her to gain his attention but all Katie could hear was her heaving breath and the steel grid ringing out beneath her rubber soles.

The Queen tooted again. The locks released and the lift climbed. The metal grid pushed up at Katie, nearly buckling her legs. She made it to the edge as cars on the other side began honking too. There was no time for debate, if she stayed on the lift, she would surely be in the biggest trouble of her life. Katie leapt and landed with a grunt on the Wisconsin side of the bridge. She ran the rest of its length for good measure as car doors slammed and drivers called after her. Once on solid ground, she glanced back. The lift was fully raised, temporarily separating "those laughing" from "those yet to laugh." The Queen's short, double toot to the bridge attendant sounded too much like mockery.

Katie called in sick for the rest of her shift and vowed not to leave the house for the entire summer. That promise lasted all of twenty-four hours when she had to go to church the next day. After services, vestibule chatter was "that crazy Van Buren girl" had been arrested for disturbing the peace. The police hadn't been able to definitively pin the school fire on Lucy but this time she was caught red-handed. Literally. There was a spray-painted message halfway down the cliff face: *L+K 2GETHER 4EVER*. No one could figure out how to get close enough to scrub it off. Which begged the question, how did the culprit spray it on?

The Van Burens paid a hefty fine and the school board felt justified in having expelled Lucy for the fire in May. Lucy turned eighteen that August (same age as her brother when he died) and motored off in her escape pod, destination: Minneapolis.

"Poor Bridget Van Buren," they'd all said.

Katie tried never to speak of it, denied anything ever happened between them. But the more she tried to erase, the more the town colored in. As did her schoolmates come fall. Seasons passed, snow fell, rain came, winds blew, and still the spray-painted message remained.

BLOGGING MY SOJOURN

One Woman's Journey from Gay to Straight

Mornings consisted of classes in your "talent offering," a skill that would glorify Christ's name. I volunteered for choir and learned a great deal from the director, Charles, who'd been booted out of the Mormon Church for too intimately inspecting the vocal cords of one of the tenors. Charles also worked in accounting, racking up some major Jesus points.

In the afternoons, Charles and I sat together in the Prayer Circle gossiping before the fireworks began. He'd found something troubling in accounts receivable and whispered that one of the boy's families had paid triple the rest of us. Math not being my strong suit, I asked what that meant. Then our group leader shushed us. Prayer Circle was payback time for the morning's frivolity. We all came together to reveal our scars, palpable or internal—a genuine downhome country jamboree of wallowing and nailing yourself up alongside The Savior. And boy had the prayer circle seen it all. Until I took off my crocs.

The bottoms of my feet are striped with scars resembling two large hash tags: # #. When I was little, I used to tell kids in swimming pools it was an Apache skin tattoo, providing traction and signifying my future as a great sprinter. The girls in my band used to play Tic Tac Toe any time I passed out. They had tournaments.

See, in the 70s, some homes were still heated by a monster boiler in the basement, with a large two-by-three foot grid above it in a central part of the home's main floor. My parents' house had one (as did this B&B). Sometimes, on those 30 below days, the middle of the iron grate glowed dark red, while dry heat blasted up from its black depths.

I was three years old when I walked across hell's ceiling. How long did I scream? Was I placed there or pushed? Is the scarred brain writing this blog post the result of haphazard pathways instantly seared into my synapses that day? Mom was so *darn thankful* it was just my feet. Because no man cares about those, right? Well, most don't. As for the boilers, they're long gone. Tiled over in Mom's kitchen. And here, in the B&B's parlor, there is a blonder patch of hardwood. But I never let her cover it with the oriental rugs. I want her to see it every day.

When I came out, they looked away. When I left home, they never tried to pull me back. I waded into a fire where all things burned true. I waited in that fire to be thrust, saved, ignored, loved. Forged into a runner of circles.

Posted by Liesl ~ 7:35 PM ~ 1 comment

Patrice commented:
How beautiful upon the mountains are the feet of him that publisheth peace; that bringeth good tidings of good, that publisheth salvation; that saith unto Zion, Thy God reigneth! —Isaiah 52:7

CHAPTER TWENTY-THREE

Samantha

"DO BALLS REALLY turn blue?" Elphaba said as she swung past Glinda.

"No, they just ache. Why, is Zev pushing third base?"

The director called down from the stage rigging. "One more minute, Samantha. We're almost done."

"Hey, no problem. This is great." She swam through the air, making fish lips at Jamie. "No, not really, but I hear guys complain about them all the time."

"Not sure I'm cool being your go-to scrotum resource."

"Well, I'm not asking Brace." She handed Jamie her cellphone.

On it was a text from Zev: Scored us tickets to M.I.A. @ Summerfest!

"Um, that's months away." Jamie skipped around a swinging Samantha. "Going to the chapel, and they're gonna get married."

Samantha could not help but laugh. "It's your fault. I took your advice." On hers and Zev's third date, she had played him some M.I.A., a Sri Lankan woman whose raps and beats were edgy and catchy enough that anyone would be intrigued. She told Zev that when she watched him and the rest of the team pile out of the locker room, then skate across the rink all she could hear was the galloping thump of "Boyz" and its celebratory rant about crazy playas. She told him: it triggers something primal and sexual, some illogical place that responds to what would make my feminist side scream. Zev's mouth had hung slightly open at that.

Jamie waved her wand in circles through the air, practicing her witchy goodness. "Is he a good kisser?"

"Yeah, he's nice. A little conservative. I could handle some tongue."

Jamie unleashed a campy giggle and batted her eyes. "Goodness, Elphaba, you really must control yourself."

Samantha's harness rapidly dropped by a foot. "Hey!"

"Sorry," the stagehand called from above. He pulled her up again, but the wires were now at different lengths and she rose sideways.

"This is making my cramps like ten times worse. Uhhh. Check my butt, Jame, I would die if I bled all over the stage."

"That would be awesome. *Wicked* meets *Madame Butterfly*."

"Shut it."

"Nope, you're fine." Jamie tapped Samantha's shoulder with the wand and said in a sweetly sardonic voice, "Simply click your heels and all your misery will be gone."

"Imma clickin' and it ain't working."

"What do cramps feel like? I would love to have a period, just once."

"Are you crazy? It feels like someone's carving a jack o' lantern inside my belly. That's like me wanting to know what it's like to get kicked in the nuts."

Jamie gazed at Samantha as they reeled Elphaba up to the rafters.

"You comfortable, Sam?" the director asked.

"Sorta."

"Think you can do 'Defying Gravity' from here?"

"It's the singing while going up that's going to be tough. I've never had to project from a rope before. It's like I don't have anything to push from."

"Well, let's try it. Take her down."

ON THE WALK home, Jamie was quieter than usual.

"I didn't mean to suggest you don't deserve a period," Samantha said.

"I know." Jamie nodded. "It's no big thing."

"You want one of my pads to try?"

"S'okay." Jamie slung a hand over Samantha's shoulder. "I can always grab one of Mom's if I want to try it. I was just thinking how shitty it would be if our parents said we couldn't hang out. We would have never been in this play together."

"I know. That would suck."

Grandma said Mom and Dad were too lenient. But Mom said it was better to bring the kids' friends into the home rather than forbid them and find out later they'd been hanging out and doing drugs. If she ended up thinking the kid was bad news, which she sometimes did, she would talk to the kid or their parents. The funny thing was, the Heathrows weren't exactly crazy about Jamie running around with the granddaughter of Senator Larson.

"It must have been hell for your mom and Lucy."

"Yeah, I guess." Honestly, Samantha hadn't wanted to think about that part. Yes, they were both snooping in on Lucy's blog and it was totally possible that her mom was the "Vicky" that "Liesl" referred to. And that eventually, Mom would—at the least convenient moment—come plop down on Samantha's bed and spill her guts, tell Samantha way more than Samantha wanted to hear to make up for the fact that she'd kept it quiet so long. *But no, just no.* Not to mention the almighty shitstorm that would ensue if Grandma ever caught wind of it.

Jamie ignored the passing stares of the shoppers as they walked the sidewalk along Main Street. "I wonder if we could help her. Talk her out."

Samantha couldn't be sure if the stares came because Jamie still looked a bit like a boy or strikingly pretty. Maybe both. "No way. I'm not talking to her about that stuff. That's way too personal, Jame."

"Not face-to-face, alexander-dum-ass. By commenting."

"Rolf68 is already trying that."

Honestly, "Liesl" staying in the closet could be better for "Vicky." But why did Samantha even have to consider this? It was no fun anymore. Sure, Samantha liked getting to know Lucy. But it was becoming too much to take in. She preferred the woman up on a festival stage holding court in ripped jeans not a church podium struggling along with the mortals.

"Did you read the last post about her feet?" Jamie asked.

"Yeah. God." Samantha nodded.

"I started a poem about her. Needs work."

"Text me it tonight. We'll figure it out."

They crossed the lift bridge. Jamie stopped midway and gazed down at the melting river, which flowed past in gray chunks. "My folks are considering Minneapolis for reals next year."

"That school with the GLBT program that Lucy mentioned?"

"Yeah." Jamie's face pinched. "Cooper."

"That's awesome." Samantha made herself smile.

"Yeah. It is."

A chill breeze blew up, glancing off the ice, and they continued to the end of the bridge.

"Maybe I could be an honorary gay and join too."

"Of course, you're totally queer at heart. Yunno, it's mostly straight kids there anyway."

But they both knew the Larsons weren't moving to Minneapolis. Ever.

"Man, it's really great, Jame. Really great. You totally deserve this."

They walked up the street in silence.

The first thing Samantha was going to tell her mom—if the woman ever got up the nerve to really talk to her again—was that you didn't have to be "in love" with someone to have your heart torn out.

CHAPTER TWENTY-FOUR
Kate

MS. VAN BUREN glowers at her soprano soloist. Her left hand rises and slowly turns, unspooling the girl's voice from her like a shimmering thread. Lucy directs the rest of the choir to remain hushed and low, while gracefully sweeping the thin baton in her right hand like a magic wand. Samantha's jaw and the muscles beneath her chin and throat tremble with vibrato, her eyes at once frightened and brave. As the girl's lungs forge into territory previously unheard by the Larson family, Lucy wistfully mouths the German lyrics in a silent duet. She extracts something nearing a swooning scream from the girl and gently lets her back down again. When Samantha crescendos to an even higher note, Lucy nods, eyes closing gratefully.

Kate pulls her pashmina shawl up over her bare shoulders. Her heart is pounding with something close to outrage, her brain telling her to calm down; Lucy had conducted the baritone in the third movement just as passionately. She glances around to see if anyone else is finding this uncomfortable. But Erik, Claudia, Bert, Brace, Jamie? They all look rapt and not the least bit disturbed so much as astounded. Samantha's voice is no longer Samantha's, or at least not what it was only months before. It is now fully-formed. Adult. Complete.

Kate sniffs at her own selfishness. There was a time, back when Samantha's face was small and round, painted with pizza sauce from cheek to cheek, and her little voice sang out across the dinner table, so sweet and clear and Kate would think, *we made this little creature.* What was the day when Samantha began to make herself? Kate doesn't know sometimes which is more worrisome: the thought of Samantha sitting in a forest somewhere with a clipboard, surrounded by silverback gorillas or walking a campus, surrounded by horny frat boys. Every day she feels whatever control she has slacken a bit more.

The next movement grows and grows into such madness—Lucy whipping the baton angrily at each vocal group—that the pianist and cellist are scarcely capable of underpinning the clamor. They watch their conductor in a controlled panic and Kate begins to doubt how much power over this multi-armed beast the woman actually has. Samantha had said that Ms. Van Buren learned choral direction at Sojourn Reclaimers, and that it was the best thing that came out of her time there, but Sojourn wasn't exactly churning out Leonard Bernsteins.

Entrenched in the cacophony, Samantha exchanges illicit grins and eyebrow flutters with Jamie. Whether or not Lucy is competent or not, they are damn near rocking the rafters. Then comes the final song, an anthem, which raises goosebumps on Erik's forearms. Kate runs her hand across them and he smiles down at her.

She had never seen Grace Lutheran's congregation leap to their feet before. They'd given standing ovations for sure, but it was usually a kind of whack-a-mole event, with everyone afraid to dedicate. But today even Brace yells, "Bravo! Heck, yeah! Bravo!"

THAT EVENING, KATE stares at the beginnings of Claudia's quilt until her eyes cross and the colors bleed together.

Screams rise from the basement. Kate tries to ignore them.

"It's possible I'm a little jealous of Lucy."

"You mean envious," Erik says from the kitchen. "Jealousy would be if Lucy was yours and you didn't want Sam to have her." The phone rings and he picks it up.

"Um, sure," she mumbles and rolls eyes.

Downstairs, Samantha's screams have turned to laughter. She, Jamie, and Lucy are playing World of Warcraft in their separate homes across town and it is difficult to concentrate with the hoots and boasts, swords clanking, fireballs crashing and dramatic Elvin music overloading Samantha's computer speakers. Kate had earlier popped her head into the bedroom to see if they needed a fourth and was met with a blank stare and then Samantha screamed out, "Heals! I—need—heals!"

I could be the healer. How hard can it be?

Erik talks politely into the phone, but there's an edge to it. Kate can see him shake his head, like, *come on, come on.* He pulls out a drawer, grabs a bottle opener, and slams it back in. He brings the phone to Kate, but doesn't meet her eyes. "It's your mom, wants to know what Brace wants for graduation."

When Kate puts the phone to her ear, her mother is still chattering, " . . . you could send him down here for a few weeks. The beach would do him good. And you know how he loves Disney—"

"Hi, Mom. Yunno he hasn't liked Disney since he was nine. But he needs a new laptop. So maybe some help on that?"

"Oh, hi, sweety. Why don't you have Erik email the specs to your father and we'll just buy the whole thing. And what about Samantha, what's she going to want for her sixteenth?"

"Hmm. She'll be getting her license, so maybe a helmet and fire retardant suit?"

"Ohhh, I remembered when you first started driving the Beetle. I never slept."

Kate sighs.

"Katie, you still there?"

"Yeah. Hey, Mom, you remember Lucy?"

"Who?"

"The girl who got expelled. The girl I—"

Her mother moans. "Dear lord, that Van Buren girl. She had some grit, that one."

"I've always wanted to tell you how much that sucked. What you did."

The line is quiet for a moment. "Well, now, Katie. Things were different back then. And frankly, if a boy had been convincing you to sneak out of the house, we would have been just as concerned. Your dad swore the two of you were ready to jump that night." Her mother chuckles a bit. "But you're right. We shouldn't have forbid you. We have a few gay friends now and I always bring that mess up when I have one too many glasses of wine. As though I'm confessing my sins."

"I loved her, Mom." Kate pinches the bridge of her nose and squeezes her eyes shut.

"Wait, you're not gay are you?"

"No. I mean, I was, I mean, everyone is not just—anyway, my point was, it was a big thing to me and you treated it like we were horrible monsters."

"Wow. This I didn't expect . . . well, I'm so sorry, Katie." Kate can hear the tears forming in her mother's voice as they always have when she wants to avoid confrontation. But it leaves her cold, hasn't worked in years. "I know that's why we never talk."

"Oh, Mom. That's not true."

But it is.

"Even after you met Erik, and we knew you were finally happy again, you weren't the same girl to us. Your father said it was just part of growing up. But that look in your eyes. Do you still hate me, Katie?"

"No, Mom," Kate says monotone, "of course not."

"You cried so much over that girl. And I blame myself. I do. But you know, memory passes such a harsh judgment. Your father and I didn't have time to think it all through, how it would affect you."

"Yeah, I know," Kate admits. The anger reserves of her youth have nearly dried up. "I've been there with the kids sometimes."

"You know, I knew a black boy in high school. And my parents forbid me from seeing him too."

"No way." Kate sits back in her chair. "You never told me that."

"It was a tragedy. He got bullied something awful. Jumped off Maiden Leap. Marcus. Marcus Robeson. He was a sweetheart of a boy. We were never that serious, mostly just friends, but I still think of him."

"Oh, my God, Mom. I'm so sorry. Wow." Kate grows silent. She had conflated the boy with the legend of Wicasa so long ago. No one talked about it anymore. He'd been lost to the ages. Conveniently.

"Well, you see why I didn't want you up there." Her mother sniffles. "But anyway, honey, when it comes to Lucy, we're doing as we were taught in church when it came to the gays."

"So, what, you don't think it's a sin anymore?"

"Oh, Katie, we don't read the gospel like that these days. We've joined a more open Presbyterian assembly, I've told you that. Now, why don't you all come down this summer? We can talk about this over a pitcher of sangria, just you and me."

"Yeah, okay. I dunno. Not sure we can afford it."

"You know you don't have to pay for much. Don't close me out, Katie. It's time we moved on from this."

"Do you still think about him?"

"Marcus? Sometimes," her mother says airily. "Marcus Robeson. More as I get older. There's a black man who works at the Publix who has the same sort of way about him, same kind eyes, and I think, I wonder if that's what he would look like now, with a paunch and grey in his curls." Her mother's voice is so thoughtful; it's like talking to a stranger, an equal. "Well, you know, he was in Bert Larson's class, he could tell you more about him."

"Oh, maybe I will. I'm sorry I let you down, Mom."

"You didn't, sweetheart. We did. Just come visit. Okay?"

THE NEXT MORNING, the tinkling bell over the Gonzo Fox's door is way too chipper for Kate's liking.

"Well, look who it is, dear," Mark says. "Didn't we used to know that couple?"

"Ha," Kate says.

Erik meanders out back to the back lot and the cache of vintage farm implements. He promised to wait until the kids were grown to redecorate the rec room with sharp, rusty tools, but the date is looming.

"We thought you were avoiding us," Ray says.

"Why would I do that?" Kate's stare darts up and down the shelves. "Been busy with hockey and the play and stuff."

"And stuff," Mark says. "I heard you had Lucy over for dinner, how did—?"

"Great. Any quilt orders?"

"Not yet." Mark wanders off toward the register and dons his reading glasses.

"Don't mind him," Ray says, "he's just a little tense with the protest coming up. Hey, you said you wanted to see a photo of Jeremy." Ray reaches into his back pocket and extracts his wallet. "Had his second birthday, last month. It's a little pixilated. Downloaded it off the adoption site."

"Oh my gosh." She turns it to make the most of the skylight. "He's beautiful. Awww, I remember that stage. So messy." Kate grins at the photo of a pudgy toddler stuffing his face with cake, a dab of pink frosting awarding him a clown nose. "You didn't say he was African-American." She immediately thinks of her mother's boyfriend—falling, falling—and wonders if things have changed enough in this town.

"I know, I know. Mark never wants to tell people. As if that one last detail is going to send everybody over the edge. Only putting off the inevitable."

Kate waves him off. "It will be fine. The Holstedts adopted two Chinese kids. Everyone treats them cool."

"Yeah, well, the Holdstedts are straight Catholics."

Mark strolls back over, throws an arm over Ray's shoulder. "Yep, we were just sitting around one night and thinking, gee, how can we make this more complicated."

"So, is it really going through?"

"We think so." Ray grins. "Thanks to our friends vouching that we won't corrupt the little guy." He reaches for her arm. "Thank you so much for talking to the social worker."

"Of course."

"Gotta be on my best behavior," Mark says. "I promised not to get arrested at the protest." He ruffles Ray's hair and turns to Kate. "You're still coming, right?"

"Yeah," she says hazily.

"You getting pressure from the senator?"

"No. She was strangely calm when I told her I'd be there." Kate scuffs her sneaker on the dusty floor tiles. "It's Lucy."

Mark groans.

Ray thumbs over his shoulder. "Um, got a new batch of estate sale crap. I'll just . . ."

"She refuses to come," Kate says, watching Ray leave and wishing he wasn't. The man is definitely Mark's better half.

"Well, of course. What did you expect?" Mark says. "She's happy in the closet. Why do you care so much?"

"Why don't *you*? You were as close to her as me."

"Yeah, and then she left and never talked to me again. And I lived through those years with you, if you'll recall, before Erik came along. You lost all perspective. Lucy just toyed with you like any senior boy would have."

"That's not true. She went to the mat for me and all I did was—"

"You only remember it differently. How about First Ave? Remember when she blew us off and went to blow some coke instead? Remember baking her that cake? You don't remember crying all the way home and telling me you'd never love anyone else?"

"Well, that's kinda fuzzy, actually." She flutters the jewels dripping from a baroque pastry stand with her fingers, where Ray stacked dozens of vinyl records to resemble a black cake.

"For good reason. Why would you want to dredge that all back up with her now?" Mark leans back on the record shelf. "Remember how I got my ass kicked in high school? Now those guys are all divorced losers and drunks who couldn't afford to buy a floor lamp from me. They wouldn't know a Tiffany from a Target. They see me today and treat me like a king. Why would I reverse that?"

"It wasn't like that with me and Luce. She suffered for me. She got run out of town."

Mark shrugs. "That's what happens when you light the Principal's office on fire."

"Lucy did not set that fire." Kate thumbs through record albums, pushing the stacks back and forth, puffs of mildew make her nose twitch.

"I can't believe you're still defending her. The night janitor barely got out with his life."

"Oh, please. He was fine. They put it out before it got to their precious gym floor."

"You sure seem to remember a lot about it."

"How could we forget? Besides, Lucy was with me that night."

Mark tilts his head. "What? No she wasn't."

"We were in the woods. We went all the way." She whispers, "It was— amazing."

"Stop right there."

Kate shakes her head. "Remember, I had just turned sixteen, and I'd been on my best behavior for over a month. Mom and Dad let me have the car 'cause they thought it was all over once Lucy got suspended. But the first thing I did was drive to her. We heard the firetruck from the park. I drove home and she did too, but . . . I guess they came for her."

Mark crosses his arms; his eyes on her grow stony. "And you didn't step up to provide her an alibi."

"I was too afraid. Ashamed. I lied to everyone. Even you, because I knew you would think I was a shit."

Mark stares out the window with the fear of their past in his eyes. "Well, she could have set it before she met up with you. Who else would have done it?"

"Who knows? It wasn't much of a crime. For all we know, Principal Juhl left one of his cigars burning and Lucy had to take the fall for him."

"He died of heart failure five years ago, so there's no asking him." Mark sighs. "Oh man. Poor Lucy." He can't seem to look at Kate now.

"You see why I can't give up on her? She deserves our friendship."

"Maybe we both sold her out." Mark grimaces. "Dammit, Kate. I don't know. Maybe it all was for the best. I remember the summer you got engaged. You changed, for the better. It was like the first time I saw you as a woman."

Kate's lip curls. "You sound like my mother."

"Well, Lucy's turning you into that kid again."

"God, you're so morose."

"Kate, you need to be careful. Lucy's—she's not all that she seems."

"Give me some credit." *This conversation is desperately in need of changing.* "Hey, what do you know about Marcus Robeson?"

"The guy who jumped?"

"Yeah. Got any old newspapers about it?"

"God, I wish I did. It was rumored he was gay."

"You think everyone is gay."

Mark looks over his glasses. "Aren't they?"

"Seriously though."

"You could check the library or the *Dispatch* online."

"I did. They don't go that far back."

Erik shuffles back in with a long, two-man saw, which sheds dust with every wobble.

"Five bucks," Mark says.

"Really? Cool." Erik opens his wallet, fishes out a bill for Mark, and gazes proudly at the massive saw beside him like he'd reeled in a prize-winning shark. He turns to Kate. "Hey, hon, did you see all those quilts back there? Looks like you got some competition now."

"What?" Kate balks at Mark, heads toward the storage room that opens to the back lot.

Mark bolts from behind the counter and blocks the doorway. "Yeah, um. Those are just some old rags I found in an estate sale."

Kate peers over his shoulder. Stacked over four feet high, there must be nearly a dozen quilts wrapped in plastic. The top one looks familiar. Although, the double wedding ring pattern *is* a popular choice. But the colors, the purple and gold she'd chosen specifically for Mr. and Mrs. Lund's fiftieth wedding anniversary . . .

"Are those all mine? Why are they here? I thought you sold those months ago."

"Um, yeah," Marks says. "They're returns."

"What?"

"Kate, they weren't what they ordered. You keep redesigning what people ask for. They're a little too—too abstract for traditional tastes." Mark shows his teeth, as if he'd eaten something rotten. "Like, Betsy Lund had no idea what that those white things were."

"They were diamonds."

"Well, she thought they looked like bird droppings."

Erik looks at Kate; she can swear he's thinking: *Gee, how do you fuck up a quilt?*

Kate pulls out her checkbook and scrawls quickly. She rips the check off the pad and tucks it in Mark's oxford pocket. "You are the last person I need lying to me."

CHAPTER TWENTY-FIVE

1988
The Twin Cities

KATIE WATCHED THE prairie fly by and turn to asphalt of St. Paul, then concrete, then off-ramps, the spaghetti junction of interstates, storefronts, and finally the high-rises of Minneapolis.

"I can't believe this is really happening."

"Me neither," Mark said from behind the wheel of his RX-7. "Wow. Why am *I* so nervous?" He took a swig from the fifth of vodka and passed it back to her.

Katie knocked back a long gulp then coughed.

Once in the nightclub, they debated the clever things they would say to the first person from their small town to rise to such a pinnacle as First Avenue—the very same stage on which *the Great Purple One* (Prince himself!) had risen to fame. Mark made use of his youthful good looks to flirt with an older man who bought them rail drink after rail drink. The energy of the crowd further heightened their anticipation.

When the Hypnogogs took the stage, Lucy looked petrified—painted blue by the lights, dwarfed by her bass guitar. She seemed electrocuted into place while the lead guitarist and singer strutted around in torn clothes, spiked hair, and makeup. When Lucy sang backup into the microphone, it was so off-key that Mark turned away, grimacing. But Katie kept on staring. She didn't care; she was simply in awe that Lucy was living out her dream.

Mark and Katie did not stay for the main act and instead waited at the side door along the sidewalk for Lucy to emerge. There they leaned against a brick wall painted black with silver stars—in each star, a different band: Hüsker Dü, The Replacements, Soul Asylum, and Prince, of course. The Hypnogogs would get a star one day, didn't Mark think? Maybe.

Eventually, the band poured out the door, eager to light up. The lead guitarist had his arm around Lucy, comforting her about her performance as she hid behind her dark, shaggy bangs. The two intermittently sniffled and wiped at their nostrils.

Lucy's first look at Katie was one of alarm. And then a wincing smile.

Before Katie knew it, she was hugging Lucy tight. She smelled different, like a head shop.

Lucy pulled away politely as if Principal Juhl were still watching them, ready to expel her all over again. "Wow. Thanks for coming, guys." She gave Mark a slapping hug, then lit a cigarette. She pulled on it wryly, more Bogart than Bacall, eyeing Katie's too-new jeans and frilly shirt with a raised brow.

"You were so fantastic." Katie could not contain her grin. She hoped it conveyed every single thing.

"Yeah," Mark said. "It was great, Lucy."

"Thanks." She shrugged, cringing a bit. "Was a little nervous."

"I baked you a cake!" Katie blurted. The sidewalk seemed to tilt at that moment.

Mark coughed and closed his eyes.

"Huh?" Lucy said, head cocked.

"For your birthday?" Katie's belly cramped and a clammy fever swept across her.

"That was last week."

"I know that, dummy. Chocolate cherry chip. Your favorite, remember?"

The other band members turned away, squeaking and snickering.

Lucy chuckled. "Well, where is it?"

"Oh. Well, I—I ate it."

It seemed to take years for Mark to drive home. He kept pulling over, rolling down her window, pleading with her not to throw up on his upholstery. She hated Wicasa Bluffs that night, hated her Lee jeans and Fleet Farm blouses. The next day, with a stinging hangover, she vowed that she would never think about that night again. And she was determined to be a woman of her vows.

BLOGGING MY SOJOURN

One Woman's Journey from Gay to Straight

For a while, Sojourn was my own little purgatorial detox facility. I guess because I wasn't born with Jesus constantly at my bedside or there on Sunday mornings, it just wasn't taking. I mean, I've always been my own personal savior so it seems a bit nosy of him. He mostly seems like a misunderstood hippie and anything good he might have said has passed through the longest game of telephone imaginable. And the bible? Eh. Although I do like this part:

Behold, thou art fair, my love.
Behold, thou art fair.
Thou hast ravished my heart.

Nevertheless, I was willing to see this process through as long as the kids around me were sure that's what they wanted too. But they all just had that look, like: *this is a dream, right? We'll all wake up, right?*

Before that man from my hometown came to speak, before I learned Sojourn had funneled money into his wife's campaign, I'd started pretty neutral on the whole thing. But then Charles sat me down one day to tell me what he figured out was going on in accounting. There were four kids with rich parents. One's dad was a high elder in the Mormon Church. One was the son of a TV minister. One was the daughter of a conservative politician and another was the son of radio show host. All of them were paying at least three times as much as the rest of us. One even paid six figures.

Maybe the payment scales by income, I said. Charles said, no, he had researched the other parents. Plenty had money. But these parents were all in the public eye. They all had a lot to lose by having queer kids if the truth got out. And the further back in the books he went, long before we ever came, the more he found.

If the truth got out.

Patrice commented:
Why are we quoting Song of Solomon? It should not even be in The Bible.

Rolf68 commented:
Something tells me this ain't about Solomon, Jesus or any other dude. Proceed with caution Liesl!

Yaweh commented:
HELLO LIESL, THIS IS GOD.
NO. REALLY, IT'S ME. TRUST ME, I'M GOD.
LIESL, YOU HAVE BEEN A VERY BAD GIRL.
ALTHOUGH I DO FIND YOU AND YOUR FOLLOWERS QUITE ENTERTAINING.
KEEP UP THE GOOD WORK.
I WILL EMAIL INSTRUCTIONS SOON!

CHAPTER TWENTY-SIX
Kate

THE AUDIENCE BANTERS as they fuss over seating in the school auditorium. She's the only one in the front row. Just like church, it's just a bit too forward for most Minnesotans. Screw them.

Kate waves back at Jamie's parents; does she look as terrified as Jamie's mother? The Heathrows (crunchy granola types, according to Erik, who lived their college years in the peace corps) look no more equipped to handle this moment than Kate. Save for this row, the auditorium is packed. Samantha had said a whole slew of Jamie supporters were coming in from the Twin Cities and Madison. *Lavender Magazine* was even sending their managing editor to cover the event.

The rumble of the crowd boils in Kate's head. Or is that her blood pressure spiking?

THE LAST TIME she sat in the front row was for *Sound of Music*, way back in the eighties. Lucy Veebee had played the part of Liesl, Baron Von Trapp's oldest daughter, whom Katie had identified with most in the movie. Mark Fox, a junior that year, played the younger brother Frederick and in a desperate twist, Liesl's Nazi boyfriend Rolf. Back then, there weren't enough boys able sing and twirl about the stage—let alone willing to.

Lucy had swept onstage in a chiffon dress, her hair in tendrils. This normally vinyl-trousered and safety-pinned girl caused quite a commotion that night. Who knew she could look like Brooke Shields and sing like Cyndi Lauper? Her mom was in heaven. Her father, hair still wet from a shower, had gaped.

Then Mark had strode on as Rolf. The crowd murmured at the sight of the boy who was supposed to be Liesl's brother. The only thing changed about him was a grey Nazi uniform two sizes too large and his strawberry blond bangs combed to the opposite side. He took her hands and pleaded in tenor, "Your life little girl is an empty page that men will want to write on."

Lucy's gaze had washed across the front row and landed on Katie. Her eyes flashed.

Oh, my God, she's looking right at me! And everybody knows it. Oh God.
Katie slid down in her chair.

Lucy wrung out her line in a syrupy alto, mostly on key. "*Tooo wriiite oooon.*"

Katie swooned with fear and shame and delicious pride. The crowd guffawed as Liesl and Frederick/Rolf began their spinning dance. Then the crowd cheered.

It was the first year the music program offered three performances. It was the start of a really good music program at WBHS.

THE SEATS FILL next to her.

Mark nudges her shoulder. "Hey you, what's so funny?"

"Oh hi. I was just remembering you in *Sound of Music.*" She leans forward to Ray. "Mark was a Nazi."

"Wha?"

"The play," he says. "I showed you the pictures. Where's Erik?"

"Went with Brace to talk to the talent scout."

"Ah." Mark looks up and his gaze turns frosty.

Lucy Van Buren stands before them in her Barbie ensemble. "Erik sitting here?" She looks around. Her mom, Bridget, stands beside her, wearing a polite smile.

"Nope. It's all yours."

Mark sits back with a sigh.

Lucy and her mom settle in, then Bridget leans across Lucy. She lays a hand on Kate's wrist. "Where are those handsome men of yours?"

Kate battles the urge to rip her arm away. She feels badly. Isn't even sure why she feels this way anymore. Water under the liftbridge, right? Gallons upon gallons.

"They've been talking to a talent scout from UW. Brace is getting a lot of attention right now. He scored a twenty-eight on his ACT, so it could go either way."

Lucy turns to Kate. "Hey, that's great. At least he's in the running. Good for him. How's Sam doing with Erik not being here?"

"She's fine," Kate says. "They'll be here for the Sunday matinee. I'm not even sure she wanted *me* here tonight. But she sure badgered me all day about whether you would be."

Bridget shrinks back into her seat.

"Really?" Lucy shakes her head. "That's crazy."

"Not really. They respect you."

"Ah, naive, impressionable youth."

"A regular pied piper," Mark mutters as the lights dim.

Kate stares at the stage too, elbows Lucy. "I know what you did, by the way."

"What's that?"

"Found that school for Jamie. The one in Minneapolis?"

"Meh. All I did was connect some people. So," Lucy whispers, "what about Claudia?" She glances around. "Is she—?"

"Late night session." Kate bows her head. "Or so she says."

Lucy sighs. "I hope it's not property taxes again. Those are killing me."

"Well. She's coming to the matinee. Even if I have to kidnap her."

WELL INTO THE first act, Jamie Heathrow stands onstage in a glittering gown and wields a scepter as tall as a shepherd's staff. Together she and Samantha (in a dull black dress and a green face) sing about defying gravity. Jamie looks genuinely awestruck, arms outstretched, as a wire harness slowly reels Samantha up into the curtains.

Jamie's falsetto is a fleeting cry to heaven. If she chooses a hormone-based transition it might remain high, otherwise those vocal cords will soon broaden. There's something extraordinary about it, something the Digicam pronged in middle of the aisle won't capture. That airy voice removes the traditionally maniacal comedy from Glinda's character. Her pleading gaze at Elphaba upends the subtext of the play, making the friendship between the girls all the more desperate, the love story between Elphaba and the boy Fiero almost an afterthought. A sort of "Yes, yes, there will be a marriage and little green babies and all that. But this is—this between *us*—this is crucial."

What if Claudia is right? Maybe Kate doesn't need to worry about Zev. It's this changeling that her daughter could be falling in love with.

Samantha's voice fires through the theater like a siren. "No wizard's ever gonna bring me down!"

The curtain tumbles inward. And at first, there is silence. It's so much to fathom. And then everyone realizes it's the polite thing to do. And then the applause grows in a *damn-that-was-something-you-don't-get-on-Channel-Five* sort of way.

At this moment, Kate doesn't care about Jamie's struggles or Claudia's flashbulbs. The girl/boy will do fine. As will Claudia. And Mark and Ray. And maybe even Lucy. The question is what Samantha is thinking right now. What does she hope will come from this? Is a trip to the *American Idol* tryouts at the Mall of America in their future?

Mark leans in. "You okay?"

The lights brighten for intermission.

Kate quickly dabs a knuckle under her eyes. "Oh my God, I'm so stupid."

"No you're not. Look around."

And indeed, Lucy's eyes sparkle and Bridget is dabbing at her own lashes with a Dairy Queen napkin.

Lucy shakes her head slow and incredulous. "Sam could skate into Julliard on her voice alone. And the stage presence? Between the two of them, it's like they've been playing those witches since childhood."

Mark grabs Kate's hand. "I need her for summer stock. C'mon, Kate."

"Just make sure she also has a summer," Lucy says.

Next to him, Ray crosses arms and nods. "I agree. She needs a life too."

"You, hush," Mark says.

Kate blows a gust. "Wow, I don't know. Let's ask her when things calm down."

DURING THE SECOND act, there are a few misspoken lines and cracks in those tired, young voices. But the unintentional humor of shy Jamie Heathrow playing the most popular witch in Oz makes the whole thing fantastic.

Along with Jamie's parents and Mark and Ray, they head backstage, but it's such a madhouse, all they can do is gape at kids running by laughing and hugging each other.

They all follow the girls to the parking lot amidst the cheers and whistles of the cast and other parents.

Samantha slings an arm around Jamie. "Dude. I'm seriously becoming a witch."

"Me too. I can feel it happening."

Kate shrugs. "Great. No car for graduation then, just a broom."

Mark takes Lucy's arm and murmurs low, "Can I talk to you for a second? Privately?"

"Sure," she says, but then she stops walking.

They all do.

Kate stares into the parking lot where a crowd has gathered. At its center glows video camera lights and the occasional flash, which imprints green dots on her retina.

"Whoa," Samantha says.

"Jamie!" a reporter calls and then they all squawk her name like gulls.

Jamie takes Samantha's hand and leads her into the glare and noise.

"Here we go," Kate says. "Now's your chance to run, Luce." She turns. "Lucy?"

But Lucy and Bridget are already halfway to her BMW.

"Great."

Mark raises an eyebrow at Kate but she looks past him. Farther down the sidewalk stands Zev, hands in pockets, not a hockey buddy in sight. Kate waves. He waves. But before she can open her mouth, he turns and strolls off. She eases into the crowd along with the Heathrows, prepared to yank Samantha from the fray the moment she says something ridiculous.

"This is a historic night, Jamie. Congratulations." And it is. The first time in this state that a trans student has played their correct gender. "How does it feel?"

"Fine. It feels fine." Jamie stares at the ground.

"But do you think this play represents a sea change for your movement?"

"I don't—I don't have a movement."

"Yet," Samantha says, her face bright and shining with the remnants of Noxzema and green sparkles.

Kate crosses her arms and grins. They are absolutely loving this. They'll remember this the rest of their lives, talk about it forever, blow it way out of proportion, even though the reporters are just from a small gay magazine in the Twin Cities, local cable, and the *Valley Dispatch*.

"Samantha, how do you feel about Senator Larson's referendum proposal tonight?" the reporter from the *Dispatch* asks. "How do you resolve Jamie's transition with your grandmother's politics?"

"Huh?"

"Senator Larson sought a vote on the marriage amendment this evening."

"Oh my God," Samantha whispers and shrinks from the light.

"All right," Jamie's father interjects. "That's enough."

Kate steps in and hooks Samantha's arm. "You don't have to say another word."

Samantha stops and says over her shoulder, "I love my grandma. We don't always agree. But I love her. Other than that? She's wrong."

Ouch, Kate thinks, that one's gonna sting, but Claudia brought it on herself.

"If there's a God, it doesn't care who we love. And it would also know that Jamie is becoming who she was always meant to be." Then Samantha nestles into Kate, and they make their way down the walk.

Mark and Ray meet them at the cars. Ray is on his cellphone, a finger in his other ear.

"The senator really pulled a fast one on us," Mark says.

"On all of us." Kate kisses her daughter's head.

"She used my night," Samantha whispers. "She used my night."

Kate locks eyes with Mark. "I'm sure it's just a coincidence, honey."

At the minivan, the girls hug goodnight. Jamie's parents briskly walk her away. Samantha gets in, and Kate closes the door.

"If we'd known," Mark whispers, "we would have bumped up the protest for tonight."

"She must have thought our family being there would do too much damage this time," Kate murmurs. "I told her we wouldn't be on the Marrisota side anymore."

Mark nods. "Probably didn't want any more run-ins with the monkey suits either."

"What do you think this means now?" Kate asks. "Will she get enough votes this way?"

"Don't know." Mark shrugs and looks at Ray, who's struggling to hear his phone. "Our friend at the Strib will let us know soon as the session lets out."

CHAPTER TWENTY-SEVEN
Samantha

SHE SPRAWLED ACROSS the couch, sucking a banana Popsicle, transfixed by one of her favorite programs on the National Geographic Channel. On screen, a lone orangutan hunched nearly motionless in a tattered jungle of leaves and ropey vines. His shoulders drooped, the amber tendrils of fur on his head gently swaying. The narrator, one of those lispy British dudes that always make these wildlife shows sound like a madhatter's tea party, seemed to know everything the ape was thinking.

"Bartholomew has tried his run at the females only to be violently cast out by his father, just like that, his food source at the preserve fiercely guarded by the others and his ribs wounded in the process. He's been like this for two days and if he doesn't find food soon, he will most certainly starve."

The ape looked up at the sparkling tree canopy. He slapped a palm on a vine and pulled himself hand-over-hand, up and out of the camera frame.

"Bartholomew may be down, but he is not out. He will return, a sort of prodigal ape, and will remember his father's slight and the other males and females who shunned him. It won't be a pretty homecoming. Orangutans are strong enough to literally tear each other limb from limb."

Mom galloped, three steps at a time, down to the family room. "Hey!" she said all happy-go-lucky.

Samantha paused the TV and looked up from the couch. "Hey."

Mom sat down on the couch arm. "Wanted to tell you again how proud I was of you the other night."

"Thanks," Samantha said quietly, gnawing a little on the Popsicle stick, she could still get a little syrup out if she sucked hard enough.

"Not just the play. The reporters too. Jamie okay?"

Actually, Jamie was getting newfound attention, not all of it good. Maddox Funk-Abel now oscillated between whistling at her in the hall and "accidentally" running her into the lockers. Brace and Zev called him out every time they were around. But sometimes they weren't. Jamie just laughed it off. And though Mom was besties with Maddox's mom, it seemed premature to take a whack at that hornet's nest.

"She's obsessing over going to Cooper now." It was odd how now that Jamie was considering leaving for the big city, she talked less about the prospect of hormones and surgery.

"Ah, that's good." Mom nodded. "I just hated to see you stuck in the middle. Your grandmother should have warned you. In fact, I'm surprised we haven't heard from her."

Samantha was no longer surprised. Grandma was skewered in the press that week for trying to rush the vote. Even half the Republicans turned down her request to vote on the amendment and called it grandstanding. Marrisota had one more chance next week at a special hearing. Mark Fox was already tuning up the Shakespeare On The Bluffs bus for a final protest.

Samantha crossed arms. "She barely said two words to me at the matinee. Except she thought it was too pagan. I know she's pissed about what I said."

Up popped the angry elevens on Mom's brow, but as the look of concern grew on Samantha's face, the elevens faded.

"Oh, honey. You could murder someone and that woman would still love you. It's just that Grandma's from another era." Mom picked up Samantha's leg by the ankle and removed one sneaker, then the other, and tossed the shoes on the floor.

"And possibly another dimension."

"She wants the best for you. But she can't exactly switch positions now, even if she wanted to, she'd lose face with so many of her supporters."

Samantha nodded thoughtfully. "Did you know the origin of 'saving face' comes from China? It's a really crucial indicator of trust in their social network."

"Where do you learn this stuff? I know it's not in school."

Samantha shrugged, tapped the Popsicle stick to her lips. "Lucy says I should consider evolutionary psychology. And put singing and astronomy on the backburner."

"Mmm. She does, does she? Well, you could do anything you wanted. You've always been smarter than you dress."

"Hey!" Samantha spun a throw pillow at her.

Mom caught it and whacked Samantha in the belly with it. "Seriously though, you've got plenty of time to decide."

"I kinda like the idea of studying what I can really get my hands on."

"And—how many primates have you been getting your hands on?"

"*Mom.*"

"What about you and Jamie? Is there something romantic going—"

Samantha grimaced. "She's my best friend."

"Yeah, so?"

"I like Zev!"

"So that's still on?"

"Well, I need to call him. He texted me after the play. We might do something this weekend. Is the protest on Saturday or Sunday?"

"Neither," Mom said. "It will probably be on a weekday, same day as the hearing. Anyway, who said you're going?"

"Come on." Sam sat up. "I could get out of school—"

"Dad and I don't want you mixed up in it."

"There are a ton of kids in PFLAG."

"It's going to be hard enough for your grandma to have me there. Mark and Ray know you support them."

"This is bigger than Mark and Ray and you know it." Samantha glowered at her mom and then looked away. "I wouldn't be obnoxious or anything."

"I said, no." Back came the angry elevens.

"Mom."

"No."

"God." Samantha flicked off the TV and bolted to her room. At that moment she hated her mom, really, really hated her. She could think of no other word for it. The feeling was like a seething ball of copper in her belly. Her tears ran over her cheeks. Why was Mom such a bitch?

Oh my God I just hated my mom in my head. What the fuck is wrong with me?
She called Jamie.

"NOPE. NEVER HATED my parents. I've hated my cousin though. Dude, I love your mom."

"I know. I think there's something wrong with me. She just told me how proud she was . . ." Sam sobbed into the phone.

"Don't take this the wrong way, but maybe it's your period."

"That's such a stereotype." From Jamie? She fought the urge to hang up.

"Sam, maybe she's right not to let you. I mean, my parents said fine, but sometimes I think they're worried if I don't get my way, I'll slit my wrists. And sometimes I think they just don't want to grow up."

Samantha wiped her eyes and fell back on her pillow. "Wish we could swap parents for a couple weeks."

"You do have better food."

Samantha chuckled. "Did you read the blog?"

"Yeah. Weird isn't it?"

"Okay, she may be crazy."

"This is what we have to look forward to."

"Let's not grow up then."

"Deal," Jamie said. "That has to be your grampa that visited Sojourn, don't you think?"

"Yeah. So embarrassing."

"At least Lucy doesn't hold it against you."

"Yeah. Hey, what did Maddox say to you today?"

"Nothing. I gotta go."

"Jame, seriously, what did he say? Did he call you Snowplow again?"

"No, just Glinda."

"Hmm."

"What?"

"That's just uncharacteristically nice of him."

"Is it such a surprise that someone might like me?"

"No. But Maddox? Talk about crazy. You could do better. Remember what he did to Amanda Barnes?"

"She was a willing participant. Just underage."

"Wow, blame the victim much?"

"Are you serious?"

Jamie sighed.

"Okay," Samantha said. "Night."

"Night."

BLOGGING MY SOJOURN

One Woman's Journey from Gay to Straight

What if my natural state is blowing things up? What if since my brother died, blowing stuff up has gotten results? What if I walked the hot grate to be seen? To be heard? All I know for sure is that I'm standing here with a stick of lit dynamite and I don't know where to throw it. When I tried prayer, there was only silence.

I've been asked to do something for "the cause." I suppose it's been a long time coming. Maybe everything we do is a long time coming.

It is a definite betrayal. So twisted, and yet, so perfect in the long run. I guess you have to capsize a sinking boat to get it to float. I only hope the ones I've come to care about don't get hurt too much. The rest of them? They're going to wish they never messed with me.

Praise Jesus

Posted by Liesl ~ 1:00 AM ~ 2 comments

InChrist commented:
Good luck! But you won't really need it. With Jesus on your side, anything is possible.

Rolf68 commented:
Please don't do anything stupider.

CHAPTER TWENTY-EIGHT

Kate

THE PINK AND green rose-painted bus full of the Civil Diss River Valley Contingent rumbles toward St. Paul. Inside, Mark Fox, the chipper skipper of this merry band, sings falsetto to Bronski Beat's "Small Town Boy," which pipes from a battered boombox. His passengers attempt to sing along with their driver even though half of them weren't even born when the song came out.

Kate steals a glance at the back of the bus, where two young women they'd picked up in Woodbury sit canoodling. One of them catches her eye and she turns back around, feeling like a peeping tom.

Anita was right, this is an away game: stuck in a sweaty bus, on someone else's schedule, everyone trying to be popular at seventy miles per hour without seatbelts. And here Kate sits with a Tupperware full of protest snickerdoodles on her lap when she should be at home, taking part in the last weeks of her son's high school years and monitoring her daughter's' love life. *Poor Erik.* He probably thinks she's completely lost it. He'd never say. Maybe he's got better things to do. Maybe she should ask. Maybe he's sneaking around with Jennifer Turnquist. Maybe it doesn't matter. He's never home anymore. And that's less disappointing than it used to be.

Across the aisle, Ray smiles and offers a knowing sigh, then returns to gazing out the window at the outlet mall passing by. *He doesn't know shit.* At least not her shit.

Kate stares at him. What must he be thinking? What sorts of arguments go on in their house? From Puerto Rico via New Jersey, Ray had come to Wicasa Bluffs for some peace and quiet. When it came to his and Mark's belated nuptials, he seemed more interested in discussing power of attorney than where the honeymoon might be. He'd gladly stayed here, put up with life in the "banal canal" as Mark called it. Their years of range-free monogamy, seemed more a testament to marriage than any extravagant ceremony Mark could whip up.

Would she really be fighting so hard for gay marriage if it wasn't for these two? If it weren't for those years of idle chitchat and bonding, while complaining about her mother-in-law? If Kate hadn't known anybody gay, wouldn't she be just another person who wanted peace, love, and harmony but left it to the activists? Or maybe even left it up to the Bible?

And isn't this trek also a mission of spite? Because way back when Claudia told toddler Brace that the dinosaurs died off because there wasn't any room for them on Noah's ark and Kate has never let that go. Truth is though, Claudia was always there as a mother-in-law, through the good and the bad. The simple things: phone calls, birthday cards, Christmas presents. She babysat many times during those early years, even though she was working long hours as a city council member and trying to launch her career. The woman was so much more present than Kate's own mom, who had stayed long enough to see her oldest safely married and then packed off for Florida as soon as her youngest graduated.

Maybe it is time to truly make Claudia a quilt. A peace offering after all this is over.

She'll probably throw it back in Kate's face.

She sneaks another glance at the two women. The bus rocks and jostles, pressing her thighs against one another, the seat tugging at her jeans, friction warming her inseam. She can't help but recall making love to Lucy in last night's dream, transposed upon the real Lucy smirking in the deli booth, Lucy wandering lost atop the bluffs, Lucy wrapped up in her new quilt and reaching out to draw Kate in with her. Kate can nearly feel herself slide into Lucy's arms before the Leap crumbles and they tumble into molten lava.

Isn't this journey also something to burnish and bring back to Lucy like a prize? Lucy might have been a great manipulator once, but Kate has learned a few tricks too. Imagine that. So, isn't it convenient, this large-scale thwarting of parental authority, a skill she had once royally failed at in front of Lucy, now recoverable by tenfold?

Maybe there would be a photo in the paper. This time with Kate on the other side.

And to what end?

You see, Lucy, I have prostrated myself before the holy mother-in-law. For Mark. For Ray. For Jamie. For you. How do you like them apples?

"Hey sad sack," Anita blurts into her ear.

Kate gulps and stares forward.

Anita scoots into the seat. "What's wrong?"

"Oh, pfft." *Think.* "Sam and I had a little tussle last night. Really wanted to come."

"Yeah? Why didn't you let her?"

"I'm not taking her out of school for this. Besides I can't do that to Claudia."

"Are you kidding? She dragged Samantha into the last one."

"Okay, let me rephrase. I can't do that to Erik." Kate slumps further into the seat. "Honestly, he and I are hardly speaking. If I had taken Sam today? No way. The press is searching for any crack in Claudia's veneer." Kate looks out the window and mumbles, "They have no idea."

Anita throws an arm around her. "I think that's why I never thought to come before. It's civil war, isn't it? Family against family. Rob's family are rabid conservatives. But now I'm thinking that if the average person doesn't take a stand, Mark and Ray are never gonna see this thing happen."

Kate forces a smile and raises her fist to limply shake it. "Yay newly politicized friend."

"Are you going to say anything to Madame Senator today?"

"Don't see how I can. What am I supposed to say? Break a nail?"

Anita clicks her tongue. "Mmm."

"So," Kate says, "how's it going with Christophe?"

"Who? Oh, the teacher-boy sandwich? He got cold feet. But we're going to try Craigslist." Anita grows thoughtful. "We've got to do something soon or Rob is going to throw out his back pretending to be our third every time."

God bless Anita Funk-Abel.

INSIDE THE CAPITOL rotunda, each side prepares its well-worn case. A representative of Civil Diss speaks first about the strengthening of gay and lesbian families through marriage.

The crowd is much more somber than last year's hooligans in animal costumes. There are claps of approval, but no yelling and no boos from the other side. The hushed echoes throughout the Romanesque building induce reverence and the curved marble walls have herded the opponents so close, the Minnesota Nice is as viscous as syrup. Under one of the dozen archways supporting the gallery, a group of teenagers holds signs, smiling with the sort of exhilaration one does when changing the world. They are dressed not unlike Samantha and Jamie, black at war with rainbows, lips glittering with fairy dust. But there's no time for guilt.

Across the circular room, Claudia Larson has yet to blanch at the sight of her daughter-in-law carrying a placard that reads, *Equality for All God's Children.* She stands studiously framed by an archway, smile on medium wattage, and shakes the hands of passing gay marriage opponents, whose signs read things like *LEVITICUS—LIVE IT OR BURN* and *LOVE THE SINNER, HATE THE ACTIVIST JUDGES.*

Bert Larson, however, has plenty to say. He slips over, pulls Kate away from Anita's side, and calmly escorts her to one of the outer columns.

"How could you do this, Kate?"

She lowers her sign. "How could *you*? What do you care if Mark and Ray want to make it official?"

"You might as well hand my grandchildren over as party favors. The next generation is at the mercy of gay propaganda."

"You should know by now that whoever my kids chose to love—"

A cameraman turns to them and they reflexively lean into each other and smile.

When the man moves away, Bert calms. "Did you forget everything you've heard in church for the past decade?"

"No. It used to be that our church didn't get involved in politics. It used to be that we did unto others as we wanted done unto us."

"You've twisted God's word to your own purposes, Kate. Do you know where your husband is while you're gallivanting around in that bus?" Bert says. "Do you? He's working hard to put food on your table and take care of his children. Do you think he wouldn't love to have a fling? Do you think he wouldn't love to go on a month-long hunting trip with his buddies? Do you think he wouldn't love to spend his money on whatever strikes him?"

"Erik and I have both made compromises."

Bert waves comfortingly at Claudia. "Because you're married."

"Yes. That's exactly my point. Everyone deserves this chan—" Kate can't even hear herself finish for the reverberating applause throughout the dome.

The Civil Diss representative steps away from the podium and the foreman announces Senator Larson. Kate returns to her friends as Claudia crosses the velvet rope with a companion in tow. It is a woman in a black skirt and white blouse, with Clinique counter flawless makeup, and long, dark hair, which is layered, like a . . . like a morning show host.

"Oh no she dint," Anita says with a groan.

Mark gasps loud and long.

"Shiiit," Ray whispers.

High above, the ceiling of the dome wants to turn and tilt. Kate tries to focus on something, anything that will alter this moment in her life. Claudia's clipped, you-betcha speechifying begins and Kate finally takes a breath. She stares— she glares—at Lucy Van Buren, willing her to look at her, but Lucy just gazes straight ahead, at the glowing red exit sign on the other side of the rotunda.

"Our friend Lucinda here once led a lesbian lifestyle. But with the help of Sojourn Reclaimers she's starting a new life. What if she had entered into one of these domestic partnerships? She would now be saddled by a false family, always unsure in the back of her mind whether she simply had not met the right man yet."

Kate tries to turn then, to leave—to run. She'll call a taxi, or call Erik. But she is blocked by a phalanx of wide-angle lenses and boom mics. When she turns back, Mark hooks her arm and supports her. He glares at Lucy, growling.

Lucy turns to him, smiling benevolently.

"What. The. Fuck. Was that?" Ray asks.

"She's high," Anita whispers. "The senator pumped her full of something fer sure. Maybe some of her buddy Limbaugh's oxycontin."

"Do you see now?" Mark hisses at Kate, "Do you *see*? This is revenge Kate. If you don't think this is payback, you are blind."

"Thanks to Sojourn, I have definitely seen the light," Lucy says. "Without the help of Bert and Claudia Larson, I would never have made it back"—She turns to her dazed smile on Kate—"back home. I mean, not that there aren't temptations—"

"Thank you, Ms. Van Buren." Sojourn Reclaimer's president, Henry Cleaver, takes the podium quickly and somberly plugs his mega-church. But his pre-packaged speech raises no more cheers or boos than anyone else.

It strikes Kate as an afternoon of eulogies rather than final arguments.

OUTSIDE THE CAPITOL, Mark refuses to wait for the vote and stomps down the broad capitol steps to the bus. The River Valley Contingent skitters after him in fear of being left behind.

Kate waits by the doors for Lucy to emerge. When Lucy does, she's flanked by Mr. Cleaver and Claudia, Bert holding up the rear.

Kate walks backward in front of them. "What the hell is wrong with you?" The granite stairs are twice the depth of normal steps, causing her to stagger and look behind herself.

Lucy stares at the ground as if carefully measuring her own steps.

"*The hell* is exactly what is no longer wrong with Ms. Van Buren," Cleaver says.

"Kate, do not make a scene," Claudia sings with a smile.

"Yeah, that's your job." Kate lets them pass.

Lucy glances back over her shoulder. "It's for the best, Katie. You'll see."

Claudia descends the steps confidently and gazes out at the St. Paul skyline. "Doesn't the cathedral look lovely today?"

IN THE BUS, everyone drops the windows down, below the do-not-lower-window-past-this-line mark.

"That bitch." Anita falls into the seat next to Kate.

"That idiot," Mark says. He drags his *Second Class Citizen!* sign wearily up the stairs like Linus with his blanket and plops down in the driver's seat.

"Maybe they hypnotized her," someone says.

"It doesn't matter. One ex-gay can't hurt us."

"Oh, great Foxtradamus," another says, "what do we do now?"

Kate stares out the window at the video lights brightening the twilight and at the crowds dispersing. The sweet scent of lilac blows into the stuffy bus and Kate lays her palm on the window. Her fingertips search for a pulse against the glass. Lucy looks out from the cluster of pundits and toward the bus, her stare washes over the thorny, twisted rose stems Mark had painted along the side.

"It doesn't make sense," Kate says. "Part of her has been erased where it should have evolved."

Mark grumbles and the bus roars to life. He slams the door shut and jerks the big wheel left. "I'm sick to fucking death of these people and their ridiculous obsession with their stupid marriages, their *hallowed* institution telling me how I have to live."

"If it's such a ridiculous institution," Ray says, "why the hell are we fighting to enter into it?"

Mark glares into the broad rear view mirror and the bus lurches forward.

Anita grimaces. "I hate to say this, but he's got a point."

"Easy for you, you'll be married forever." But Mark continues to balk at Ray. "So, what exactly are you saying?"

The bus rolls away from the capitol and toward the onramp to the spaghetti junction interchange.

"I'm saying that I moved to Minnesota a decade ago to be with the man I love." Ray sits with his legs in the aisle, looking around at everyone. "I didn't sign up for a war. If I wanted a battle, I could go back to my old family."

"Don't you want your son's parents to be married?"

"I want my son to come into the least stressful environment we can give him. Maybe we should move to the Bay Area and forget this war with the Snow Queen."

"Wait," Anita says. "Back up a second. The Great Foxtradamus says Rob and I will be married forever?" She seems genuinely puzzled by this.

"Of course," he grumbles. "Your wrinkles mirror each other."

Anita grabs her face. "What?"

Ray rolls eyes. "Mark thinks if you sleep facing each other, you'll stay together. You get wrinkled more on the side you sleep on. Husbands always sleep by the door, so—"

"*This* is your science?"

Wind picks up inside the bus and the windows go back up to slits. A rumble fills the interior. Kate watches the city fall away to suburb and then to bean field. She opens her purse and pulls out a mirror.

CHAPTER TWENTY-NINE
Samantha

SHE TIPTOED UP the stairs and into the darkened kitchen.

Her parents thought they were so sly with the sexing. Every Saturday, after Dad got home from golfing they'd wait until the kids went to bed, then they'd shut their door and lock it.

Jamie liked to joke that her parents only had sex once, just to make her special. *Har. Har.* But Samantha had seen so many nature shows she couldn't even kid herself. In fact, it had recently become quite handy, this Saturday night business. It had become her "meat night" when she could scour the fridge for random samplings, enough to slake her cravings but not so much that anyone would notice. Unfortunately, the only meat in the house tonight besides frozen deer was one ragged slice of roast beef. Samantha stashed the deli bag under her t-shirt, gingerly closed the fridge door and slipped quietly downstairs. She opened the sliding glass door to the backyard, walked out to the patio, and sat down on an iron chair, the mesh chilling her thighs. The night sky was clear. The air smelled green and peppery like geraniums.

Samantha unfolded the bag. What was she going to do with the evidence? She couldn't bring herself to flush it. But leaving it in any of the trash bins might get it noticed and then the puckhead would guess who took the last slice and boy would he be proud of himself. No, she would take the bag to school and trash it before she met up with Jamie.

She looked to the stars, dangled the slice above her mouth, and slowly lowered it.

Sweet, sweet meat.

The kind that gets stuck in your teeth.

What a treat. Meat.

"I'm sorry cow," she said to Orion. "And I thank you."

Behind her, the sliding glass door hissed.

"Sam, what are you doing still up?" came mom's soft voice.

"Hmmm?" Samantha wiped the grease from her lips with the back of her hand. Her tongue rapidly scoured her teeth. "Just stargazing."

"Thought I heard someone in the kitchen." Mom and Chuck walked over. She sat down on the glider and he loped off to pee in the new hostas unfurling along the fence. "Wondered if we could talk for a few minutes."

"Oh! Sure. Yeah." *Frak.*

"I feel like you're holding onto something.

—*Double frak*—

I mean, not that I need to know every little thing, but you're skulking around like a thief these days."

Samantha leaked a muffled chirp with a shrug.

"I think I know what it is." Mom stared up to the sky and then leveled her eyes back on her daughter. She looked kind of severe in the mostly dark.

"Awww, Mom, I'm such a fraud."

"What? Sweety you could never be that." Mom kept her voice low, glancing at the neighboring windows. "I only want to know that you and Zev, and you Jamie are being—safe."

"Huh? Mom." Then Samantha hushed her voice too. "How many times do I have to tell you I'm not a lesbian? I only like Zev."

"Okay, okay. I'll never mention it again." Mom chuckled and drew her fingers across her chest in an X as if that were somehow holy. "But you and Zev need to be safe."

"Of course, Mom. We've only kissed."

Mom squinted at her but Samantha had nothing to hide—when it came to Zev.

"Wait, what makes you a fraud then?"

Down the alley a basketball hit a backboard and then came the rubber splash of dribbling. Again, the basketball hit the backboard and the hoop twanged.

Samantha pulled the waxed-paper deli bag out from under her thigh.

Mom bit back a smile. "Wow, roast beef." She held out her hand and Samantha tossed her the bag. Mom balled it up in her fist and tucked it in her robe pocket. "That's like, the heroin of meat." Her eyebrows danced.

"It's not funny. I feel terrible."

"Your grandmother could be right. You may be anemic. Think I'll schedule your physical earlier this year." Mom dangled her legs off the glider and pushed it back and forth with her toes. "Blood will spill, Sam. It spills every day. With or without you."

"I don't want to be complicit. All the mechanized slaughter? All those lives started—and then stopped?" Samantha held herself. "This world is just madness sometimes."

"Oh, honey." Mom patted the glider. Samantha came over and sat down, leaned into the terrycloth robe and her mother's breast. Mom draped an arm around her. She smelled like home, would always smell like home. "It's beautiful too sometimes. The best thing going. You know, your dad and I spend a fortune buying only organic stuff for you."

"I know. But it's not enough. Once you learn about animals and how they think, it starts looking like a holocaust."

"God, you sound like me at your age. I like how you remind me of the ideals I forgot. Maybe it's time we all ate less of it." Mom's head lolled back so she could see the top of the sky. "Yunno, you don't have to be exactly like Jamie to show solidarity. Is she pressuring you—to go full vegan?"

"No. Not really. Well, maybe." All those stars, so far gone in space and time, made tracers with the motion of the glider. "Didn't Lucy pressure you to try new things?"

"Sure." Mom looked away. The glider slowed. "Everyone shapes us, I guess."

It was probably time to tell Mom about the blog, but she just couldn't find the words. She sensed it would change everything between everybody. They sat silent for a while. The basketball player had stopped. A few blocks down a small dog was yipping. Chuck stopped sniffing around and grumbled.

"You know how people who wear glasses look sorta bleak when they take them off?" Samantha asked. "Lucy kinda looks like that." She set her mother with a casual stare. "Except when she's around you."

Mom drew in a deep breath and let it out slow. She surveyed the yard like a queen appraising her queendom. "Luce and I had a special bond. Like you and Jamie."

"Kinda, but not quite. Like more, right?" Samantha crossed her arms. "Jamie's dad told her that Lucy once sang for you up on the Leap."

"Yeah, it was totally embarrassing." Mom laughed easy and low. "I loved it. And then I hated it."

"And did you love *her*?"

Mom's nose wrinkled. "I was too young to understand that stuff."

"I understand love. You were my age."

A tiny gust parted her mother's lips. She shook her head as if somehow she was surprised by this. "Yeah. I did. I really did."

"I'm sorry she's letting you down."

"She's letting us all down, Sam."

"But mostly herself."

"Mmm."

BLOGGING MY SOJOURN

One Woman's Journey from Gay to Straight

Got back from the Family First Expo yesterday. Hoped I'd return to more business on the horizon but, apparently, one must have the patience of a sloth in heat to run a Bed and Breakfast. We have guests trickling in and exactly one reservation for a month from now. Anyway, I met lots of well-meaning people, scored a huge bag of swag: pencils with Bible verses, clappers for Jesus, sunset-filled bookmarks, CDs of inspirational rock that's actually well-produced, etc.

In the trash it goes.

What they have done to us, the young ones in particular, I cannot forgive. I can almost forgive those people who tried to erase me from their lives back when it was the norm, but to know it's still going on decades later?

Sorry, not sorry.

I mean, hell, what else is there to do around here? Repent? Please. If there's any praying to be done, it's to pray that I still have the courage to pull this off the right way.

I think the town may have a betting pool on when I'm going to jump from this bluff. Honestly, I have never felt more alive. I don't get depressed in the traditional sense. Sure, I've been abused, taken drugs, been robbed of my hormones. But none of those things cracked my core. And my core runs hot. I'm not going to drop off a cliff like some cold stone. I'm going to burn out in the sun's corona.

Anyone who truly knows me knows that. I thought Vicky knew me but she is no longer mine to hope for. Unfortunately, I don't think there is anyone else who truly knows me. I've never been sure how to reveal myself to others but through art and mirrors and acting out.

So I think it's more disappointment than depression actually. Yeah, I'm existentially disappointed that people haven't lived up to their worth.

Praise Jesus?

Posted by Liesl ~ 3:00 PM ~ 2 comments

Patrice commented: It's all I can do to keep reading this blog.

Rolf68 commented: And yet here you are.
You're waking up, Liesl. Rub your eyes some more. And get back on the carousel. Have you lived up to what you could have been to Vicky and her family? Her friends?

CHAPTER THIRTY

Samantha

SHE WAS EXHAUSTED, her eyes dipping nearly closed and her head weighing heavily as she ran the electric toothbrush over her teeth in a perfunctory swipe. There was still puckhead laughter coming from the rec room, but it was moving upstairs. She rolled her eyes. At least Maddox was finally leaving.

The end of Brace's high school year was arriving fast and furious with people coming and going, freedoms won for the new man of the house. A half-dozen of Brace's teammates had been over watching *sportsball* highlights of some kind. They'd all shaved off their hockey mullets and now looked (and sounded) like they were ready for boot camp—or a zoo. Meanwhile, she and Jamie were trying to study for end of semester tests. Zev kept popping in, making sexy eyes, except she was dressed in her rattiest sweats, and besides Maddox would also sometimes follow him in and try and steal things off the shelves and make fun of the loser-quotient of her collectible figurines and stare at Jamie.

Jamie had gone pink in the face and she looked somewhere between spooked by Maddox and electrified by his presence. Sure, they had talked about the hotness level of guys before, but this was the first she'd seen of this side of her best friend.

Meanwhile, Mom had been carting down buckets of Pizza Rolls and liters of sodas, which, while keeping Mom distracted from her growing list of dramas, was fueling the obnoxiousness coming out of the rec room.

Samantha had finally shut the door to the entire lot of them, so they could actually concentrate. They didn't even have time to read Lucy's blog tonight, a first. And anyway, Samantha was a little exhausted by the woman's unpredictability.

Now, with everyone gone, Samantha settled into bed. She tossed around for a while, thinking of increasingly hotter and hotter scenarios of her and Zev just happening to run into each other around town. Trying to find just the right locale in which to complete the fantasy, she began to drift.

Her phone buzzed across the room from her desk.

Sigh.

She stumbled out of bed, snatched it and climbed back in.

    GLINDA: hello?

    GLINDA: where are u?
    ELPHABA: bed zzzz
    GLINDA: very funny i'm waiting!
    ELPHABA: ?
    GLINDA: u said go to leap
    ELPHABA: no I didn't!

Samantha scrolled up her feed. Meet me on leap @10:30

    ELPHABA: i didn't write that!
    GLINDA: wtf
    ELPHABA: hello?

    ELPHABA: HELLO

But Jamie did not write again.

Samantha ran to Brace's room and shook his big slumping frame awake. "Hey, puckhead! What did you do?"

"Whu?"

"You use my phone to punk Jamie?"

"What are you talking about? Lemme sleep."

"Did Maddox open my phone? Hey! Did he?"

"No!" He scoffed, then squinted at her. "Wait. Maybe."

Samantha sprinted up the stairs to her parents' bedroom.

CHAPTER THIRTY-ONE
Kate

ERIK WHIPS THE truck into the gravel lot next to the clearing. Rob Funk-Abel pulls his Audi up beside them. They hadn't called the Heathrows, gambling that this was all a simple misunderstanding, but halfway through the drive, Anita texted that Maddox was not answering his cellphone.

Even without headlights, the lookout point of Maiden Leap is much brighter than the last late night Kate had been here, what with the streetlamps next to the Gainsborough manse and a nearly full moon.

As the parents emerge from their cars, a rocking guitar blares from the turret room of the old home. The music stops and starts over and over again, reverberating from inside. Lucy must be writing.

At first it seems no one is at the lookout point, but as Kate, Erik, Rob, and Anita ascend the clearing, they make out two figures at the very edge of the bluff, out past the fence, struggling.

All four sprint forward, Erik leaping the fence.

Maddox has Jamie by the wrists, trying to pull her up, yelling, "Come on, push!"

Jamie is bent in half, her belly on the main slab and legs standing on an outcropping a couple feet below.

Erik drops and scrambles out onto the craggy rock. A scream rises in Kate's throat, but she pushes it back down.

"Oh God," Anita says. "Oh shit. Oh fuck. Oh God."

Erik grabs Jamie by her armpits while Rob grabs Erik's legs to steady him.

Kate gingerly steps out onto the rocks and as they drag Jamie up, she helps hoist Jamie by the belt hoop until her feet can find purchase. Anita goes to her son, who stands mute.

As Jamie clambers onto the relatively level shard of stone, Kate looks out and down, knowing it's probably the only time she ever will take the opportunity. Through the brush, the road and river below seem to rise up at her. And, of course, no Wicasa or Chelee to be found. Her vision tilts and she turns away.

Jamie scrambles up onto her knees and collapses back down sobbing, her butt on her heels.

The men stand up panting, hands on knees.

Maddox bends down, softly apologizes to Jamie, and she smacks his hand away with a low growl.

Kate pulls Jamie up to her feet. "Are you hurt anywhere, honey?"

"No." Jamie sniffles. "Well, maybe my arm."

"What happened here?" Erik demands.

Rob violently pushes his son in the chest. "What the fuck were you doing?"

"We were just playing and got too close."

"I wasn't playing anything. I could have died!"

"Oh, you weren't going to fall."

"Fuck you!"

"I said I'm sorry!"

"Everyone calm down." Kate piles her hands on top of her head as she catches her breath.

All is silent. Even the stop-starting song from the Gainsborough. The light in the turret is out.

A dark figure walks quickly toward them and then slows. "What the hell—?"

Jamie runs to Lucy, weeping and mumbling into her shoulder. Lucy turns her away from the group and walks a few steps, brushing Jamie's hair back and searching her face; imploring her to repeat herself. Jamie whispers quickly and then quiets.

Lucy turns back, her eyes sharpening on Maddox. "Thought she was fair game, eh?" She fake laughs. "Thought she'd be eager to become a woman? You think you're the only guy to get his rocks off pulling this pathetic shit?" She looks at Rob with a scoff and shakes her head. "It never ends."

Lucy pulls Jamie to her and walks her up the path to her driveway. She helps her into the passenger seat of her sportster and they drive off down the bluff.

Rob yanks his son down the gulley by his arm, Anita trailing behind in tears.

All grows silent on the clearing. Save for the boil of insects. Twenty generations of crickets and cicadas. Thousands upon thousands.

"This place is cursed," Kate says.

Erik rubs his beard growth with shaking hands. "Or maybe people just suck."

Kate goes to lean against him.

AT HOME, AFTER speaking to the kids and calming Samantha down by omitting just how close to the precipice they actually were, Kate and Erik crawl into bed.

It's well past midnight. He is still shaking.

Kate holds him tightly and rubs his scalp with her nails until he is snoring. She stares at the popcorn ceiling. The man had thrown himself at the bluff with only a millisecond of calculation, simply assuming he wouldn't go sailing off—for someone he wasn't even related to.

She envisions the empty space just beyond the bluff and how it beckons. How it pulled on her that night so long ago and how her parents just left Lucy standing near it in the dark, Lucy's red face shrinking in the taillights. How easy it would have been for Lucy to simply jump and cause the biggest uproar imaginable. And how has Kate not even thought about this possibility until just this very second?

What was the invisible quotient that stopped Lucy, but not the boy in the 1950s?

Maybe Lucy had already been too strong to give up, too strong to give in. Sure, it might have made a good legend to leave behind, the Leap was due for another suicide people had darkly joked. But no, Lucy would have wanted to see how it all ended. Maybe, if she could have faked her death like a magician, she certainly would have tried. But to actually jump to her death? No way. She would leap someday, but Evel Knievel-style all the way to Paris.

The only real lovers you've ever had can hurl themselves right at an edge without a thought, while you've done your best to skirt it.

Kate whimpers a sleep sigh. Just as her mind tumbles forward into slumber, she wonders if the Robeson boy didn't jump either, but was pushed like Jamie nearly was.

THE NEXT DAY, the Heathrows file a police report. As suspected, Maddox had tricked Jamie up to the bluff and had tried to get her to perform oral sex. When she had refused, he had dragged her to the edge, made her promise not to tell or he'd throw her off. He hadn't meant it really and Jamie hadn't thought he had either. He was just embarrassed. But then she'd slipped.

Like any self-respecting small town family, the Heathrows don't press charges. Jamie won't let them and they easily concede. None of them want the mark on the family reputation, even as victims. It's enough to bear witness to an official in a government building.

As far as Samantha is concerned, they do something much worse. They begin house hunting in Minneapolis.

BLOGGING MY SOJOURN

One Woman's Journey from Gay to Straight

This town knows how to hold onto its secrets. And if those secrets don't play nice, it flings them off the bluff. *Good-bye!* Even the victim is in on the game. Complicity. Complacency. Fear. Shame. Same as it ever was, right?

When the school forced me to come out to my parents, I told them I was leaving town. My mother cried for a bit, but went cold. My dad? He shrugged. So go take a flying leap like the black fairy, he said. The black fairy was the boy from his class who had committed suicide off the bluffs.

And right then I learned so many things. The boy hadn't just jumped because he was bullied for being black but also being gay. I learned my dad might have had something to do with it. And I learned that if my dad hadn't been so drunk and ashamed of me, it would have stayed a secret forever.

If our cells truly do regenerate every seven years, then I have shed my past—I have shed my entire body—at least two times since I was flung from the bluff. So, if I'm a different person nearly three times over, why is it I still dwell on this stuff and my feelings for Vicky still cut so deep? She is the river that runs through this town. An honest woman. A giver of life. And me? I am but a logjam.

I think it's time to move on down that river.

Praise Jesus

Posted by Liesl ~ 2:00 PM ~ 1 comment

Patrice commented:

Yes. It is definitely time to move on. I pray for you every night Liesl. Do not squander it.

CHAPTER THIRTY-TWO

Kate

KATE AND ERIK lie facing each other—blinking in the half-light, chuckling into the folds of pillows.

"This is ridiculous."

"Who goes to sleep looking at each other?" Erik asks.

At this proximity, his face looks like one of those enormous Easter Island statues. "Well, apparently Anita and Rob. She says they talk late into the night about all sorts of stuff."

"Yeah, probably what mental institution to put Maddox in."

"So," she ventures, "do you think my quilts are awful too?"

His mouth twists to the side. "They are a little weird. But if it makes you happy . . ."

For some reason this reminds Kate of how Erik used to brag ironically that he was going to keep her barefoot and pregnant. And everyone laughed because no one said that sexist stuff anymore, so somehow that made it funny. But it also made her kind of sick.

His eyes open. "Close your eyes, you're making me nervous."

"You first."

"On three."

"One. Two. Three."

Erik is out within a minute, bottom lip sputtering.

I really need to stop with the afternoon coffee.

Stranded, Kate considers reaching for the remote.

Someone else has considered the same thing. She can feel it. Somewhere in the house, someone else is awake. She's had this ability ever since the kids were born. Sometimes it's the high-pitched hiss of a TV tube, but she could swear sometimes it's merely the sound of eyeballs blinking.

Kate slips out of bed. When she reaches the downstairs rec room, blue light glows from down the hall.

Please don't let me walk in on Brace jacking off to porn.

Couldn't be; his laptop is dead. The glow is coming from the room across from his.

Please don't let me walk in on Samantha jacking off to porn.

"Sam, it's late."

Her daughter jumps in her chair and clicks the mouse, furiously closing windows.

"What are you looking at?"

But Samantha doesn't respond. Just keeps glaring at the screen clicking.

"Sam? Is it Jamie? She okay?"

"Yep. She's fine." Samantha's voice comes small and quiet.

"What are you hiding this time? The Outback Steakhouse website?"

And then Kate remembers again her parents storming in, turning the room upside down, reminding her that nothing really belonged to her at all. She hovers at the door, now fully understanding their fears and the illusion of her daughter's autonomy—hers to give, hers to take. For now.

Samantha sighs, shoulders sagging. "Come on in."

Kate hasn't been officially invited in here in over a year. The kids were in charge of cleaning their own rooms at fifteen. Army surplus netting with plastic leaves hangs from the ceiling and the green light fixture above casts a dim jungle shadow all over the walls and bed. Kate battles the urge to pick up the dirty clothes strewn across the floor. It seems Samantha moved most of her stuffed animals to the upper shelves and they need a good dusting. Her lower shelves now house library books on primate pack dynamics, McFarlane action figures of rock stars and ghouls (difficult to tell the difference), sunglasses for every occasion, empty nail polish bottles.

"Can I see what you were looking at?"

Samantha grimaces. "Not sure that's a good idea."

"Why don't you let me help decide that?"

"Mmm, I dunno, Mom." Samantha looks nauseous, but she opens the window back up. She sighs. "I guess you have a right to know."

Kate leans in to peer at the screen and recognizes the sparse page format.

"That's a blog."

"Duh, Mom. Look closer."

Kate drags over the ratty *Spongebob* ottoman that her daughter has had since age seven. She sits on it and takes over the unfamiliar Mac mouse.

"*Blogging My Sojourn.* Hmm." Kate roots around in her molars with her tongue.

It's a simple site—no pictures or graphics—with only one link: Sojourn Reclaimers, but the visitor stats are in the thousands. Kate reads the profile.

Fits the stereotype: middle-aged woman, lost and alone, failed lesbian relationships, various addictions, a damaged childhood, all contributing to the type of personality that goes from one extreme to another. Like most blogs it's a rambling, narcissistic confessional.

Kate bounces around the week's entries. With Samantha watching her, she feels more like a voyeur than she usually does online. She can't focus.

Samantha huffs, takes the mouse back, and heads for the archive. "I got curious about Sojourn a while back. Wondering what the heck they were doing to Lucy." She scrolls up and down until she finds it. "Listen to this, Mom."

> . . . the girls remind me of us at their age. Rangy little minxes who want to watch the stars and change the world. They're already itching to get out of Dodge and sing their own song. Make it big. The age-old cliché. How can I tell them that the flip side of the cliché is that all they want to do out there is drain the brightness? They've already had a small taste of that cruelty. It will steal the magic parts they should never give away. It won't want the real *person*, it will only want the product.
>
> Music has forever been an opportunist. It's always there, ready for an ear, waiting for the energy of release. These girls are just a new instrument.
>
> I don't know, maybe they'll make it. Maybe they're stronger. Vicky and Ed are better parents than mine were, after all. And at least their girl isn't a lesbian. Got a hockey-jock for a boyfriend. But still, I'm scared for that little baby goth."

"I'm sure it's only a coincidence," Kate mutters, though her skin tingles.

"No. There's more."

"I'll bet. Give me that." Kate takes command of the mouse again and frantically clicks all over the screen to find the *Close Window* button. Apparently the *Escape* key on a Mac is only for decoration. "I don't want you to read any more of this," she says with a hiss.

"Mom. I'm the one—"

"You're not to read one more word."

Erik and Kate have kept an eye on their kids' social media accounts, but they'd never thought to protect them from something like this.

Kate finally locates *Shut Down*. "I need to make sure this is okay for you to see. Promise me you won't read any more until I do."

Samantha groans and murmurs, "I promise."

"All right, honey." She kisses Samantha's forehead. "Get to bed. Everything's going to be fine."

Kate creeps to the kitchen, grabs one of Erik's pale ales, and pads downstairs to his office. The computer dongs its greeting like Cinderella's first stroke of midnight. As she opens the web browser, fascination and horror crawl over her same as they did when she sprinted across the lift bridge to outrun the Wicasa Queen.

Shit.

How is it that she, Katherine Louise Andern Larson, someone so ordinary, should have this thrust upon her? If the blog was this easy to find, it won't be long before everyone knows about it.

BLOGGING MY SOJOURN

One Woman's Journey from Gay to Straight

Near the end of my stay, my group leader had decided I was a lesbian because I'd been molested by a man. They wanted to hypnotize me, vacuum out the details. I wouldn't let them. Guess I didn't want them to be right. But either way, I wasn't letting these people that far into my head.

While my parents were visiting me at the Sojourn campus, my group leader encouraged them to offer whatever they could think of. So Mom spilled what she thought was the *magic* moment.

Apparently, when I was five, my parents left my brother to babysit me while they went to a party. When they came home, my brother was passed out drunk on the couch. And I had wandered in from my bedroom to sit in front of the TV watching his porn. The women were "doing bad things to each other," Mom said.

—Do you know how hard it is not to laugh when your mom says stuff like that in front of other uptight people?—

Anyway, that night my dad beat my brother "within an inch of his life" and kicked him out. I don't remember any of this, but the whole story was enough to send Mom bawling out of the therapy session to sit in the car.

Until that day, I'd never realized that's why my brother left. He went to work on the ships that year. So, in a way, his death is my fault. We all had a hand, our crappy little family. Suppose that's another reason why I stayed away for so long and why I'd stayed in Europe when I knew my father needed bone marrow donors. That and the fact that I became his punching bag after my brother died, while my mother stood in the kitchen. Of course, I didn't mention any of that to the group leader. Something about my parents always left me tongue-tied, as if to acknowledge their fuck-ups made it all so absolutely true.

Posted by Liesl ~ 6:00 PM ~ 3 comments

Patrice commented:
Finally we know. Satan has had his hooks in you for a very long time. But you can get back on track. If you can just hang in there, the kingdom will be yours.

Down4Jesus commented:
I'm beginning to see what an uphill battle this is for you. I'm a little conflicted here. Don't get me wrong. I think we can all change with God's love. But I'm not sure this is right for you. There's something off here.

Rolf68 commented:
I don't know what to say to this Liesl, except it wasn't your fault. None of us here wanted any of this for you. And I'm sorry there wasn't someone else better to help you process it. But we're here for you now.

CHAPTER THIRTY-THREE

Kate

HER QUAVERING BREATH catches with a tiny croak.

"Luce," she whispers.

Kate cowers stiff-necked in front of the monitor as Lucy's words and her own imagination drag her down dark halls and sharp corners she'd never known existed. After reading the latest entry, she rams the keyboard tray back under the desk and the wireless mouse tumbles to the floor. Her entire body shudders in the damp, sub-floor air.

She'd spent the night inside an archive of self-loathing, the family having risen and fed themselves. Erik had come down to have her sign tax forms for Taken4Granite. Eyes mostly trained on pixels, she'd grunted through a couple brief conversations.

So now she knows for sure how Lucy feels about her. But the rest? The ugly rest? The abuse, the neglect, the guilt, the *cancer*? There's no room for satisfaction here. Little Katie Andirons had been a respite. But in the end, she'd betrayed Lucy too.

Kate rubs her eyes, fingertips digging in harder than they should. It's nearly ten on a Saturday morning. The family must continue to make do without her. She takes the stairs two at a time, showers, and dresses quickly.

She is out the door and in the minivan when Erik emerges from the garage, wiping grease from a wrench.

He mouths, *Where the heck you going?*

She waves and returns the mime, *I'll be right back.*

He sets his jaw, continues polishing, and shuffles into the garage.

THE VEGETABLE AND flower garden on the south lawn of the Gainsborough estate is nearly the size of the home's footprint. The air is fresh and clear up here beyond the traffic. Kate crosses the grounds and draws a calming breath. She grinds crumbs from her eyes, wondering if she looks as exhausted as she feels.

Lucy has clearly been in the garden for a while for she has passed the kneeling phase and sits cross-legged in the turned black soil, trying to untangle delicate netting. She's wearing a bill cap, tight T-shirt, and hospital scrubs pants, but also wearing what looks like a black compression sock midway up her left arm and a gardening glove on just that hand.

"Hi," Kate says hoarsely.

Lucy pushes back the brim of her cap and squints up. "Well, hey thar, stranger." She tosses aside the netting with a sigh. "I'm starting to despise cute fuzzy bunnies." She wipes the side of her face with the back of her wrist. "What's up?"

Kate searches Lucy's face for recent signs of torment but Lucy grins, flushed and glistening with perspiration. The mink brown hair at her temples curls in wisps same as it did back in high school when girls' P.E. played softball—except now a few silvery strands have made inroads.

Lucy stands and shakes dirt from her scrubs. "Something wrong? Is it Jamie?"

"No, I—" Kate had planned a moving speech for a woman standing with razor blades hovering over wrists, not for a woman perfectly contented to be frustrated by rabbits. "What is that? Did you get hurt?"

Lucy's face goes pale. "Oh! This?" She pulls off the glove, rolls the arm sock down her wrist. "Nah, it just aches sometimes. Are you okay? You look kinda tired." She cocks her chin to the house. "How about some coffee?"

"I—I'm trying to quit."

"Wannasoda?"

"What?"

"Do you want a pop?"

"Oh. Sure."

"All I got's diet."

"Whatever's got caffeine in it."

Lucy chuckles and shakes her head.

Kate follows as Lucy crosses the broad lawn and heads toward the back door of the ominous three-story, butter-colored Queen Anne. She breathes in the air of sweat and nitrogen-rich soil emanating from Lucy. *Like spring water tastes.* And something else, the same intangible scent from the night of the Christmas concert and years before at the First Avenue concert. Like India ink. Earthy. Mossy. Pungent. Nature condensed.

Kate stops. "Patchouli!"

"Whoa. What?"

"You wore patchouli that night at First Ave."

"Oh, yeh?" Lucy starts walking again. "Spilled a whole vial of it in my suitcase a long time ago. Mom's going bananas trying to get it out of all my stuff. Says the house smells like a hippie den."

Kate walks a step behind and to Lucy's side. After all these years, Lucy's body remains lithe. Her arms and legs are long, her shoulders and hips evenly broad, her short torso slim. The cropped sleeves of the T are mere triangles off her sculpted shoulders. When they were kids, Katie had only seen Lucy completely nude in the daytime from behind; once in the locker room shower, wet hair snaking down the curve of her back in dark tributaries, her buttocks glossy with soap. Her breasts—*Are they new? Were they taken from her?*—sit high and firm, though there's no relief of a bra strap under the shirt. Why does it feel so forbidden to simply stop and hug this woman?

Kate straightens her posture, growing self-conscious of her own body, which is—though technically younger and randomly attended to with yoga—something less than a masterpiece by today's impossible standards.

"I keep forgetting soda's called pop 'round here." Lucy wipes hands on her already dirty scrubs and leaves stripes of newer, darker mud on the hips. "And hot dish? All my friends out west call it casserole. Guess my language changed too." She opens the storm door and the scent of fabric softener whooshes from the house, *Springtime Breeze* erasing its namesake.

"You were always good at acclimating," Kate says.

They enter the upward sloping back porch, an all-purpose room off the kitchen. The tumbling sound of a clothes dryer and chamber music leak out from deeper within the house. A black-cherry colored cat basks on the arm of a sagging couch. It melts into Lucy's touch and shuts its eyes. Next to the couch leans a TV table, topped with tomato seedlings in plastic containers. A battered, tweed guitar case peeks out from under the couch slip.

Lucy hurries through a vigorous hand rinse in an iron washtub basin and shuffles over to a stumpy, retro fridge with a chrome lever handle. She throws an arm over it and gazes in for an agonizing amount of time, as long as Samantha does before Erik yells to "stop air conditioning the house!"

"So how about you? Do you and Erik travel much?" Lucy extracts two cans of Diet Coke Lime and whispers with a pinch of the cheek, "Goes well with Mom's joy juice."

Kate smirks, nods. "Oh, just trips to Florida. You know, Orlando." She cracks the can, takes a sip. *A little rum wouldn't hurt right now, actually.* "Okay—I know, I know—Epcot is *not* France," she says with a drawl.

"You should see Euro-Disney, it's totally bizarre."

"Hello, Katie," Bridget calls from the laundry room.

Kate's shoulders clench. "Oh. Hi, Bridget. How are you?"

Bridget ambles in, eyes aimed over her glasses at Kate and a half-smile pasted on. "Well, I've still got that breathing problem."

"Sorry to hear that. Maybe you should see a specialist."

"I have, three already. They can't find anything. Quacks. Lucy's driving me to Mayo . . ."

Ah, the Mayo Clinic in Rochester, every Midwestern baby boomer's rite of passage. As Bridget chants her litany of ailments, Kate sneaks a glance at Lucy.

Lucy's eyes slowly cross and it's all Kate can do to maintain her mask of intense concern for the older Van Buren. Lucy tucks hands in pockets. She rocks back and forth on her track sneakers and, in the melon incandescence of the sun through bamboo window shades, looks about seventeen again. "Mom, we're gonna sit out front."

"Did you stain those rails yet?"

"I was waiting till it cooled off."

"You said you'd have it finished before the Sandersons arrive."

"I will."

"Do you need some help?" Kate asks.

"Uh, no." Bridget walks between them with her clothesbasket, forcing them to take a step back. "Thank you, Katie. We know you've got your own home to attend to."

Lucy rolls her eyes, thumbs at the door to the kitchen. Kate follows the invisible trajectory. They make their way past the French Country ideal she'd been fantasizing about at the Gonzo Fox. *Ooh, check out the ginormous brass and iron stove!* Her mouth waters. *Oh,* the breads she could bake, the roasts, the parties.

And then there's the dining room, floor-to-ceiling oak paneling and glittering crystal. The table is set for eight with china that speaks nothing of Lucy save for small painted roses, which resemble those on the trellis at the side of the house, the ones she likely pricks her fingers on.

Kate grows dizzy as they walk. The floors are not level. Either that or she's having an attack of vertigo. In Lucy's presence, anything is possible.

Beneath its stately veneer, the Gainsborough exudes something un-house-like and unmoored. From the moment Kate had stepped into the back porch, it was as if she'd boarded a vessel. Not because of anything as tacky as sailing décor, no. It was the questing jut of the foundation high on the bluff, the leaded windows shuddering against a swift breeze, this floor creaking beneath her feet. And perhaps, the ghost of a young sailor.

In the front parlor, Lucy abruptly steps left to avoid an invisible obstacle.

Kate looks down as she passes over a yard-long rectangle of lighter oak. Where the heating grate had been.

"Oh man, Luce—"

"Sorry about Mom." Lucy walks over to a green velvet settee, picks up the acoustic guitar lying across it, and sets it in its stand by the fireplace. She plucks a letter opener from a nearby writing desk.

"Did she move in?" Kate asks quietly, still staring at the rectangle.

"Might as well have." Lucy sighs. "You know though, I think this venture is really bringing her out of her shell. She's drinking a lot less. Getting up early, out shopping and chattin' with the locals."

"Well, that's good." Kate shakes her head. "Every time I see Bridget, I think about the time our parents got together in the principal's office."

Lucy halts at the door. "After all this time, that's all you think about when you see her?"

"Actually, I don't see her that much." Kate grips the soft drink can tight enough for the aluminum to pop. "But it was an unforgettable day, you have to admit."

"I try not to think about it." Lucy opens the door to the porch all the way and takes in a deep breath of bluff air.

Oh, yes you do and for all the world to read.

Kate stops at the door with a short gasp. When she'd arrived, she'd gotten out of the minivan, marched up the yard, and hadn't even thought to look behind herself.

If this home is a ship, here at the high front porch stands the prow. It's actually set a bit higher than the Leap itself. Across the bluff on the Wisconsin side, farmland stretches for miles, some of the same wheat fields her father had once owned. Clouds above and the river below fling rippling shards of light into her eyes, makes them water, makes her yawn.

"Sorry. Didn't get much sleep last night." She looks back into the house and murmurs, "Lucy, this house is a genuine treasure."

"We'll see." Lucy leans against the doorframe, digging at soil beneath her fingernails with the letter opener. She cocks her head toward the parlor. "I tried shabby chic, but Mom thought everything looked a wreck. She bought me *The Complete Idiot's Guide to Running a Bed and Breakfast*. Wasn't that sweet?"

"Well how hard can it be?" Kate gazes at the expanse of it. "I'd love to do this."

"Yeah?" Lucy taps her chin with the letter opener. "Hey, maybe you can help me with it after the kids graduate. Do you have a plan?"

Kate shrugs. "I don't know, garden more?"

"It would drive me crazy not to have a plan. How can you not have a plan? Why don't you go back to school?"

"I'm too old."

"Katie, you've been too old since the day you were born. Stop doing that to yourself. Unless you are physically unable, you go for it. Always."

"I'm not sure Erik would—Okay, I see your point," Kate says. "But you're one to talk. Don't know if you still care about your coolness level, but um, Sojourn dropped it by a factor of five." This was a lie, of course, and they both knew it. Any forty-year-old who could hang with school kids and it not look ridiculous was, well, cool enough.

Kate gapes at a pony hair wingback across the room. "Is that—the quilt I made you?"

"Yep."

"It's supposed to be on your bed."

Lucy digs the letter opener under her thumbnail. "Mom took it off. Says it's too nice for me to actually use, thought we should display it. You know like a contribution from a local artist." She raises a hopeful smile.

"It's a com-for-ter! You were supposed to use it."

"All righty." Lucy shuffles back in, takes the quilt, unfolds it. She capes it over her head and wraps the remainder around her body, looking like a refugee from a children's fable. She roams the front room covered like that, adjusting picture frames, inching vases one way, then the other. "Maybe you could make us some more for the guest rooms. We'd pay well."

"Got a few I can donate," Kate mutters. "No charge."

Bridget walks through with a stack of folded sheets on her way to the grand staircase.

"Hi, Mom."

"What on earth are you doing?"

"Using my quilt."

"It's eighty degrees out."

"It's *comforting* me." She winks back at Kate.

Bridget mumbles unintelligibly as she suffers her way up the stairs.

Kate's cellphone buzzes at her groin. "Oh, crap, that's probably Erik. Sorta left him in the lurch." She pulls the phone out and nods. "I should go."

"Well, wait a second, what did you want to talk about?"

Kate chews at her lip. Is there time to bring up the blog? The cancer? It would take all day. Why splinter all this good humor? "Oh, I just wanted to see how you were. We hadn't spoken much since . . ."

"The capitol." Lucy winces.

"Yeah. That." Kate rolls eyes. "I feel like there's a few things we could straighten out. I feel like—"

"Let's have a picnic next week."

"Okay. Here?"

Lucy peers back up the staircase. "God no."

"The Leap?" Kate says quietly, her eyes widening.

Lucy's cheeks go pink. "Sure. Next Tuesday?"

"Yeah, that sounds great." Kate sways a little. A breeze blows in from the bluff. Tubular chimes ring out on from the porch, the harmonics playful in their randomness.

> Music has forever been an opportunist. It's always there,
> ready for an ear, waiting for the energy of release.

Lucy grins—the trickster. As if she knows. *Everything.* As if she planted the thoughts and was just waiting for them to sprout. She looks Kate up and down. Just like she used to. "I'll see you around noon."

"Yep." Kate rushes down the steep front steps, blood pounding at her temples. "Later." She feels Lucy's eyes on her, a tingling down her back, as she crosses the lawn to her car.

ON THE WINDING drive down the bluff, she drums her fingers on the steering wheel, leans into every turn. If that was the old knowing in Lucy's eyes, it was certainly in her own. Must she swear Samantha to continued secrecy? Making an accomplice of her own daughter is something Anita Funk-Abel would do. But if Erik finds out about the blog, he's going to tighten the reins. *Do I have a fucking bit in my mouth?* Still, it's only a matter of time before everyone finds out. At the very least, she's got to ask Lucy to stop, to take it down. But how can she? It's Lucy's only voice.

Kate yawns deep and long. The van rocks back and forth from switchback to switchback. The backyard hammock is definitely calling.

To sleep, perchance to dream.

She widens her eyes, forcing them to stay open ten more minutes.

The stoplight on Main stays red for longer than usual. And Kate pulls away out of habit, engrossed in the remembrance of Lucy standing there grinning goofily beneath her quilt.

But Kate is wrong. The stoplight always stays red this long from the Bluff Road direction, a direction she rarely drives. She only has time to realize the gravity of her mistake and trade the fond smile for a flinch before a broad flash of white t-bones her van. The world slides sideways and then spins like the view from a Tilt-A-Whirl.

BLOGGING MY SOJOURN

One Woman's Journey from Gay to Straight

My last week at Sojourn was filled with prayer services and dances, social engagements for men and women reborn into a world that would soon be transformed into God's kingdom.

And what a party it was. The strangest I'd ever been to. And I've been to some doozies. Imagine a meeting hall filled with bright fluorescent light, the slap of laughter against aluminum walls, the smell of cheap cologne co-mingling with onion dip. Desperately sober, we faced each other smiling blind and clutched onto our one conjoining happiness: the fact that we had made it without cracking.

And we had made it under the wire, just in time for the rapture. God was sure to come any day. After all, the towers of Babylon had been brought down in New York and a smooth-talking Anti-Christ from Illinois had his sights set on the White House. It was time to release the new believers into the world.

Fly! Fly my pretties, *FLY!*

Praise Jesus

Posted by Liesl ~1:00 PM ~ no comments

CHAPTER THIRTY-FOUR

Samantha

SHE HAD FOLLOWED Mom's minivan on her bike at a surreptitious distance until she watched it climb Bluff Road. Then Samantha hotfooted it on over to the Heathrows' geodome house to wait out the drama and distract herself.

"Okay, but what if, the best way to create change was . . . to stay?" Samantha lay on Jamie's bed, walking her sock feet up the wall. "No one besides Maddox was all that mean to you and he won't even be around this fall. We'll rule the school."

Jamie did in fact seem over her near death aspect of the experience and agonized more over having been humiliated by a boy she kinda sorta liked. She'd never been one to make a big deal out being called Snowplow in grade school but this was ten times worse. Still, she seemed to prefer it never come up again. Samantha couldn't help wondering if that was a remnant of her "boy" side, that fear of being perceived as weak. And because no charges were filed, few knew about it anyway. In fact, the only family member who still talked about it was Mom, though even she called it "Maddox's stunt" as if he'd merely gone bungee jumping off the Leap.

"That's not the point, Sam." Across the room, Jamie talked into the mirror and delicately brushed the brown mascara up her already full lashes.

"What *is* the point? To only have queer friends? To march in a bigger parade?" The dome shape of the house created large triangles in the walls and the sun through the skylights sliced through them like an algebra problem. Sam placed her feet on two triangles at a time, walked to another. "We could march with the Civil Diss River Valley Contingent this summer."

"Mom warned me you would go there." She turned to Samantha. "Eyeshadow. Too blue?"

"Whoa, yeah you gotta gradate it, soften the edges. What do you mean, *warned* you?'

"That you'd get all moody about this. Yunno, you can't guarantee next year isn't going to be hell. I can't do the guys' locker room anymore, Sam. I need neutral space to decide what path to take."

Samantha sneered and mouthed *neutral space.*

"Listen, dude," Jamie said, "we're going to see each other every weekend."

"No, we won't. Oh my God, you are such a sucky liar."

Jamie added even more eye shadow, dragging it angrily across her eyelid.

"Whoa," Samantha said. "Stop. You look like a . . ."

"Like a drag queen?" Jamie screeched, then her voice cut low. "Just say it."

"Actually a ho was what I was gonna say. But you wanna look like a drag queen too, go ahead." Samantha sat up and shook out her hair. "I'm outta here."

"Oh, that's mature."

Samantha stalked to the door, opened it and was met by Jamie's mom, who looked wide-eyed at her.

"Your dad's here, honey."

Samantha skated past her, across the cork floor in her socks.

Dad stood in the Heathrows' entryway, still dressed in his short-sleeve dress shirt and tie, looking as stunned as Jamie's mom.

With her lip curled and voice still perturbed, Samantha asked, "What are *you* doing here?"

"Put your shoes on. Your mom's been in an accident."

She's dead. Shesdeadshesdeadshesdead—

He quickly moved to her. "She's gonna be okay, kiddo. It's all right. We just need to get to the hospital. I didn't want to call and upset you. I put your bike in the truck."

"Sam." Jamie ran into the room and crouched down—one eyelid blue, one bare. "Call me as soon as you get news, okay?"

Samantha nodded quickly, her fingers spun through the laces of her shoes.

CHAPTER THIRTY-FIVE

Kate

KATE ROUSES IN a foreign, yet disturbingly familiar white room that smells of iodine. There's a TV attached to the wall by a long metal arm, never a good sign. On screen, a woman warms her hands on a cup of coffee and then proceeds to Irish stepdance around the room.

No, Folgers, the best part of waking up is knowing you're not dead.

She senses the beginnings of a massive headache and stiffness throughout her shoulders, but it mostly feels like living. The sun is still up. Someone has her hand. She squeezes. Something is stopping her from moving her head. Plastic. Around her neck. She moves her eyes.

Erik turns to her with a smile, but it flattens. He draws a thumbnail down the cleft above his upper lip a few times. *Not good.* When he used to have a moustache, this gesture indicated impending disaster in his latest business venture or that he was about to confess that one of the kids got injured on his watch.

"I want you to stop seeing Lucy," he says.

Kate blinks. "I must not be dying."

"Concussion. And don't try to move your neck. They want to do a scan as soon as you're ready. I asked the kids to give us a few minutes too. We need to talk."

"The van."

"Totaled. We needed a new one anyway. But, Kate. I saw the blog."

"You know, I never liked the gold," Kate says. "Let's get a red one, so everyone can see me coming."

"Kate. Lucy's still in love with you."

Kate's lips are crisp, her entire mouth dry, her tongue a foreign object.

Erik sighs. "You didn't clear the history bar."

Kate regards the window. "You're sure good at clearing it I noticed."

"What does that mean?"

"You think I don't know you look at porn?"

"Oh come on. I was checking out Jennifer's new business. It's nothing. But I figured you'd get weird if you saw it."

"Erik," she mimics his stern tone, "Jennifer's still in love with you."

"Quit changing the subject. Is there something you want to tell me?"

"What? That Lucy's still a lesbian? Everybody with half a brain can see that." Kate rolls her eyes. "Except Lucy."

"I want to know how *you* feel."

"I care about her, Erik. If you read the blog then you know why."

She feels dirty saying this half-truth.

"What if she's stalking you? Remember before Dale got divorced? His crazy mistress?"

Who could forget? Dale and Jenny had woken up in the middle of the night to a woman standing over their bed with a lacrosse stick.

"Oh, come on, Erik. She's got better things to do."

A familiar alto sing-songs down the hall, "Three oh five? No, no, that's not it, Bertil. Here we are. What on earth are you kids sitting out here for?" Kate has never been so glad to hear Claudia's voice. "There she is. Oh my garsh. Do you know how worried I've been?"

Claudia and Samantha flank either side of Kate and bend down to kiss her on the forehead. Samantha's eyes are swollen, fearful. Kate squeezes her hand. Samantha squeezes back. Bert and Brace follow along, chuckling about something. Erik stands and backs up.

"Hey, Mom, how you feeling?" Brace says. His forehead gathers, eyes round and anxious. This reminds Kate of the night he cried himself to sleep, pudgy little arms tight around her neck, after she came home from the hospital with his new sister.

Kate smiles gently at them. "Well, I had this dream, it seemed so real," she raises a fist and points her thumb around the room, "and you were there, and you were there, and there was a scarecrow, and a lion—"

No one laughs.

"Does this mean we get a new car?" Brace turns to Erik. "'Cause I'm voting for a Jeep."

Samantha raises a hand. "Prius."

"Priuses are fugly."

"Jeeps are destroying the planet."

"Kate," Bert says from the end of the bed, his hands jingling the change in his pockets. "I don't want you going back up there anymore. That bluff is bad news."

"I can't believe this." Kate crosses her arms. Same shit, different family.

Claudia looks to him. "It was near that stoplight where the Robeson boy landed from Squaw Leap, wasn't it?"

"Mmm, hmm." Bert's lips thin and his bushy white eyebrows gather. He shuffles over to the window to gaze upon the hospital campus, his pockets jangling louder.

"Such a dreadful night," Claudia says. "We were all out cruising Main. Your grampa and I had just started going steady. Marcus landed in . . . pieces. Oh, the pall that boy cast on our prom."

"Wow, how rude of him," Kate mumbles. "What was he like, Bert? Mom said you knew him."

"Oh, not all that well," Claudia interjects. "You probably barely remember him now, do you dear?"

"No. Hard to picture him."

"Maybe he thought he would turn into steam like Wicasa," Brace says faintly.

"In our day, that wasn't how the tale went." Bert shakes his head. "It was the same story up until the firing of the arrow. But the way we told it, Chelee was a lightning fast sprinter; he beat the arrow. He grabbed Wicasa and they landed on an outcropping. No bodies were ever found because they escaped, not because they turned to steam."

Brace scoffs. "Either version is impossible."

"Not to mention there's no such thing as an Indian princess," Samantha says. "So racist. The Dakota say the white man just makes up Native American stories they wish someone would tell about them. And Gramma, we don't call it Squaw Leap anymore."

"Oh, sweetie," Claudia puts an arm around Samantha and gazes wistfully out the window too, "I remember when I used to be politically correct just like you."

Samantha eyes bulge.

Now seems a good time for Kate to feign unconsciousness. The voices grow hushed but continue discussion as to what new vehicle to procure. Bert offers to take the kids out to Pannekoeken for supper. And soon enough, the soreness, the horizontal posture, the dark, all of it envelops Kate. The bed seems to turn counterclockwise and she slips back into sleep.

WHEN SHE WAKES again, the room is darker, sun going down. To her side sits Claudia, slowly blinking at her.

Kate swallows. "Where's Erik?"

Claudia fills a Styrofoam cup with a straw in it with water from a Styrofoam pitcher. "Went to grab something at the cafeteria. Grampa took the kids out for a nice dinner." She hands the cup to Kate and rubs her own arms. "It is absolutely freezing in here. Aren't you freezing?"

"No, I'm burning up." Kate downs the entire glass. "Here, take my blanket."

"Wouldn't dream of it. Maybe if you sat up."

"I'm okay—"

Claudia reaches out and grabs the bed remote. The bed rumbles to life and folds Kate into an upright position.

"Um, thanks."

"I blame myself."

"What? How could this be your fault," Kate asks with an exhaustion that belies the fact that she's now crammed with energy, enough to catapult from the bed and sprint home. "I wasn't paying attention. I never drive that direction."

"All this with Mark and Ray has been way too upsetting. You know, one can take this PC thing too far. They are grown men after all, capable of handling themselves."

"Well, of course." Kate's voice rises. "But it was pretty cruel to march Lucy into that rally. I told you how worried I was about her."

Claudia's eyelids flutter. "She came to *me*, Kate."

"Huh?"

"I thought you wanted me to embrace her?" Claudia shudders. "Do you know how hard that was to do? When I knew she might be, you know, *wanting me?*"

"Oh, brother." Kate holds her head in a vise grip. "Please don't make me laugh."

"Listen, I was on the school board in the eighties. I remember very well when that girl was suspended. She was a spitfire if ever there was one."

"Wha?"

"Oh, yes, I was one of those who decided that case after her parents tried to fight it."

"You never told me that," Kate says, her eyes locking onto Claudia.

"Mmm." Claudia tsks. "Mr. Van Buren thought it was *unfair*, said he could discipline his own daughter. That if we suspended her, her scholarship chances would be ruined. *As if.* Lord, I've never met such a belligerent man in all my life. I was studying for the bar at the time, and it felt like my first big case. And now I know we did the right thing. For you and all the other girls. That's the problem with public schools, all the angry unfortunates dragging down the ones with potential. Damaged children are a contagion, Kate. Every parent knows this, even the liberal ones pretending it isn't true. Still, with prayer, look at her now—"

"Oh my God. Claudia, you know Lucy didn't graduate with her class. She had to get her GED later on."

"Well, it was her own doing. She set fire—"

"Nobody ever proved that." Kate's fingers tremble as she palpates her dried lips. "Did she—does she remember you?"

"Oh, I doubt it. I was blonde back then. Natural, you know."

"So you knew about her and me?"

Claudia raises an eyebrow. "Well, when Erik first brought you to meet us, I didn't make the connection. I'd forgotten all about it. And then, by the time I remembered—well, Erik was so crazy about you. And you were such a nice, quiet girl."

Kate blinks hazily. "So much for that, eh," she mumbles. "Did you ever tell Erik?"

"No, and he doesn't need to know, Katie. Sweetheart, I love you as my own daughter. Everything I have done, I have done to protect you and my son and my grandchildren—and their children too. Even before I knew you I protected you. Just imagine that."

A young man in burgundy scrubs enters pushing a wheelchair. He crosses arms, stands by the closet, and smiles politely. "We have an order for a scan on Mrs. Larson."

Kate's mind goes soft. Something is wrong here.

"Ah, middle age." Claudia commandeers the bed remote again. "It's all about making sense of the stories you were told."

BLOGGING MY SOJOURN

One Woman's Journey from Gay to Straight

I am giving the local hospital one star on Yelp. They won't even let you inquire about the patients, let alone visit them if you're not family. And if you ask a few simple questions, if you challenge the staff, well, out come the orderlies.

So Vicky was in a car crash and I know it's down to me. She had come to visit, to talk, but something stopped her. She's frustrated with this ex-gay thing, much more than I expected her to be. I thought she'd filed me away years ago. But she still cares and now I'm really screwed.

When I returned to the hospital this morning to drop off some flowers, she'd already been released. So, at least she is going to be okay. But it was my fault. I know it was. Everything I touch seems to burn. Why does this happen to me? I used to let it go. I used to move on. But I feel myself slipping, falling, dragging everything down with me.

Do not touch the hot grate. Do. Not. Touch!

Posted by Liesl ~ 11:00 AM - 2 comments

Patrice commented: I'm out.

Rolf68 commented: Oh, Liesl, my dear girl. Every action has an equal and opposite reaction.

CHAPTER THIRTY-SIX

Samantha

SAMANTHA STUFFED SIX reject quilts into the Burley, the bike carrier on wheels her parents toted the kids around in when they were small. She attached it to the back of her mountain bike, rode across the bridge to Wicasa Bluffs and inched up the hill to the Gainsborough B&B in granny gear.

Lucy helped carry Kate's quilts into the house and laid them out on a shimmering red davenport. "Want some lemonade?"

"I'm good." Samantha took a perfunctory swig from her water bottle.

"Hey, can you or Jamie use this?" Lucy reached into a worn suitcase, pulled out a suede vest with fringe, and tossed it to her.

"Oooh, cool." Sam slid her arms through and shrugged it on. The vest was lined with satin and cut high, would be perfect on top of a ratty old v-neck T, with cut-off jeans and boots.

"Yeah, it's kinda retro, isn't it? Needs somebody young to pull it off."

"Thank you." Though Brace would call her on the hypocrisy of animal skins . . .

"No problem. So. How is the patient?"

"Fine," Samantha answered quietly. "Better I guess." She really hoped this wouldn't turn into a gross Mom-as-romantic-lead-in-eighties-movie sort of conversation.

"She was here right before it happened." Lucy stared out past the gravel drive and clasped hands on hips, contemplating it. "That hill is so steep and it ends right at the stoplight. It's always been dangerous. You gotta be careful riding down it. You got good brakes?"

"Sure." Samantha remotely knew she should ask if Mom had confronted Lucy about her blog and if she had been upset. Asking Mom right now was totally out of the question, she was all zoned-out on painkillers. She knew if she hadn't shown Mom the blog it would have never happened. She'd cried all the way to the hospital, thinking she'd killed her. But now she convinced herself Jamie would want to be here when they told Lucy they had read the blog and had been forbidden from reading anymore.

"Hey, you okay," Lucy said, she reached out and poked Samantha's long bangs behind one ear. "I heard that Jamie's blowing town. When I suggested Cooper, I didn't completely think it through. I'm sorry, kid."

"Whatever." Samantha shook out her hair, walked out onto the porch, and sat on the step. Everyone was always trying to pull it out of her eyes. Didn't they know she looked like every other girl with it all flat behind her ears. Surely Lucy of all people knew that. "I've never said this to anyone before. But I think it's really selfish."

"Selfish of her to leave?" Lucy sat down too.

"That and the transition. Everything is about *Jamie*. And don't get me wrong, I am so in her corner, but it's like my brother says, nobody notices when you're just regular."

Lucy was quiet for a while. "It is going to be rough next year without her and Zev. But Jamie won't always be this focused on herself. Once she grows comfortable in her own skin, she'll be able to give more back. And if you're not into Zev, it's best to let him go."

"I am into him, but he might be done with me. Took his cousin to prom."

Lucy made a wincing face. "Ouch. Did he give you a reason?"

"She's got some bone disease and they've always been close. He wanted to show her a good time while she was in remission. I'm fine with it. He's a great guy. And we're all still going to Summerfest together . . . but he got accepted to Columbia, so it's getting a little frosty. Probably for the best."

"That's your Mom talking."

Samantha looked out past The Leap. The wind was picking up, pushing clouds above them eastward. "And really, what are the chances that Jamie and I are going to end up in the same college either?"

"It happens. All the time. And the way the Internet works now, you can talk to anyone halfway around the world like they're in the room with you."

"Gee, thanks for the technology update."

"Smartass. Hey, I lost a lot at your age too. It's unavoidable. Everyone is in transition, not just Jamie. Talk to her. Tell her how much you're going to miss her. Forget your pride. It ruined everything for me when I was your age. And I thought I was somehow valiant putting up such a front."

"Yeah?"

"Yeah. Disappointment burns like an ulcer if you let it. Does a ton of damage. You and Jamie need to have the best summer you can imagine. Save the tears for September."

"Ooh, song name."

Lucy mock-gasped. "Yeah. I'll get on that."

"Who's the smartass now?" Samantha stood up. "I gotta go."

"Hey, got something else for you." Lucy hopped up and went inside for a minute. She came back with her huge pair of astronomical binoculars.

Samantha raised her hands. "I can't."

"Sure you can." Lucy pressed them to her. "You use them more than I do."

"Then I'm only borrowing them." Samantha tested their heft in her hands. "Wow."

They walked to Samantha's bike.

"Hey, you got a little red bump there." Lucy nodded at Samantha's cheek. "You get stung?"

Samantha let her hair fall in her face again. "Oh? Oh, that. I get those sometimes."

"Hives."

"Yeah. That's what it is. When I get anxiety."

"See what I'm saying? You can't run away this stuff. You'll bury it and inflict it on yourself."

Enough of this. "You gonna join a band again, someday?"

Lucy hesitated, taken aback. She looked out over the river valley. "Yeah, probably. I'm writing. Not giving up." She turned back to Samantha. "Neither should you."

"Right, *Tears for September.*" Samantha chuckled and then remembered the book. "Oh!" She went to the Burley trailer, grabbed *Song of the Lark* and held it out to Lucy. "I liked it. I liked that there wasn't a big moral to the story. Most books we get in school have happy endings or bad endings with a lesson we're supposed to learn. It just felt like real life."

Lucy crossed her arms. "Keep it. Reread it in ten years." She smiled broadly. Were her eyes glistening with tears? Why was she giving stuff away? Was the cancer back? She didn't look sick. But cancer was weird that way. Jamie said her aunt had been fine one day and was dead the next week of a brain tumor.

"You're going to be amazing, kid," Lucy said. "Just take your time. Take it all in."

Samantha shrugged and grabbed the bike handlebars. Without permission her body let go, ran back to Lucy, hugged her really quick. Then she got back on her bike.

"See ya," she said and rolled off, the wind flapping the fringe of her new vest as she sailed down the hill. A fullness and confidence emanated from both within and all around her at the same time.

LATER THAT NIGHT, Samantha took a break from Frans De Waal's *Chimpanzee Politics* to browse her mother's yearbooks for Lucy Van Buren. There at the end of the senior pages, Lucy hung in her little oval, grinning goofily, her hair spiked and looking like an artful assemblage of crow feathers. Below her name: *Class Clown.*

Samantha landed next on Mom's unfortunate sophomore photo, the girl-woman looking weightless and fairy-like, thin-necked with sparkling eyes, a glistening smile. No angry elevens in sight. Katherine Louise Andern had yet to grow into her nose. And oh, those questionable fashion choices: plaid blouse with puffy sleeves and a curly bob parted flat in the middle?

Whatever.

Samantha flipped through the unprinted pages in the back that were interspersed with big ballooning handwriting in various marker colors. Stars, XOXOs, hearts from a dude named Gary and some indecipherable lettering that looked half Japanese, half Martian:

FOREVER, L

Brace ambled over to Samantha's bedroom door, all humid from the shower but still a little stinky, like mold or jock itch or whatever happens to a puckhead's feet when they're locked in skates all the time.

"Dad is so pussy-whipped."

"Huh?"

"Mom's making Dad take you on the fishing trip this summer."

"Um, no, he asked me to go."

"Yeah, right. She made him ask."

"Prove it," Samantha snapped. "Dad asked me all by himself."

Brace looked down his nose at her. "Thought you hated fishing."

"Well, maybe I'll just observe. Don't worry, I won't tell Mom about the beer."

"Great." He rolled his eyes and turned to go.

"Hold on a second. What's so awful about being pussy-whipped? I find it fascinating that you're threatened by female anatomy."

"Don't bonobo-analyze me, dude."

"I can't help it." Samantha shrugged. "Once you start seeing the ape in everyone it changes everything. Besides, bonobo males are total mama's boys. It's a great life. They don't have the violence of other ape societies. Women handle the food and keep the men in check with sex. Each male is as popular as his mom."

"So, that would make Dad the top guy in town, since Grandma is like the alpha female."

"Well, yeah, technically. If Grandma had a clearer majority, he would be top male. But he'd still be under the other top females."

"Like Mom."

"Yeah. He'd probably be above me, but you'd be below me."

Brace shuddered. "Scary. And there'd be no hockey."

"Then you'd have to be a chimpanzee I guess, and risk getting cannibalized. Maddox is a total chimp. But in bonobo society, all the daughters have to leave the troop eventually and find new troops. So I'd be out of your hair anyway."

"Hmm. Nice. Still, sounds like a buncha bullshit to me. There's a reason they're still in the jungle and we're not."

"Yeah, that's the million dollar question. We're still looking for the missing link. It's not a perfect science. Every researcher comes to the table with their own biases. And a lot of it happens in zoos. Animals act differently in captivity."

Brace leaned against the door and shook his head. "Least you know what you want to study."

"Jamie says you can't go wrong with a business degree."

"Eh, what does she know? Her parents are freakin' socialists who live in a geodome."

"Um, they make a ton of money selling solar panels." Samantha shot him the get-out-of-my-room-puckhead look, glaring at the division of beige hall carpeting and her purple carpeting. At least he referred to Jamie in the feminine this time.

His stare softened. "Heard she's not going to be in school next year."

"Nope. Moving to the cities."

"I'm sorry, Samster," he said quietly.

Do not *cry in front him. Do* not.

"Yeah. Me too."

CHAPTER THIRTY-SEVEN

Kate

"MY GOD, KATE." Anita stares at the new quilt hanging off the wall. "That is like the second coming."

"Is that's good? Or bad?"

"Bad for us sinners. Perfect for Claudia. I've never seen anything like that."

The first week of her recovery, Kate had sat up in bed, her throbbing head dulled by vicodin, with her colored pencils and a pad of grid paper and sketched it all out. The result was enough for Samantha to exclaim that it looked like something out of a William Blake painting. Hopefully, that meant she was on the right track.

Samantha had helped her deconstruct some of the de-commissioned quilts she'd bought back from Mark. The ripping felt like hari-kari but she wasn't going to spend another dime on this bogus hobby. And there was a lot of good material here. The slick satins on the outside would impress her mother-in-law's ostentatious side and the soft flannel underneath would keep Claudia's lean body warm. Claudia might be expecting a quilt with some symmetry to it, a saw tooth or a Jacob's ladder perhaps, but with this design she would constantly face complexity. It was dangerous, of course. At what point had Kate gone from an obedience to craft to nosy confrontations? *No wonder no one wants to use these things.*

Kate feels feverish. "I'm not starting over. I can't do this anymore. Last one."

"Kate, I'm serious. It is beautiful. Like a thousand pieces of shattered glass, and sunbeams and color, and—it's fantastic—I'm not lying."

"It's weird though, isn't it?"

"Who cares. Claudia should be fucking honored. You poured your soul into this."

"Actually that and about twelve pots of coffee." Kate tears open the Velcro of her neck brace and moves to the middle of the room. She lowers to the carpet and takes up a crossed-legged position on the floor, then lightly sets her wrists on her knees, closes her eyes, and exhales. Her neck slowly drops sideways, ear to shoulder, as the air flows from her lungs and out her nose.

Anita cracks her toes on the floor and joins her.

Two minutes later, they reverse the pose to the other shoulder for another breath. And again Kate brings her chin to her chest. Her pelvic bones finally come to relax on the ground. Chuck Norris joins them, interrupting every quaking position with a lick on the cheek or closed eyelid. Anita collapses, laughing in a heap, unused to his affections.

After forty-five minutes of Hatha postures specifically assigned for the spinal column, they gather themselves back into the lotus position and bow to the quilt.

"Namaste."

"Namaste."

AT THE DINING room table, over green tea, Kate blurts, "I'm bisexual."

Anita snorts back a sip. "Um, random. But okay."

"I mean, whatever that means, you know?" Kate says softly. "I love my husband but women are cool too."

"Wow." Anita stares into her cup. "This reminds me of *The Hours*, when Julianne Moore leans over and kisses Toni Collette in the kitchen."

"Agh. I'm not trying to come on to you, 'Nita."

"Phew." Anita wheezes a chuckle. "I mean, you're"—She wiggles eyebrows and with her palm makes a window-cleaning semi-circle motion at Kate's tight lycra tank—"But no."

"Right. Moving on. I'm talking about Lucy."

"Veebee." Anita clicks her tongue. "Yeah, I figured that out months ago. You ladies got it bad. You were like a couple of warped lovebirds in school."

"Erik kinda sorta knows too. I keep avoiding talking about it completely. And he lets me." Kate sips her tea. "Do you think it's possible to love two people at once? I mean, not just sex, but love?"

"Sure. It's the details that screw you up. This is exactly what pisses people off about bisexuals. You're not supposed to love two at once."

"Well, how do *you* do it?"

Anita scoffs. "Did you invite me over here to teach you cuckoldry? Got no time for that anymore. It's all I can do to keep peace around the house, let alone outside of it."

Kate lays a hand on Anita's wrist. "Is everything all right?"

"Well, I don't think Maddox should get off scot-free do you? Rob's a mess. Thinks everything turned out fine in the end. Nobody got hurt and he wants him to get to play hockey in college. But I can't get through to him. Kate, I think there's something wrong with my son."

Kate can think of nothing else to do but give Anita a little squeeze of the arm. She hears Claudia's voice, *damaged kids are a contagion,* and she knows she wants this woman's son nowhere near her own anymore. But she also thinks of Samantha and her youthful challenge to the hypocrisies of adulthood: *Are we really good people if we're only good to the people it's easy to be good to?*

"Maybe we all just need to keep a closer eye on him," Kate offers, as much to convince herself as Anita.

"Yeah, I need to focus on my family right now. Stop fooling around. For a while."

Kate nods. "Guess we all do."

"Girl you're just getting started. But maybe I'm some sort of lesson. Dear lord. Anita, the cautionary tale."

"Do you do therapy?" Kate swirls her tea around. "I mean, I've thought about it, but I don't want to freak Erik out."

"Girl, therapy isn't going to freak him out near as much as catching you with your head up the choir director's skirt."

This makes Kate chuckle because of course she has to picture it. Now that she's cooled down a bit, she releases her hair from its hairband and shakes it out. Anita does the same.

"You're going to have to talk it out," Anita says. "Probably with both of them, at some point."

"I know. But the thing is, I'm not sure what it is I'm going to be telling them. In the first place, what if Lucy is like, back off."

"Well, there is that little matter of her being an *ex*-gay."

"Oh, that's all a lie. She's still in love with me."

Anita sits back, blinking. "You know, I kinda like this new, confident, sex-positive friend of mine. What if you suggested a threesome?"

Kate gently bites her lip. "Maybe." *Why can't you consider sharing?*

Anita leans back. "Are you sure this isn't just about closure with all that high school crap? I mean, I've never known you to be attracted to other women."

"Sure, I have. A few times. Nothing serious. I always closed it off. Same with guys. But Lucy is special."

"Oh, she's special all right." Anita laughs. "Although I will say, she saved my ass on the Parade of Homes tour. She's opening the Gainsborough for us. It'll be our last stop. *Le pièce de résistance.* Do you know how long I've been trying to get in that place?'

Kate sighs. "Listen, it goes without saying that you'll swear secrecy, right?"

"Of course, Kate. *Please.*"

"Lucy wrote a blog. It's really dark. I need you to read it and tell me what it says."

"Why can't you read it?"

"I promised Erik I wouldn't."

Anita cackles. "Well it's sort of the same thing, isn't it?"

Kate cringes. "Oh, I hate this. You know, if she had never come back I probably would have just buried it further. Why did she have to come back?"

"I think you know the answer to that."

"Okay, go to bloggingmysojourn.com on your phone. I can't here."

"Now?"

"Yeah." Kate rises and brews them two more mugs of green tea. She brings out a batch of peanut butter bars made with a new recipe using Stevia instead of sugar. They are awful of course. Anita takes one bite, sets it aside, and starts reading.

Kate leaves her to it for a half hour, to get the broad strokes, and starts supper. Two lasagnas. One with spinach, the other ground beef. It is slow going.

"Hold on," Anita says. "Have you read these comments?"

"Yeah, but they give me anxiety."

"Didn't Mark play Rolf in *Sound of Music*?"

"Yeah?" Kate returns to the dining room table. Anita hands her the phone.

Liesl, you came home for Vicky, not God. Be careful.

"What the heck?" Kate scrolls back to Liesl's first entry. Rolf68 has been commenting from the beginning. Kate stands in solid shock, mouth open.

"You think that's him?" Anita rises, gathers her hoodie, and yoga mat.

"If it is, I'll kill him." Kate's jaw hardens. "Anita, I'm so tired of always being the last to know stuff. Why does everyone think I can't be trusted with the truth?"

"You need to let off some steam girl, and downward dog ain't getting it." Anita zips up her hoodie. "How about a night on the town?"

Kate and Chuck follow her to the door. "Erik and I are going to dinner this weekend."

"No, I mean a girls' night out. We'll go to a gay bar. If you are unmoved by the abundance of queer T and A we will call this thing with Lucy a false alarm."

"Um, I'm not sure that's how it works but—"

"Oh, yes. I am so down for this. Then I can screw around vicariously through you." Anita opens the door, steps onto the walk but then halts. "However—"

Chuck starts out the door, Kate holds his collar. "What?"

"You have to tell Erik."

Kate groans.

"You can't sneak, Kate. It's too dangerous. Toxic. Bad karma."

THAT WEEKEND, KATE and Erik re-christen date night at the Sailing Club restaurant overlooking the riverfront. It's a perfect evening on the back deck, the air as close and warm as baby's bathwater and charged with the community joy at having survived another winter and a tricky spring. A polka band plays its merry swing inside the adjoining bar.

Erik fills Kate's glass with a second shot of cabernet.

She twists off a hunk of French bread and mops up some olive oil.

He meets her glass with his frothy pilsner. "One kid down. One to go."

"Cheers." She takes a sip. The wine tastes smooth and smoky. "Did it seem like he grew up too fast to you?"

"No. Not really," he says.

"Me neither." Kate lays a fork into her salmon; the flesh is succulent and jeweled pink in the middle, a whole different beast from the canned variety. "The kids took the right amount of time. Why does everybody say it goes so fast?"

"'Cause they don't make the best of it I guess. Life isn't all that short when you think about it." Erik loosens his yellow and navy striped tie. "We just waste too much of it."

"What did you waste?" she asks.

"Not much." He charges into his filet mignon. His hair is nice tonight, neatly trimmed, tousled with a little wax. He always knows how to keep and dress himself without any henpecking. His mother pecked enough to last a lifetime.

"Oh, come on," Kate says. "Anything. How about Jennifer Turnquist? If you had the chance to sleep with her again, would you?"

"Who says I haven't had the chance?"

"Funny. I mean if I didn't mind."

"Does it have to be Jennifer? I mean couldn't it be . . . Scarlett Johansson?"

"Excuse me, she's way too young for you." Kate picks up a roasted asparagus stalk with her fingers and chomps it like a French fry. "Sorry, that's wasn't fair, was it?"

"S'okay. I'll revise. Catherine Zeta Jones."

"Mmm. Maybe. She is pretty hot."

Erik's fork hovers mid-air. "You think so?"

"I wouldn't kick her out of bed." She knocks back another slug of wine.

Erik stares. Kate feels her cheeks redden, further enabled by the wine.

"Who else would you approve of in our bed?" His white teeth flash in the candlelight.

This is going to be an interesting night. "Patrick Dempsey?"

Erik doesn't flinch. "Needs a shave."

"You could handle a guy?"

Erik searches the air. "In theory. All's fair. But he's not getting near my ass. No. Way."

Kate sputters a thin spray of wine into her palm.

They are quiet for a while. Enjoying the meal, the paper lanterns, and the bells of the sailboats clanging on the river. A Harley Davidson rumbles past on the main drag.

He looks up. "You been back to her blog?"

"Not exactly."

"I guess it's not my place to say what you can and can't look at."

"Maybe it is. Maybe it isn't." Kate looks down at her plate. "I want to go back to school."

"Huh-uh. We can't afford it yet."

"I'll take out a loan," she says, sounding like a pleading teenager. "Borrow from my parents."

"Let's get Brace out of college first. Sam into it. It's not *that* far off."

She looks out over the river. Of course, he makes sense. He always makes sense.

"Anita and I. We're thinking of hanging out in Minneapolis next weekend. A girls night out sort of thing."

Erik nods. "Sounds fun." He leans back and finishes off his beer. "Just a drink or two though."

"Yeah, I know. So we're gonna check out the Kitty Kat Lounge."

He laughs. "Sounds like a strip club."

"A lesbian bar actually," she says quietly.

He slowly sets his glass down, cocks his head. "No."

Kate sighs and gazes around at the other tables, to those who are laughing and gorging themselves, wondering why she ever listened to Anita. Anita, who couldn't even raise a single child right telling her how to talk to her husband. *Well, just fuck that.* Of course Erik was going to say no. She wonders if she is well and truly going crazy for real this time. What is she doing to herself, to her marriage? Why can't she let this thing go?

The waiter approaches with the dessert menu.

"Just the check," Erik says.

The drive home is silent. The house dark and quiet, both kids still out on their dates. Brace with a girl he met on the docks, Samantha with Zev.

They don't turn on the lights. Kate follows Erik to the backyard to let Chuck outside. They stand, staring into the night.

"You can go," he says. "With Anita."

"I was going to anyway."

He turns to her in the shadows, and she can't see the prevailing emotion: shock or anger. She can think of nothing else to do but reach up and kiss him.

IN THE BEDROOM, Kate straddles Erik, hands gripping the headboard. Every time he tries to turn her over, she pushes him back. For once, he submits. He doesn't look away this time and stares at her with wonder.

Jeez, this daily yoga thing is really paying off.

Kate never thought her marriage would evolve into a plot between two stubborn people to see their portion of an ancient pact through to the end. Daily forgiveness, implicit accountability, Erik will never betray her. Sure, he's probably masking a few things to save her feelings and the marriage itself. But Kate is okay with that. She's doing the same.

Erik's body draws tight as an oak. He holds her hips still for a moment, eyes rolling back. His fingers find her and soon she begins to climax. But the tickling joy goes on and on and he removes his hand too soon. She collapses onto the bed, left with a dull ache.

His hand slowly falls upon her thigh and he drops quickly asleep in the same splayed position in which he came.

Kate stares at the ceiling.

I want . . .

There is no heterosexuality. There is no homosexuality. There is only sex, sometimes an indulgence, sometimes duty. And love is a bond radiating from primaries to secondaries, tertiaries and beyond. She doesn't need to go enlightening anyone about the perfect simplicity behind the man-made drama, not Claudia, or even her own daughter, who will surely find it out sooner than she had.

BLOGGING MY SOJOURN

One Woman's Journey from Gay to Straight

F. Scott Fitzgerald once said that an artist has the ability to entertain two opposing viewpoints at the same time. Clearly, I'm no longer an artist.

This was all much harder than I thought it would be. Not just the small town, or Mom or the run-ins with my old teachers—though fuck knows those are awkward. It's Vicky. She's more of a temptation than if I were to walk into a nightclub and have three young hotties fighting to give me a lap-dance. I am hopelessly drawn to a woman rockin' the mom jeans. What the hell? It's probably just limerence interrupted, you know, but there it is.

I tell myself Vicky's not my concern. Better that I should grow fallow on this hill because she sends a shiver down my spine with that deep green stare and those timid shoulders. That she's not the awful person I thought she'd be makes this task ten times harder. I'm so pissed over the time I wasted. Plenty of people to blame. But none of it turns back the clock. I am tempted. She is discontented. I could take her like Boulanger took Madame Bovary.

Best to keep my distance. After all, why does sex have to be the ultimate end? If nothing else, Sojourn taught me that. Vicky's age and wisdom endear me to her in a way young lust could not possibly maintain. She's an amazingly strong woman, but will she still be at 80? Will Ed still be there to hold her elbow on icy sidewalks? I cannot divorce myself from that care. I don't think I have to, do I? It isn't all lust. It's also care for another human being. I've rarely experienced that. Rarely wanted to see a person grow up and outwards even if it didn't include me. I've rarely wanted to do everything I could to keep someone I love close to my heart. To make sure they are happy.

I'm still trying to figure out how to hit the restart button on my life. Step one? Going out to the only place in the city that serves girls like me. Guess I'll have to settle for hotties instead of mom jeans. At least this, I deserve.

Posted by Liesl ~ 5:00 PM ~ 2 comments

InChrist commented:
It's time somebody made herself a sojourn back to Texas.

Down4Jesus commented:
Liesl have you ever considered Ativan? Our family doctor prescribed it for me. Just one Ativan and a conversation with our Lord and I'm right as rain.

CHAPTER THIRTY-EIGHT

Samantha

THE NEXT FRIDAY night, she and Jamie had the house all to themselves. Brace was out with Zev and Maddox. Dad was out with his golfing buddies. And Mom was out with Anita Funk-Abel.

The two had cranked the stereo for an hour, dancing around the rec room. Chuck Norris howled until they stopped to play foosball. Now Jamie lay on Samantha's bed, cramming her face with Goldfish crackers and Twizzlers, slurping pineapple Crush from a can, playing Nintendo—all forbidden fruit in the Heathrow household.

Samantha sat at her desk, checking her Warcraft auctions, but she couldn't hold out any longer and snuck a peek at Lucy's blog.

The charade was crumbing; Sojourn had failed and Lucy was set to jump back on the girl train at some lesbian bar in Minneapolis. And while that should be grounds for celebration, Lucy's thoughts about Mom were disturbing on too many levels. There was also the matter of Sojourn's corruption and her grandparents' link to it.

A niggling little bug had been buzzing around in the back of her mind, growing in annoyance since the last Civil Diss protest at the capitol. Lucy's sudden desire to break Sojourn rules had brought it to the forefront. Where were the Simian Avengers these days? Why didn't they show up at the capitol, when there were no other SA protests going on that week?

"Something wonky is going on." Samantha got up from her computer.

"Eh, she's finally going out and letting her hair down," Jamie said, furiously punching buttons on Samantha's old Nintendo Game Boy as the Tetris blocks fell faster and faster. "I think that crash really woke your mom up."

"No, I'm talking about Lucy." Samantha walked down the hall to the rec room.

"Well, her too for that matter," Jamie called after her. "Sure wish we could go."

"Soon, young Padawan. Soon." Samantha flipped through her parents' old record albums. Dad was particular about his, even though he wouldn't dare put them under a needle anymore and had repurchased most of them on iTunes. The entire shelf was alphabetized except for Mom's slight stack, which was relegated to the end and tilted in the opposite direction. Her music was a decade newer and of questionable quality in Dad's opinion. The Go Gos, George Michael, The Cure, Prince, plus all Lucy Veebee's bands: The Hypnogogs, Lucy & the Leapers, and CDs of Cake for Horses.

Samantha turned to the back of a seven-inch dance mix of the Leapers song "Urgent Wishbone" which had been in a hair color commercial in the late nineties. In the photo, Lucy's band stood around arbitrarily in an abandoned lot, trying to look like thugs. Lucy's young face was smooth, her eyes underlined with heavy black kohl. The sneering blonde drummer was leaning her back against Lucy, drumsticks a spinning blur in her hands.

That sneer though.

Samantha shuffled through the albums. Though the other band members changed, that same blonde was on every album and CD cover with Lucy. She looked too familiar. Tammy Tom-Tom, read the liner notes. Could they be more than friends?

Samantha walked back into her bedroom and opened a new window on her iMac.

There were a few old Leapers videos circulating on YouTube, "Urgent Wishbone" the most popular. She hit "play" and the band sprung to life, clothed in black on a white backdrop. Lucy rocked on her heels to the beat and layered a slippy groove beneath the blonde's balls-out percussion and the guitarist's screeching. The copper-haired singer commanded the center of the monitor and shrieked random insults.

"I love this one," Jamie offered, jutting her head back and forth.

Samantha muttered, "Mmm," her eyes fixated on the screen.

Throughout most of the song, pixilated Lucy hid behind her brunette mop and worked diligently at her bass. But near the crashing end she began to strut around. She slinked up to the camera and grinned with a shameless intensity that Samantha only saw after the Grace Lutheran choir had set the church on fire with the *Requiem*.

Then the camera zoomed in on the drummer.

Samantha recognized that look of fury. "Oh boy."

Jamie sat upright. "Wut?"

"She's the ape." Samantha poked the blonde woman's face on the monitor. "She's the lady who got arrested at that rally last winter."

She scrubbed the video back to Lucy staring into the camera. Samantha closed her eyes and overlaid the image with those twinkling black eyes in the other gorilla costume, the one who came up to boogie with her. Samantha raised her fingertips to her lips, softly tapping. "Oh man. Oh man."

"What is it? Sam?"

CHAPTER THIRTY-NINE

Kate

AT THE NIGHTCLUB entrance, a large woman with short, shiny black hair holds up a flashlight and extends a hand. "IDs ladies."

"This is my ID." Anita splays fingers around her face.

Kate pats her shoulder. "It's a compliment."

Anita's frown reverses. "Oh. Well, hells, yeah. Here you go." She presents her driver's license as if it's a platinum account.

"Actually, ma'am, we card everyone."

"Hrm." Anita's shoes click as they wander down a darkened hall, toward the thump of bass speakers interspersed with siren sounds. "She called me ma'am."

"Well *I* think you look young." Kate appraises the posters on the walls for bands and special dance nights. She's heard of none of the headliners.

"Really? Is the blouse a little see-through for this crowd? I don't want to start anything tonight."

They push through a heavy set of red velvet curtains and into a white glare. There's a spotlight aimed at the curtain. They immediately stumble into each other and shuffle to the side of it blinking.

"I think we just failed our big entrance." Kate struggles to adjust her eyes to in the dark perimeter. The rest of the nightclub is dimly lit. There are two bars to the left and right and on top of each is a girl in fishnets getting friendly with a chrome pole, which impales the bar and rises up to the ceiling.

"Jesus, Mary, and Saint Joseph," Anita says.

The dancer twirls down to accept a bill from a patron, who tucks it in the strap of her black garter. The woman slithers back up the pole.

"Wow."

Kate forces herself to look away, into the crowd mingling in the middle and to the back, where another velvet curtain backdrops the dance floor. Along the walls, there are risers with booths and chairs. Women decorate every corner of the nightclub—beautiful women, cute women, tough women, angry women, light women, dark women, laughing women, freaky women. Some are dressed like the dancers: in miniskirts, camisoles, and chunky stilettos. Some sport massive dreadlocks and piercings. Some wear tank tops and cargo pants. Some are in oxfords with popped collars and tailored pants with perfect cuffs.

Kate spies the bathroom hall past the dancefloor and an adjoining lounge with pool tables and video games. "Ooh." She clasps hands. "They have Centipede. Let's play."

Anita hooks her arm. "Hold on, Ferris Bueller, I need a cocktail."

"Oh, yeah."

"And um, we're not hiding in an arcade. I intend to busteth a move."

"No one says that anymore."

"I says it."

The bartender in a tight pinstripe vest, her breasts ready to spill out, leans across the rail. "What can I get you lovely ladies?"

Anita taps nails on the bar counter. "Vodka gimlet and a cosmo for junior here."

The couple next to them is having a squabble. One is kissing the other's neck, trying to make up for flirting with the pole dancer.

"If you're going to stare," Anita whispers at Kate with a spitty hiss, "try to be less obvious."

Kate raises hands. "Well, you just don't see that every day."

"It is kinda adorable."

"Yeah." Not to mention vaguely tingle-inducing.

The drinks arrive, and Kate claps. "I've always wanted to try one of these." She gingerly slides the iced pink drink from the bar top and takes a sip.

"Well?" Anita asks and knocks back a slug of her cloudy lime cocktail.

"I think she accidentally poured me a glass of Pinesol," Kate rasps.

"Yeah, it's great isn't it? You'll be loose in no time." Anita tips the bartender generously.

Kate peers around, a full scan of the room. On the drive to the city, Anita mentioned that "Liesl" was headed out to the bars tonight. But although Kate had already glimpsed a few of Lucy's doppelgangers, the real thing was nowhere to be found. Maybe it had all been wishful blogging on Lucy's part. "You sure this the right place?"

"This is the only bar left that has a lesbian night. Apparently, they're all off having babies nowadays." Anita stands on her tiptoes. "Could be she likes to show up late."

"Or maybe she already went home with someone."

"Well, forget Lucy. The point was to get the lay of the land. I'll bet you dinner for four at Lagerheads you won't be attracted to anyone."

"You've already lost the bet."

"Yeah, there is something affirming about this place. I could totally slum it. Hey." Anita whirls around. "Let's dance." She grabs Kate's arm.

"Whoa." Kate carefully balances the glass as Anita threads through the crowd.

God, Anita is so conspicuous. The trick is to play this as a joke, right? Because what mother of two would actually dance to this electronic hammering noise? But no one is watching them, the music providing an aural cover. Wait. There are a few, here and there, smirking from Anita to Kate as the two set down their drinks and walk onto the polished floor.

We could be your mothers. Look away. Look away. Cute though. Okay, let's see. I suppose I could kiss that woman with the nose chain. Ooh, that lady looks too much like Claudia; that would be completely weird.

The room grows warm and close, scented with sweat and hair product. Kate slides into the groove. The cosmo hits bottom as the music thumps along, coaxing pelvic thrusts from even the most conservatively dressed. She fights that ridiculous urge with what's left of her dignity and tries not to look too much like a hen scratching around. A few riot grrrls scoot away from them. Maybe she and Anita are doing this wrong. It's certainly not the easiest thing to do with jeans too tight and a pair of Spanx under that. Fortunately the new push-up bra is doing its job, despite having appeared rather flimsy when she first put it on.

The club fills with even more women and the occasional male sidekick. After a second round of drinks and another shot at dance fever, a slow mix takes over.

Anita wanders to the opposite bar this time. She scoots a stool aside with her hip. "Oh, barkeep."

"Just Diet Coke for me." Kate stares wistfully at the game room. An hour passes and under the influence of two martinis it seems like fifteen minutes. "Can we play pool or something? I might need to learn that."

"Meh." Anita scoops up her drink and slurps at it as if parched. She scans the room. Her head juts from side-to-side to the beat and then locks to one side.

"Oohhh, yeaaah," she sings baritone.

"What?"

"Look-at-the-door, look-at-the-door, look-at-the-*doooor.*"

Where the hell did they put the door again? *Ah*, Anita's now facing away from it with bulging eyes, as if looking at it again might turn her to salt.

Kate looks past the crowd to the spot lit velvet curtain.

The woman stands there, gazing around. She's no longer a ghost, or bleak, or Barbie; she is at maximum wattage, in tight cobalt cords, torn tunic, with shaggy blades of hair and thick eye makeup more West Hollywood than Clinique. All along the bar, heads turn and a few women scoot out their barstools but do not rise. One girl holds another back, giving the musician some space. But the stares keep at Lucy Veebee as she moves through the crowd.

Another woman with a blonde pixie cut follows behind her. She looks familiar, like one of the band. Kate recognizes her sardonic sneer from photos. Apparently it is permanent. The woman's thumbs furiously type into her smartphone.

Kate gulps. There's a heart in her chest somewhere, but it seems to have shriveled and dislodged. The music hammers at her ears. Anita nudges her, but Kate can do nothing but stand there frozen as if a wildcat were creeping by unawares.

Lucy and the blonde walk up to some young fans and she hugs each of them. The blonde leans back and holds her cellphone up. Lucy and one of the girls hold each other, cheek-to-cheek and smile into the flash of the cellphone camera. They all titter as the blonde photographs Lucy with all of them this way. The blonde departs to the bar, shaking her head, thumbs back to typing.

Anita laughs incredulous. "What do you wanna bet she's been coming here every Saturday night before church?"

"Stay here, 'Nita. Don't leave, okay?"

"Why would I do that?"

Kate pushes off the bar and maneuvers through the crowd. She can't think of one clever thing to say. The young women clustered around Lucy glance at Kate, eyebrows raised. *Awesome.* She probably looks like the suburban housewife she is, judged somewhere between "sexless frump" at "trying too hard" in her push-up bra and baby-doll ombré blouse.

Lucy glances over her shoulder, directly into Kate's cleavage. Her gaze rises to meet Kate's eyes and she does a triple-take.

Kate smiles, mouth open, and rapidly waves.

Lucy turns away from the group, takes Kate's arm, and walks her back to the bathroom hallway, lit crimson with bare red bulbs and painted brick.

"What are you doing here?" she asks calmly.

"What are *you* doing here?"

"Katie, did you follow me?"

"Anita figured out that this is where you'd be tonight. We know about your blog. Samantha told me. Just look at you." Kate smiles coyly. "You're back on brand."

Lucy pulls the tunic shirt away from her chest and stares down at the hideous mug of Iggy Pop screen printed across it. "It's hard to fight. What do you mean my blog? I never told Sam about a blog."

"No. She and Jamie found it."

Lucy squints, her head tilts. "Sorry? The band destroyed my right ear."

"That's your left." Something flutters in Kate's stomach. "I said, the girls found it. *Blogging My Sojourn*? Took me a while but I read every word. Your Daniel entry? My God, Luce. I'm so sorry about—"

"You got the wrong person." Lucy walks toward the bar and signals the bartender. "Jack, straight."

"Sojourn considers lying a sin I'll bet," Kate says. "Liesl? C'mon Luce. How obvious is that? And do I seriously look like a Vicky? Victoria?"

Lucy squints. "You sound kinda crazy right now." She slaps down some bills, knocks back the shot, and smacks the glass down.

"Luce," Kate stares frightened at the empty glass, "we can work this out. I don't know how, but we can." She slides it aside. "Without that."

"I am working things out. I—I give all my problems to the Lord. It's taking a while, but—but it's gonna be fine."

"C'mon, listen to yourself." Kate shakes her head. "Luce. Just stop. Let it go."

"This is so not right," Lucy mutters and starts from the bar.

Kate grabs her arm and holds her there. "I'm sorry, Luce." She wills Lucy to look at her, but she won't. Lucy glowers at the ground like a petulant child. "But I'm also sorry for me. I missed you so much. You don't know how hard I cried for you. How many times I thought about you over the years."

Lucy continues to hang her head. "We were never—very close." She tosses her shoulder. "Not like best friends or anything."

"Close enough to fall in love."

"Yeah, well, that's how our bodies tricked us I guess."

Kate leans closer, her lips brush Lucy's ear. "I'm still tricked."

For a moment, Lucy doesn't move.

What did I just say? Oh God, there is no going back from this—

Lucy gently pulls away.

Maybe it's time to let her go.

But Lucy doesn't head for the door. Instead, she slinks backward, moving through the dancing crowd and into the flashing lights. Her nimble right arm outstretches, forefinger beckoning.

Kate's feet give her no choice but to follow.

The rest of the dancers move fast, arms akimbo, flickering in the lights. But Lucy sways slowly, cutting the beat in half. Kate begins to dance too. She keeps a safe distance until Lucy speaks so quietly, Kate has to lean in.

"What?"

"I said, what perfume is that?" Lucy's nose dips into Kate's hair and her breath tickles. "It's nice."

"Really?" Kate yells. "I—I don't know. Nothing. Sam used up all my perfume."

"It's good. Like lavender or something." Lucy dances backward, her presence clearing a small quadrant of the dance floor.

"Oh. Yeah." Kate follows and trips forward. "That's um, Palmolive, aromatherapy."

Lucy catches Kate's nervous hands, pulls her close. "Just to confirm. Dish soap?"

"Yeah." Kate's forehead falls onto Lucy's shoulder as she snorts out laughter.

Lucy's body shudders in her arms; it feels orgasmic.

"Shut up," Kate says.

"I'm sorry. You're such a mom." Lucy smooths her arms. "I love that."

They lean into each other. *This is the girl*, this is the body Kate remembers. There's no denying how wonderful it feels. How right the luxurious surge from foot to scalp. She pulls back a little and smiles. In these arms, a lost portion is found again, in the sultry warmth of her first love, the electricity in her touch. There are few things besides dancing which turn two into one. Dancing will have to do.

Kate feels Anita's stunned stare from across the room. She twiddles her fingers in a wave over Lucy's shoulder. Anita lifts her cocktail with a wry smile.

"What would Henry Cleaver say?" Kate asks.

"A girl's gotta relax. Let her hair down."

"This is my fault. All my fault."

"It isn't." Lucy cranes her head back, holds Kate directly in her dark stare. "Whatever happens, don't think that. You are a good person. Okay?"

"I give up, Luce. If you came back to torture me, mission accomplished."

Lucy's blonde friend dances in the space near them and holds up her smartphone, scanning the dance floor, landing briefly on them. Lucy stiffens, glaring at the woman, and shakes her head. The blonde looks Kate up and down with disgust and something that even resembles fear, then storms for the exit.

Lucy's gaze follows the woman out. Then she smiles softly and murmurs in Kate's ear, "I came back because you're a psychic projector."

"A mind reader?" *God*, it's hard to have a lucid conversation so incredibly close to this woman.

"Psychic projectors don't actually read minds." Lucy moves them around the floor, her hands smoothing across Kate's hands, entwining with them, pressing them onto her warm body. "But their thoughts are so powerful, average people sometimes read them like orders."

Kate gulps. "Sounds like hypnotism."

"Nope. The majority of psychic projectors don't even know they're doing it. That's why it's rarely been documented."

"So I called you back here?"

Lucy shrugs, her eyes sparkling. "Maybe."

"Sometimes I wish—" Kate cocks her head, searching for the words. Her cellphone buzzes in her back pocket.

"What do you wish?" Lucy runs her hand up Kate's neck. "I'll make it happen."

"They'd have let us have one date. You know, something average, like dinner and a movie." She pulls out her cellphone. "Ooh, this is Sam. I should take this. The girls are all alone in the house." She reluctantly pulls out of Lucy's arms and walks back to the bathroom hallway.

"What is it, honey—Sam, I can barely hear you. Are you all right? Well, can't it wait? Yes, Lucy's here. That's none of your business. What the heck are you talking about? Gorillas? Just, stop it. Alright. I'll ask her. I'm hanging up now. Jesus."

Lucy leans on the wall, her head cocked to the side. "Everything okay?"

"Oh." Kate rolls eyes. "Sam thinks you're a Simian Avenger." She laughs and pockets the cellphone, growling. "Ugh. Why I ever thought I could drive just twenty miles away from my family and expect to have my own night—just one night—clearly the delusion of a pathetic woman."

Lucy looks away, licking lips.

"Lucy?" Kate stops. "*Lucy?*"

"Kate, you're a Larson now. And you need to be ready," she reaches out.

"Oh my God." Kate's mind reels as connections form, she squints as if it might help make sense of the past six months. She bats Lucy's hand away. "Is that what all this is? You're coming out to prove them wrong?"

"Yeah, but, there's a lot more. Sojourn extorted a ton of—"

"I trusted you. Sam trusted you. Jamie—"

"Come on, I'd never hurt those girls."

"This will hurt *everybody*."

"I didn't start this, Katie. *They* started this a long time ago."

Kate's chest shakes with mounting disappointment. "Why couldn't you just let it go? You had such a great life." She paces the hall, while others come in and out of the bathrooms gawking at them. She points at Lucy. "You're a dick, you know that? This isn't high school. You can't just play games and be excused because your parents sucked."

"Um, I was never excused."

"You were until the fire," Kate says. "You set it didn't you?"

Lucy's hand wanders up the brick wall, finding cracks, tracing them with her fingers.

"Oh, my gawd. I defended you."

"Oh, no you didn't." Lucy sighs. "Okay, listen, you were a kid, so forget about that. Besides it wasn't the fire, Katie. It was *us* that screwed me and you know it. And now everyone wants to pretend we never happened."

"That's true. They do. You know why? Because half of them are gone or dead and the other half are too old to care or don't want to remember their mistakes. There's only the two of us who even give it a second thought."

"You still do?"

"You know I do. Dammit, Lucy. Shit." Kate stalks out of the hall. Where the hell is Anita?

Anita is laughing with a group of women, a bit too loud, a bit too wobbly.

Kate takes her arm. "We have to go."

"What? I thought—"

"Please now. I'll drive." She drags Anita clicking, stumbling, toward the curtain. Anita digs for her business card holder, handing out cards along the way.

Kate rips the curtain open.

Lucy is chasing the blonde from earlier down the hall. They are wrestling with something, a phone. "Please don't do this," she says to the woman.

The woman leers at Kate as she passes them. She's actually quite pretty, with deep blue eyes.

"Kate. Wait, please." Lucy puts one hand out at Kate, but turns back to the blonde. They wrestle for the phone again. "Would you give me that? I swear we are done if you do this." It flies into the air, scrabbles across the floor.

"Dammit, Lucy," the woman yelps.

Anita hiccups as they bang through the front doors. "Wow, catfight. Do you really need that kinda drama?"

"No. No. Definitely not."

A fine mist has gathered, weighing down into rain. The night sky of Minneapolis glows amber. Kate piles Anita into the passenger seat, gets in, and familiarizes herself with the elaborate instrumentation.

There's a tap on her window. It's Lucy.

Kate starts the car. Lucy taps harder.

"Please, Katie," comes her muffled voice.

Kate locates the window button and stabs it. "Stop calling me that."

"Can we still get together and talk? I want to explain."

"I don't know. I don't know anything anymore." She looks to Anita for assistance, but her friend has reclined and dozed off.

Lucy's feathers have fallen from the rain. She reaches in, clasps Kate's shoulder. A drop of water runs down her fingertips, past Kate's collarbone, and between her breasts. "I'm sorry."

Kate clutches the wheel for strength. Her knuckles turn pale. "Did you know . . . Sam's birthday is the day after yours?"

Lucy lets go. "Whoa, really?"

"Yeah, by an hour. I tried, to push, to make her arrive in time. But she was big. Erik told me later that I was so out of it that I said—I said, I baked you a cake." Kate's voice quakes. "He thought I meant for him."

Lucy's eyes close, her mascara running like a gunpowder misfire. She swallows hard, wipes water from her face with her shoulder and looks away, toward the blonde woman glowering by the door.

"I would have named her after you if I could have," Kate says.

Lucy stares into her. "Do you know how much that means to me?"

"She thinks you're awesome, Lucy." Kate punches the window button. "Don't ruin it."

BLOGGING MY SOJOURN

One Woman's Journey from Gay to Straight

Well, I've failed this ex-gay thing, clearly. Despite what so many liberal psychologists and conservative Christians say, I'm not sure any good comes of turning yourself inside out and riffling around in your psyche or soul. But I gave it a shot, as I always do. I gave Sojourn a chance, albeit one from a biased perspective, but I stayed the duration.

Okay, just past graduation. But still. I wanted to see. I couldn't help but look. I'd be Lot's wife for sure.

Most people run for the basement when the funnel cloud drops. Me? I got to stand at the window. One of these days the glass is going to shatter.

Posted by Liesl ~ 8:00 AM ~ 2 comments

InChrist commented:
You've given up far too easily. Was this just a joke to you?

Liesl commented:
My heart wasn't completely in it, if that's what you mean. I wish you all the best, but this organization is going down. Pick up a *USAToday* and see for yourself.

CHAPTER FORTY

Samantha

ZEV PULLED AWAY from the kiss. "Whoa, where did you go?"

"Sorry. Jamie and I were up way late last night." Samantha blinked wide and then snuggled in closer to his musky t-shirt. She drew her hand across his thigh, fascinated by the solid thickness of muscle. According to her research, to guarantee sex, chimpanzee males beat all the young females until they submitted. There were no dates, no proms, no walks along the beach. She couldn't imagine it. Her brother was right, not everything was reducible to chimps versus bonobos. There were too many gaps that needed filling.

"Samster. Take it easy."

"Please don't call me that," she whispered into his ear. "Brace calls me that."

"Sorry. It's just that, you're making me . . . yunno."

"Shit. I'm so sorry." She scooted back to the passenger seat though she really wanted to run her hands up under his shirt and feel the cut of his chest and abs.

"Nah. It's okay." He peered out the window and down Bluff road. "We shouldn't be up here anyway."

No lights were on in the Gainsborough manse.

She'd asked Zev to take her to the Leap mostly so that she could spy on Lucy, make sure she wasn't headed toward the female parental unit. That same parental unit had come home the night before, armed with angry elevens, and stormed straight up to the bedroom. And frankly Samantha was fine with that. Mom was levelheaded. Well, historically speaking. She would do the right thing. *Wouldn't she?*

It wasn't fair that Samantha would have to choose: Lucy or her grandmother. Why couldn't adults get along?

Zev started the Ford, turned it around, and inched it down the hill, gravel popping under the slow moving tires. "So, I'm thinking of joining Brace and Maddox at UW."

She sat up. "What? Really?"

"Yeah, think I'm gonna undergrad there and then do Columbia for my masters." He shrugged. "Dad says I should be prepared for it all to change once I actually get in. But that's where I'm at right now."

She grinned out the window, up at the waning moon, and calmly ventured. "Wow, so maybe we'll see each other sometimes."

"That's what I was hoping too. But—"

"You should totally date other girls," she said rapidly.

"Huh?" He stamped the brakes, which slowly pushed them forward in their seats.

"Well, I mean, there will be so many at college and it's not fair to expect—"

"Are you wanting to date other guys?"

"No."

"Neither am I. Girls, that is." He chuckled and pushed up his glasses.

Samantha grinned at him, tucked her hand in his. Zev was no chimp, definitely a bonobo. She sighed as they passed over the sparkling St. Croix. It was the hardest thing in the world to dial her feelings for this guy down to a medium setting even when it was the most logical choice.

CHAPTER FORTY-ONE

Kate

ERIK GAPES AT page 2B of the *Star Tribune* spread across the dining room table:

EXTORSION AND SEX SCANDALS
MARR LARSON CAMPAIGN

A fuzzy cellphone photo of the daughter-in-law of Senator Larson dancing with the graduate of an ex-gay program spans two column widths. If Kate and Lucy were any closer they would need to be horizontal. Inset within is a sharper photo of Kate with Senator Larson under the Marrisota banner at the state capitol.

"I didn't think you'd really do it."

Kate sniffles. "We didn't actually *do it*. I talked to her for five minutes."

"Wow, she's a close talker," Erik says. "You've already cheated on me in your heart. So what does it matter?"

"Then we cheat a hundred times."

"That many, aye?"

"Oh come on, Erik." *God, these new chairs are uncomfortable.*

He shakes his head. "I guess part of me still thought it was just this innocent flirtation thing that women did sometimes. But, hell, I know what you're like in bed. What would make me think it would be any different with her."

"What is *that* supposed to mean? I told you we didn't do anything." Kate's eyes sting with dried tears. She mumbles, "At least you finally get what she meant to me."

"I already got it, all right? I got it a long time ago." Erik grips the table and coffee splashes up out of their cups. "And now so does the rest of the world!"

"*That's* not my fault. But I'm sorry. I really didn't plan—Well . . ."

"Kate, I look like a real idiot. I gotta go to work with this? On top of the Sojourn allegations, Dad's doing all he can to stop Mom from swallowing a whole bottle of Xanax." Erik slumps back in his chair. "What the hell's happening with us?"

Kate rubs her eyes. "I don't know, Erik. I don't know."

The door is closing on the girls again—the Andern car pulling up to the bluffs, its lights striking the clearing of Maiden Leap with a harsh glare.

She heads straight to her sewing station, wraps the kaleidoscope quilt in plastic, and tapes it closed. She latches the cover on her sewing machine, closes her kits, and carries them down to the storage room. It's time to make the living room livable again. She straps the package onto her Schwinn and sets out.

A film of humidity has settled in the late summer air, making the distant oaks more blue than green. Cicadas whir electric in the shadows and aggressive yellow jackets have officially launched their campaign of annoyance and fear.

Kate coasts without braking down the hill to the lift bridge, daring another crash. The thick breeze across her perspiring body feels delicious and perhaps the only thing closest to joy she will feel today. On the Wicasa side she passes the bustle of Main Street—the fudge shop, the Irish pub, the hat store—and climbs Center Street, a mile long hill that connects the old bluff town to its newer subdivisions widening on the prairie. Her quadriceps ache but her lungs are strong, her heart damn well up to the challenge.

Senator Larson and her husband live in a modern three-story colonial up here beyond the bluffs in the Pine Creek golfing community, where everyone knows everyone because they look exactly like each other. *And there goes Bert and Claudia's daughter-in-law rolling by on her rusty bike, you know the bisexual who makes those bizarre blankets?*

CLAUDIA SITS IN her robe with the new quilt on her lap, her hands smoothing across the satiny shards of color. "Ah, it's a rainbow, God's promise to Noah."

Kate plops down beside Claudia on her in-laws' pristine white couch. "Well, actually, that wasn't—okay, just promise me you'll use it."

Claudia's face squinches up and tears rolls down her cheeks. "Gracious," she dabs eyes, "everything's making me cry today."

"Claudia, listen, I'm so sorry about that photo."

"Yes, yes. I know. It was perfectly innocent. Erik already told me. It was a birthday party and everybody was acting like teenagers. I've got bigger fish to fry right now. Bert and I are on our second day of fasting." Claudia eyes the silver tray of butter cookies with disdain. "Just pray the Lord's advice comes soon."

"You're really not mad?"

"Oh, psst, I know how these things go when alcohol gets involved. But anytime you walk into one of those places, you put so much in jeopardy, Katie. Don't you realize that?"

Claudia's pupils are dilated mostly black with just a slight frost blue ring of iris. She's higher than a screech owl in a cottonwood. Kate has rarely seen the woman so unhinged. There were glimpses, certainly. Once when Brace's diaper leaked onto her pastel twinset in church. Or the time she misspoke Revolutionary war dates on Channel Five's *Face Off* and then after, in the green room, continuously struck her own forehead until Bert yanked her wrist away. There was a brittleness there that required protection—like saving the flesh from a bone's compound fracture.

Today all Kate had to offer was her last quilt. She fills her mouth with a butter cookie.

Claudia nods, gazing out the window. "One must always behave oneself in a small town, Katie. You never know whose child is going to grow up to be a novelist."

A few crumbs blow from the corner Kate's mouth.

"I realize now Ms. Van Buren has had it in for me. For years. And probably you too, Katie." Claudia hands Kate a school form copied from an old Xerox machine. In the notes section at the bottom:

> I do think the Andern child would make a good mentee. She's a straight 'A' student, save for her time in contact with the defendant. But I would not consider sponsoring the Van Buren girl. While it is true that a 'B' student can be more clever than an 'A' student (who tends to learn by rote) they are less malleable. WBHS would be better served if Ms. Van Buren were isolated from the other children.
>
> My recommendation is expulsion.
>
> —Claudia Larson

Kate hangs her head. "This changed her life, Claudia. There were no adults looking out for her."

"Perhaps I was too harsh. Perhaps my mistake was believing there was only room for one powerful woman in this town." Her voice rises, quavering. "Or, perhaps Ms. Van Buren is an actual witch, who has cursed the Larson family name."

Despite the day's excruciating events, Kate turns away to bite back laughter.

"My poll numbers are cratering. All thanks to her and Sojourn extorting those families. But it is a test for us, Katie. A test of our faith."

Kate nods. *Oh, it's a test all right.*

"Now I know you would never hurt Erik, so let's not ever let that happen again." Claudia looks at Kate, her upper lip quivering over her tall teeth. "Because—because there would be hell to pay, for all of us, now wouldn't there?"

A cottony lump lodges in Kate's throat, making the dry cookie even tougher to swallow. She reaches for the tea. "Are you threatening me, Claudia?"

"With what? With what do I have to threaten you? It is not me that stands in final judgment. I know there are temptations. There are choices. But I have seen the Lord's good works first hand. People can change. This family has survived, was built, from the power of change."

Kate frowns. "You mean, you think I changed after high school?"

"Certainly you. And others." Claudia draws a sip from her cup. "Others have changed and never looked back."

Kate nods, pondering it. Who are these others? She glances back at Claudia. "You?"

"No. Goodness, no, don't be ridiculous." Claudia shudders. "But trust me, I have seen it. You'd be surprised what the Lord can change if you really want him to." She pats Kate's knee. "We'll get through it, Katie. When the Lord returns, it will all be old news. You'll see."

KATE RIDES SLOWLY up to her house, her legs loose and rubbery, ready to give out.

Erik is on the lawn, watering the blue spruce bushes that border the foundation, his stare casting aimlessly about the yard.

She lays her bike down in the driveway, stumbles up, and throws her arms around him. He drops the hose to hold her but his stance feels like that of a man ready to leap.

BLOGGING MY SOJOURN

One Woman's Journey from Gay to Straight to Gay

It doesn't take a fancy shrink to figure out why I hate bullies. But someone had to stop them, didn't they? Why don't I feel any better?

Posted by Liesl ~ 8:00 AM ~ 4 comments

Rolf68 commented: As much as I loathe conversion therapy, you lowered yourself to their level.

InChrist commented: It's in the Lord's hands now.

WildeRosemary commented: You don't fool us, Liesl. I know you are soft on the inside. Have you considered the correlation of not being able to forgive and the onset of inflammation, of cancer? You've got to break the cycle if you want to survive.

Andirons commented: Looks like you're the bully now.

CHAPTER FORTY-TWO

Kate

FURY GRANTED KATE the first peace she'd had in months. At first, she felt torn open. She couldn't even claim to be as gullible as a teenager when her own daughter figured out that Lucy had played them all for fools. Soon the hole left behind filled with outrage. That burned hot and quick and flickered out, smoldering with her disbelief in the human capacity for cruelty. It didn't matter anymore whether Lucy meant to be cruel or not. In the end, Kate was a bit thankful. Lucy had taken with her the possibility of a choice.

Now, when anyone mentions that name, Kate's blood runs cold as snowmelt. She can almost see why her mom never talked about the Robeson boy jumping from Maiden Leap. The Robeson boy, the Van Buren girl. *We dare not speak their names.* To take one's life, to rip oneself from the pack, cuts short any chance for understanding and provides every opportunity for supposition. And then? Dismissal.

The family prepares for the wedding with solemnity, the men in gray pinstripe, the women in sage green satin. Brace got a haircut, actually trimmed his golden bangs for Mark and Ray. Kate beams—*so handsome, his own man now.* Samantha seems more nervous than she was for the play. But even if she makes a mistake, she'll still nail it.

Kate paces by the door to the garage, running over the lines of her toasting speech one last time. Erik stops for an inspection. She kisses his cheek. He smiles a bit. It's taking him a while to warm back up to her. She must be patient.

"Brace," Kate calls out. "Do you have the keys to the church?"

"Yep."

"In your pocket?"

"Yes!"

"All right, guys, I'll see you at the park."

"Okay, Mom."

"Bye, hon."

Kate carefully slides into the new Camry, its interior polished and still smelling of the showroom. By the time she reaches the lift bridge she can already see the decorations brightening Wilson Park, rows of white folding chairs, sheer linens flowing in the breeze.

When she arrives in the dressing tent, there's not much to do except receive the requisite touch-up by the hair and makeup stylists. Then she joins Mark for moral support.

"Hey, look at the ceiling." She reaches up to his left nostril and plucks a rogue hair.

"Ow!" His eyes water.

"Sorry, I didn't think it was attached."

Mark sneezes. "Bullshit. Do you do that to Erik?"

"Of course. I'll have a talk with Ray about technique." Kate brushes off his white satin lapels.

Mark raises his chin and looks down at her. "Lucy's here."

Kate straightens a tie that doesn't need straightening.

"Did you hear me?"

"Yeah, I know. So what?"

Mark searches Kate's eyes with his level gaze. "We had a long conversation. She fought hard to keep that picture out of the paper. She was only in this to take down Sojourn and Marrisota."

"Or so she says. I can't believe you're suddenly defending her."

"You gotta admit, she's one hell of a method actor for the cause."

"Are you kidding? She didn't fool me for a second."

Mark grins his knowing grin that says, *yeah she did, but not the way we're talking and so I'll be a pal and won't mention it.* "Well, you need to talk to her. Soon."

A bitter laugh escapes. "Not today I'm not." She had not expected this from Mark. Maybe it was because he was too focused on the romance of his wedding day but he seemed to have lost all vitriol in the past weeks. "Why didn't you tell me about the blog?"

"I was trying to protect you."

"I didn't need your—"

"Stop stressing me out on my big day."

"You brought her up."

"Now, listen, she said she wouldn't stay for the reception, cause any trouble. But she won't be in town much longer."

Kate shrugs, looks at her phone. "Looks like you've got twenty minutes."

He bites his lip. "What do I do with twenty minutes?"

"Run. Run for your life."

"Very funny."

"Come on." She hooks his arm. "Let's watch the riverboats."

MARK AND RAY stand under an ivy-covered trellis, Kate to Mark's right and Ray's brother to his right. Between the two pairs, the female pastor from Minneapolis Unitarian welcomes the crowd with a short benediction.

Samantha rises from her chair and steps to the side of the trellis. She faces the audience and slowly, quietly begins "Somewhere" from *West Side Story*. It's surely not lost on anyone here that there *is* a place for Mark and Ray, that their someday is near, no matter what the Claudia Larsons of the world try to do. Samantha's voice rises and rises, out across the wind and well past the crowd. She holds the final high note, eyes closed. Kate fights tears knowing the havoc it will wreak on her makeup. When Samantha finishes with a simple smile, Kate looks to Erik, who does not appear worried about makeup.

Everyone turns to the pastor. There's something about wedding ceremonies that make Kate's mind wander. This one is no different. It's the same sermon, always. An attempt to describe the magic that holds two people together. Promises that are damned difficult to keep for years on end. Ray's vows are succinct, Mark's go on and on. Kate struggles to pay attention to the back of Mark's head, but soon her gaze meanders into the crowd.

In the second row, Lucy Van Buren sits in a strapless, cream dress beaming at Mark, as proud as a sister. It takes great effort not to steal too long of a look at her chest, where the hint of a tattoo arcs above the breastline. If Lucy had stayed in Wicasa Bluffs, it would be her up here supporting Mark. The two of them had an affinity long before Katie came along. But Lucy let him down by not sticking out the small town life, never writing or calling, and then by coming back the messed up way she did. Everybody had their reasons; everybody had their little spites, wounded kids, the whole crowd of them. On this day, as Samantha just sang, she should find a way of forgiving. Mark seems to have.

The pastor spreads her arms. "I now pronounce you husbands for life. You may now kiss."

Ray clasps Mark's neck, his thumbs resting on Mark's jaw and his fingers part the back of Mark's curly, orange hair. He kisses Mark deeply without hesitation. Then, as he draws away, Mark stumbles a little, eyes blinking, and everyone chuckles. The rest is a blur of people and noise and the procession to the Crystal Ballroom conservatory up the well-manicured footpath.

THE SOFT CITRUS scent of eucharis and rosemary herbs fills the sunlit ballroom. Mark and Ray take up their places in the middle of the wedding party table, flanked by Kate and Ray's brother.

After the first course, Kate stands, she relaxes her hand on the cordless microphone and channels Samantha's confidence:

Let me not to the marriage of true minds
Admit impediments. Love is not love
Which alters when it alteration finds,
Or bends with the remover to remove:
O no! It is an ever-fixed mark
That looks on tempests and is never shaken;
It is the star to every wandering bark,
Whose worth's unknown, although his height be taken.
Love's not Time's fool, though rosy lips and cheeks
Within his bending sickle's compass come:
Love alters not with his brief hours and weeks,
But bears it out even to the edge of doom.
If this be error and upon me proved,
I never writ, nor no man ever loved.

She looks down at the husbands. "Ray, this lover of Shakespeare here next to you was not born to be a minstrel. But he is a seer and a truth-teller." She lays a hand to her breastbone. "How do I know this? Because the day he met you, he called me from New York at four in the freaking morning and told me that he just met the man he was going to marry." She allows time for the chuckles and the *Ahhs*. "I've taken him at his word ever since.

"It feels odd in a way, to welcome you to a family of friends that you joined long ago. But we—all of us here—want you to know," she laughs through the rest, "you're not getting out of Wicasa Bluffs alive."

Applause fires around the ballroom and Mark cackles with glee. Ray stands up and hugs her. He whispers in her ear, "Mark was right." He sniffles. "It was worth it. All these people bearing witness. We needed this. Thank you, honey."

The tumbling peal of church bells rolls down the bluffs. People turn in their seats. "That's Grace Lutheran!" Mark says with a yelp.

"Whoa." Ray turns to him. "How'd you swing that?"

"I didn't."

"Guess someone up there loves you." Kate looks out at her daughter and husband. Erik winks at her. Hopefully, Brace will make it back in time for cake.

LATER, KATE DANCES in Mark's arms to big band swing. They twist sloppily back and forth, cheeks reddened by champagne. Nearby, Erik dances stiffly with Ray, Samantha dances with Zev, while Brace and Jamie stand on the periphery making polite conversation.

When the music slows, Mark sighs. "Well kid. The Great Foxtradamus has put away his crystal ball."

"No."

"Two of the couples I thought would stay together are getting separated. And it looks like Barb and Randolph are getting back together. Totally goes against my sleep-side theory."

Kate clicks her tongue. "Some people. Can't predict 'em."

A vague cynicism rains down on Kate as she releases Mark to his husband.

Social Services may or may not award them a little boy to raise as their own. If it does, it will not be because Mark and Ray were married by the pastor of a hippy-dippy church, but because the child needs parents and these two men are his best shot. Mark spent a fortune on a gorgeous ceremony and filled everyone with prime rib and cake and liquor until they were rolling around with appreciation. After the bouquet is thrown and the last slice of cake is frozen, where will the guests go, but back to their insulated lives and legally sanctioned marriages?

Kate steps out into the flowered courtyard for a breath of fresh air and squints up at Maiden Leap. A figure in white stands at the edge then turns and walks away.

BLOGGING MY SOJOURN

*One Woman's Journey to Whatever
I Damn Well Please*

I have no idea why two people want to staple themselves together for life. My parents' marriage ran at extreme temperatures: icy disdain and scorching hate. Fought like cats and cats. And now my mother is this lonely old woman still pining after my crazy dad and hasn't got a clue how to date again.

Still, you have to admit, when even gay people are trying to marry it must be a proclivity with some value, right?

If Vicky's daughter was speaking to me right now, she would have the answer.

Posted by Liesl ~ 5:00 pm ~ 1 Comment

Elphaba commented: Gibbons are the only apes that mate for life. They're even more consistently monogamous than humans. But they live alone together and don't belong to a troop, to protect against interlopers. Nobody knows yet which is the better approach, in a pack or in isolation. It varies species to species.

My vote is for pack. And the pack wants you back.

CHAPTER FORTY-THREE

Samantha

"TEN AND TWO," Dad said.

She wasn't taking it personally that her time behind the wheel on their drive up to the cabin had been mostly silent. Brace might be fearing for his own life but he'd get over it. Dad was still fuming from an altercation with Mom. He'd gone from guardedly annoyed after Mom's crash earlier in the year to blowing up at the slightest thing since the newspaper article.

The kids had been waiting in the truck with the windows down and heard him yell, *Ya better decide what it is you want!* He didn't yell often, and when he did, he didn't do it so loud the neighbors could hear. Until now. It made Samantha sick inside that their home might be turned upside down like she'd seen happen to other kids' homes. And it had fixed Brace's jaw in angry solidarity with his father.

She focused on the award of getting to drive. Then, when they hit the one lane roads of northern Wisconsin she almost welcomed Brace correcting her every move. After they arrived and unpacked, orders had to be taken and Brace started goofing around, Chuck had wandered off into the wild berries, Dad got antsy because the sunlight was waning, and little by little Mom got set aside.

The three of them headed down the wooded path to the dock and Dad attached the electric motor to the fishing boat. They trawled out to a quiet section of lake where waterbugs skipped and long-legged spiders lurked in boxy webs on low hanging branches. Chuck barked from the shore, then swam out and scared all the fish away. They hauled him into the boat and he napped in a puddle.

Brace caught three walleye, Samantha caught one herself, and Dad yanked out a big pike but threw it back after they took a picture. Back at the cabin, she volunteered for cleaning the fish. She felt it her duty to feel the guts of her own meal slide through her fingers, to become immune to the rank smell, before she enjoyed its flesh. Of course she did not say this, because Brace would have launched into some bogus Native American chant, but it felt right all the same.

After dark, the three of them relaxed in the hot tub, which was essentially a giant wooden rain barrel atop a firebox full of coals. Brace and Dad drank Miller Lite and though Dad offered her one, Samantha said no. She didn't want to drop Lucy's binoculars in the water. The sky was so black here that the stars provided enough light to see the smudge of the Andromeda galaxy. How many earths did Andromeda have? One? One hundred? None?

"When I met your mom," Dad broke the eerie silence, "there was this whole fourth of July hubbub going on around us—the fireworks and the bands and the carnival. Yeah, I know, we've told you the story a hundred times."

Samantha looked to Brace, expecting the sarcastic eye-roll, the annoying huff. But he only waited on his father's words.

"It was the most magical night of my life. The strangest thing was, she had just been standing there, all alone. Like someone delivered her there. No one else next to her, no family, or friends, or boyfriend. I remember I could see the lights of the carnival in her eyes. She was beautiful. Sweet as can be. Couldn't believe my luck. We said hi to each other and we never shut up." He shook his head and took another swig.

Without phones or clocks or TV or video games, minutes stretched like years out into the void.

"I didn't understand it at the time," Dad said. Brace startled and the steaming water sloshed. "I had no idea your mom's heart had already been broke. And I guess you kids know all about that now, but it's important for you to try to understand. Hell, it's taken me years to get it and I'm not even sure she does completely. There are people who marry their high school sweetheart and stay together forever. They never got that chance."

Dad was silent again for a while. "When you're married, yes, you belong to each other." He looked to his children. "But you don't—you don't own each other. Does that make sense?"

Samantha and Brace slowly nodded. She looked to her brother, who lowered his head. She could not be sure if it was condensation on his cheeks.

CHAPTER FORTY-FOUR

Kate

KATE STANDS ATOP Maiden Leap. The afternoon air is dense, weighted with thunderheads and smelling of wild onion. "It would be just my style to take a lightning bolt right now," she murmurs. Over the past couple of weeks, she and Lucy had swapped glances around Wicasa Bluffs, and then waves, and then it felt ridiculous not speaking. So when Kate got the email with the subject line: *Meet me at the Leap*, a mere five minute debate waged in her head as to whether she would go.

But Lucy is late. *Typical.* Another reminder of the liberties she's taken, the havoc she's created. "Why the fuck am I giving her the satisfaction," she whispers. "She's probably sitting up in her crow's nest laughing."

"Thanks for coming," Lucy says from behind her.

Kate turns, feigning calm.

Lucy stands barefoot in jeans and a black tank top. She cringes a smile and wraps arms around herself. There's something about her today that seems as fragile as burnt sugar. She might be the same unpredictable creature she'd been twenty years ago, but now she lacks the blazing force of youth to hold her in one piece.

Still, that's no longer Kate's concern, is it?

"So, I've wondered about something for a long time." Kate stares back out over the St. Croix, to the thatch of trees hugging Riverton; she can make out the Objibwe burial mounds from here. "Did Wicasa jump for love? Or freedom?"

"Hmm, I don't know," Lucy says. "Maybe when you're an imaginary Indian princess it's hard to tell the difference. So, how's Erik handling things? And the kids."

"Fine. They're at the cabin. Fishing. House is really quiet."

"Peaceful?"

"No. Unsettling. You wanted to talk?"

"Yeah. Thought we could have a picnic up here," Lucy squints at the fast moving sky, "but it's probably safer indoors."

"Never safe around you," Kate says under her breath as she joins Lucy and they walk toward the Gainsborough. "Where's Bridget?"

"At the old house. Won't come back 'til I get rid of the bats."

"What?" *Stop laughing.* "How bad is it?"

"Well, we had this one up in the corner of the dining room and it freaked out our supper guests. If I'd just left it alone, we'd have been fine but Mom made me chase it all around with a butterfly net. And then she starts screaming that it's gonna pee in the gazpacho. So then it got tangled and was screeching and everyone was running to their rooms and packing their bags."

They slowly climb the creaking porch stairs.

"I'm no expert," Kate says, "but I think every time you catch and release one, it just flies back in. And they're endangered so you can't kill them either."

Lucy shakes her head. "What the hell am I gonna do?"

"You gotta seal off their den with these little one-way doors so they can only get out. And then hope they find another home. I know a guy who does it, give you his number."

"Cool. I should call him before I go. How do you know this stuff?"

"I used to feed an orphaned bat down at the vet."

"They're kinda cute. Like little foxes."

"Mmm. So, you *are* leaving. Are you coming back?"

Lucy taps the thermostat, turns up the ceiling fan, and walks around opening windows. She leans against the towering archway between the front parlor and dining room.

"Do you want me to?"

Kate tamps down a more indignant response and quietly says, "Of course."

"Six months probably. I have to testify on some Sojourn stuff in Texas. And then there's this group of women writers, poets, performance artists. They're going on tour this fall to combat climate change. I'm going to manage them into the new year. Got the connections."

So Lucy was already done with LGBTQ rights and on to saving the planet. God help the planet.

"So restless," Kate murmurs.

"The gypsy side."

"Maybe you've got too many sides."

"See how well you know me?"

"Wish I didn't." Kate sighs through bared teeth. "Lucy do you even understand how much you've put me through? And now, my family? My kids. No—I am fully aware how much blame I deserve—but do you even grasp the full impact of your little charade? Both of them?"

"I do."

"You can't possibly. You don't even know how hard it was for me after you left town. Two years, Lucy. Two looong years of high school. High school. You know how kids are." The blood pounds in Kate's skull and her eyelid twitches. "All the talk and the jokes behind my back? Having to prove to Gary over and over again that I wasn't creepin' on his sister?"

Lucy winces, fingers wiping something invisible from her mouth. "I'm sorry for how I handled it back then. But I'm not sorry about us." She paces the Oriental rug, straightening its tassels with her toes. "If I could go back and only be your friend and let things take their course, you know? If we could have somehow waited. I know women that fell in love in high school and didn't officially date until they were eighteen. Why didn't I just—?"

"Because you're Lucy. And I loved the way you romanced me. But you shunned me after that. At First Ave. Remember? I tried to call you so many times after I graduated. Is it because I never stood up for you?"

Lucy looks sourly at the floor. "Um, yeah. A little. Guess I hoped you would *sacrifice* yourself for me. Somehow. It's like, I jumped. And . . . you weren't there." She cringes, disgusted with her self-pity. She sighs. "And then the older I got I realized how impossible it had been for you and then it became all the more embarrassing to come back. You were everywhere—on the streets, by the school, in the fields. On the Leap." She glares at Kate now. "In the park. By bikini tree." Her searching eyes and sharp intake of breath proves it happened. That night was not a dream. Not imagined.

Warmth spills down the length of Kate's torso and into her thighs.

"And then," Lucy says, "you did what any normal person would do. You met someone better." Her chest heaves and she shakes her head, refusing the tears.

They stare dumbstruck at each other. *We won't cry about this anymore. Because that's what platonic girlfriends do: they cry and makeup and dab their eyes and laugh and exchange little patting hugs and then go home to their husbands and forget all about it. But we're not quite that. Are we? We are a lifetime thing.*

"I think I—" Kate says. "I came up here for the same reason you asked me."

Lucy gulps and steps back. "Hold on, Kate." She raises a hand.

"See how nice that sounds? Say it again."

"Kate." Lucy says the more mature name so quietly it's only a small wet click in the middle of her mouth. "Slow down."

"It's already been twenty years. How much slower would you like?" She steps forward. "Let me see your feet. You never showed them to me."

"Wut?" Lucy backs toward the wall and into a floor lamp, and fumbles to right it. Kate goes to her, bends down, clasps Lucy's ankle, and gently pushes it backward, bending Lucy's leg back and up at the knee until her calf meets her thigh, then the other. As if she were inspecting a horse's hoof. Lucy places a hand on Kate's shoulder for balance. A few blades of grass and the indents of pebbles cross the scars, but the white hashmarks are there on the left foot, fainter on the right, as if toddler Lucy had raised that one up, hoping to take flight.

Kate slowly climbs the length of her and gently presses her forehead to Lucy's temple.

Lucy stares straight ahead. "I don't want a pity fuck, Kate."

"Maybe I do."

Lucy looks to her then and whispers, "How does one pity the goddess?" The corner of her mouth turns up.

Kate's heart lopes as she takes hold of Lucy's tank top.

Lucy stops her hand. "They're gone. Silicon. Really. They—you don't want, just—"

"It's okay, Luce. It's okay."

Lucy bites her lip, the hard plank of her belly clenching. Kate waits for her to relax and slowly pulls up the tank.

"Oh."

From Lucy's bellybutton grows a vine of ink that splits in two and becomes an amazing inferno of green fire and black thorns. With her fingertips, Kate traces the tattoo as it weaves and winds up, over and around two nippleless mounds, crossing but not obscuring two five-inch long scars, which are still purple in parts, still healing. It's difficult not to get lost in the confusion of it, the defiance of expectation—what Lucy sees every time she looks in the mirror.

Kate pulls the tank on up and over Lucy's head, exposing the short, wine-colored scars in Lucy's left armpit, where a masked marauder in white stole her lymph nodes. Kate raises that arm and lays her first kiss there. Lucy exhales into Kate's hair and her fingers thread into Kate's curls, pressing and tugging at her scalp, as if this the first time someone has done this.

HOW LONG HAD she been kissing Lucy's soft intent mouth? Five minutes? Fifteen? Fifty? Kate hasn't been this wet since her twenties. Their quiet moans are a song she hasn't heard in ages. When was the last time she had sex in daylight? She hadn't wanted Erik to see the aging body of a mother. He stopped wanting her to see his face when he came. But now that's exactly the point on this day. To break the membrane of mystique, to ruin it, to wallow in whatever awkward mess spills forth. Defang the beast.

Lightning brightens the windows, followed by a tearing sound high above.

Lucy rolls off the wall shivering. She takes Kate's hand and leads her up the stairs, holding tight to the thick oak banister.

Lucy's room is like an antique hotel room, a transient's nest, with open suitcases half-packed and toiletries strewn across the old dresser. Under the influence of desire it's merely a whirl of southern sunlight and scents: leather and wood polish and patchouli (of course, because that stuff never goes away).

Lucy brings her to the tarnished brass bed and pushes back the rumpled crazy quilt.

Lay lady lay.

They climb up onto the tall mattress, slide across the cool sheets, rise up on their knees, and face each other. How easy it is. This undressing. This entwining. This skin on skin. Why is this enough to wreck a home? Maybe because there is as much of a stranger here before Kate as the girl she once knew. A face lined with knowledge, no longer innocent. A lithe body at once familiar and foreign. Lucy's soft skin is still pale but the mole at her collarbone is larger than it used to be. Her hips are still teardrop shaped but her baby fat is long gone. She's thin enough for the cool clothes but too thin without them, needs a solid month of home cooking.

Kate gently throws her weight forward, pressing Lucy down and kissing her concave belly. The skin of her thighs is as silky as it used to be. She makes Lucy come twice in quick succession, her cries inspiring, her scent maddeningly delicious. It's nearly too late to savor her own climax by the time Lucy rises up, flips Kate onto her stomach, her hands deft, stealing back everything that was once so briefly hers. With her cheek mashed into a goose-down pillow, Kate watches their fading glory in the wide mirror over the dresser. And with Lucy's every stroke a year's worth of tension melts away until a soft explosion floods Kate's body and mind.

Outside, rain pours perfectly vertical in thick drops. It spatters on the sill and drips onto the floor.

KATE WAKES FROM their catnap to Lucy staring at her in the copper light of the newly exposed sunset. Kate pulls back the quilt and runs her fingers over Lucy's new breasts. They are cool to the touch, the ink of the tattoos fresh and bright, not yet bleeding out of the black outlines.

"Do you feel a phantom nipple?"

"Was hoping I would but no."

"Eh, nipples are so last year."

"Although, when I see you touch me like that, I can feel it in my head." Lucy closes her eyes. "I could have some shaped, but they wouldn't feel the same. I sure wish you'd gotten to know them. Before. They were pretty awesome." She reaches down, and with slow reverence, strokes a hand across the soft bulge of Kate' belly, across the stretch marks left by birth.

"Lucy, tell me you're not going to die," Kate says in a choking whisper.

"S'okay. I'm clear. Or I will be in three more years." She raises her arm, makes a fist then shakes her fingers out. "That's why you caught me with that sleeve on. It aches some days and I have to protect it from infection."

"How is Bridget handling it?"

"Eh, I haven't told her. Losing Dad's too fresh. Although on some level I suppose she knows. We talk around it. The Van Burens are prone to growing stuff, we run rampant even on a cellular level." Lucy chuckles. "Sometimes I wonder what cancer my brother would have ended up with if he'd made it to middle age."

Kate lays her head on Lucy's chest; minutes pass to a quiet beat.

"Do you ever think about the people who you'll see die?" Kate asks. "And the ones who'll see you die?"

"Wow. Um. No."

"Maybe you should."

THAT EVENING IN the kitchen, Kate mixes up a rich waffle batter with canned peach chunks and pecans then pours it into the steaming iron. She proudly presents a stack neither of them could possibly finish.

But Lucy stands rigid, staring upward. Kate waves a hand in front of her face, then traces her line of vision up in the corner of the tin ceiling.

There's something dark and furry lodged up there.

Lucy resolutely walks from the room and returns wearing a raincoat, bicycle helmet, and wielding a broom. Kate scoffs and volunteers for duty, wearing only an oven mitt. They make an awful racket dragging over first a stepstool, then a chair, and finally a ladder. She climbs it, Lucy supporting her legs, and pulls the little flying fox off the wall. They stand looking at the terrified creature, Lucy peering over Kate's shoulder. Sorry dude, Lucy says. And then Kate releases the bat out the back porch.

Starved by the day's events, they greedily fill themselves up with waffles and maple syrup and fresh butter and whole milk. Kate calls the Larsons' voicemail. There are no messages. Lucy takes the quilt from her bedroom, throws it over one shoulder and they walk hand-in-hand out to the clearing next to the lookout point.

They talk into the night about their parents: Lucy's father, Kate's discovery of her mother and the Robeson boy. The moon rises.

"There's something I've been meaning to tell you about that," Lucy says. Kate turns to her as Lucy stares at the dome of heaven. "Since I got back, Mom and I have been talking, going over stuff about Dad and the kid who jumped off the Leap."

"You said he was gay in your blog."

"Yeah. After that night happened with Jamie and Maddox, I started to wonder if maybe Marcus didn't actually jump. Or maybe if he did, maybe my dad was there."

"Like he got bullied into it?"

"Yeah."

"Mom said Marcus was a sweet guy," Kate says quietly. "A smart guy. Do you think your dad had it in him to do that?"

"Man, I wish I could say he didn't. I asked Mom and of course she brushed me off, but she had that look." Lucy turns to Kate to show her the hollow stare. It gives Kate a chill. "It's been the dirty little secret of their generation. But, Kate. The other thing is." She looks back at the sky and sighs. "Dad called *two* guys fairies when I was coming out. And last week, Mom confirmed who the other guy was. He was friends with Marcus. Close friends. Real close."

"Who?" But Kate knows. It makes perfect sense now, who Claudia saw *change*. "Can't be. Bert was already dating Claudia when it happened."

"So? You dated Gary and saw me on the sly."

"But they got pregnant with Erik that year."

"You could have gotten pregnant too. Claudia was Bert's beard, like Gary was yours."

Kate clasps a hand to her mouth, contemplating the circumstances of Erik's parentage. If Bert saw his lover die, he probably thought that was in store for him too. She remembers the shame she felt. His would have been even worse thirty years previous. She sits up. "Oh my god, you're going to out him."

"No. No. I mean, I'm not gonna lie, I considered it before our photo in the newspaper. But no, I didn't even tell Simian Avengers because I knew they would use it. I knew it would be the final straw for your family. And really Sojourn is going down. I don't think Claudia is going to win this marriage thing either. It kinda felt like overkill, yunno?" Lucy searches the air. "Anyway, could be Marcus jumped because Bert chose Claudia. Could be my dad and some other guys pushed him. We'll probably never know."

Lucy rolls into Kate's lap and Kate combs fingers through her hair.

"I'm so glad you didn't jump," Kate says quietly.

Lucy's teeth shine bright in the night. "I'd rather defy gravity."

They talk about Daniel's death on the Bonnie Saint. How she probably had PTSD the whole time they knew each other in high school. They talk about the search for justice as a veneer for revenge, never quite fulfilling any need, and that love seems to be the only obvious answer in the world. Lucy says she doesn't believe in God, never had really, though she wishes she could. Kate believes in something, perhaps a God borne of human imagination or something that defies imagination with no beginning or end. One thing is for sure, it cares little about their struggles, at least not in a human way. Unless God is simply love.

Kate lies back down beside Lucy, gazing into her moonlit face, her searching eyes. How easy it is to ponder everything and nothing again, the biggest things and smallest, as if Lucy had just finished telling the story of Wicasa and Chelee. Lucy's hand slides up Kate's wrist, her palm filling Kate's. Their fingers intertwine and silently speak as if these hands are autonomous. *This is our place, our clearing, no one else's.* Lucy's fingers smooth Kate's flesh and walk up and down, pressing into the tender middle of a palm that arches beneath it.

Kate says she finds it hard to imagine Lucy stuck in a hospital bed and wonders who was there for her. Was it her drummer, Tamara? Yes. She even tried to marry Lucy in San Francisco. But it wasn't Lucy's thing, kids or picket fences. Why would she bring more Van Buren DNA into this world or subject adopted children to the Veebee madness? This squashes a notion Kate had compiled over the years fed by what she saw other lesbians doing . . .

. . . A notion of young Lucy having stayed put in Minneapolis for her. Kate going to vet school at the U. Riding on the back of Lucy's Harley in the Pride parade. Those years dressed as a peasant girl, working the scotch egg booth at the Renaissance Festival while Lucy hawked non-refundable Tarot readings. The vicious arguments they'd have, unhindered by the marriage sacrament and Kate's resulting escape back to Wicasa Bluffs to cry on Mom's shoulder until Mom and Dad moved to Florida. The affairs Lucy had with her groupies but then the drama-filled coming back together and buying the bungalow in Powderhorn Park. The insemination. The kids that resembled Sam and Brace, but not quite them—a little like Mark because he gladly delivered sperm to their house when her follicles were dilated. Getting Lucy into rehab. Watching Lucy play in the park with their Not Sam and Not Brace. The big, reclining chemo chair in the cancer center that swallowed Lucy like a child. The pain pills. The nights spooning Lucy, the nights facing away from her. Every night until the end.

Before they walk back to the house, she casts the old fantasy out over the Leap. It's different now. Today transformed everything. For better or worse.

Kate senses her largest marital transgression that night is to actually sleep in Lucy's bed. Or at least try to. Instead of Erik's large comforting sighs, Lucy occasionally whimpers and then tosses around. The only thing that quiets Lucy is holding her, which Kate gladly does but not without thinking of others she has comforted. She sees Erik alone in the rustic log bed with straps for springs, underneath their scratchy Hudson Bay blanket, sleeping sound despite the loons on the lake hooting their crazy warbles. Brace and Samantha are nearly tumbling out of the bunk beds that they'd earlier fought over. Chuck's nails are scratching the wood floors as he dreams of chasing rabbits.

AFTER SUNRISE, SHE quietly raids the fridge and fries up a potato hash with ham, bell peppers, sea salt, and thyme, generous amounts of oil. Lucy shuffles in, hugs Kate from behind, and kisses her neck.

"Hey."

"Hey, yourself."

On the burner next to the hash, Lucy sautés some morel mushrooms she'd hunted down in the forested section of her acreage the day before. They dance around each other at the stove and then slow dance for real. Then Lucy tries unsuccessfully to squeeze two full glasses of juice from a half dozen oranges.

"They're lining Claudia up for a run at Washington," Lucy says as they sit down to eat. "You knew that right?"

"Yeah, she is considering it." Kate nods. "Erik and I wish we could stop her. But you can't tell her anything. She's a force."

"I really wanted to hug you that day at the capitol, when you stood up to me and Claudia. I was so proud of you. I'm sorry I dragged everyone into this."

"We were already into it, Luce. I just hope for all your efforts, we win the vote."

Lucy shrugs. "Vox populi, vox dei."

"Yeah, that's what worries me," Kate says. "So, is Tamara still in town? I'd like to meet her sometime."

"Back in Oakland. Not your biggest fan."

"Mark told me she took the photo out of spite."

Lucy clicked her tongue and nodded. "She knew about what happened between us but I think it kinda took her aback when she actually saw us together. She thought I could come here as an ex-gay and that would provide some sort of barrier I guess. She's really a good person though. Strident. Reminds me of you." She grins. "Tam's the glue. The strong one. She always figures out the details." She laughs. "Hell, she was willing to help me see you again if it would set things right."

"Erik was willing too."

"He's great for you. I hate to say."

Kate reaches across the table, and Lucy meets her fingertips. They close eyes. There it is. The pounding pulse. A breeze blows in through the back porch screen and lilts their hair.

They make love in Lucy's big clawfoot bathtub, giggling under the tap stream until the water runs cold. Then they dress quietly and walk downstairs to the parlor.

At the porch steps, Kate turns back, walks into the room, and picks up the acoustic guitar from its stand by the fireplace. "Sing me to the car. I haven't seen you play in years."

Lucy nods. "Got something new, actually. Still working out the lyrics." She strums the guitar, alternating with finger-plucked leads.

Kate slows her walk.

> *I fall asleep dreaming of Maiden Leap, Maiden Leap.*
> *Arms spread wide, I step off. Falling slow, falling slow in flashes.*
> *Stomach lurch, building speed. Head turned down, to auger in.*
> *But then I catch the upward draft. Sailing out, sailing out o'er the river.*
> *Low and fast, out and proud. Beneath the bridge, back up again.*
> *Climbing out, out of the rift—the glacier's rift that the angels missed.*
> *Up and up and up and up and up and up and up and up.*
> *Cross the prairie, cross the land. Aim it West, overdressed.*
> *Cross the prairie, cross the land. Aim it West, under-blessed.*
> *My shadow paints, so briefly paints,*
> *My shadow paints the world.*

At the car, Lucy leans on the door and closes her eyes as she strums the last chord.

It is this one simple song, above everything, that tells Kate this woman will be all right. As long as she can conjure the music, she will keep on emerging into something new. And ever unbreakable.

Lucy slips the guitar from her shoulder and lets it slide down to the grass. They hold each other. All is silent but the birds. Kate tries not to kiss Lucy too deeply, knowing it will only start something they have no time to finish. It is one of those moments when you know, something very bad could happen—another car crash or an awful diagnosis—but at the same time you know everything is complete and all is as it should be, because nothing was left unsaid, nothing left undone.

After Kate starts the car, Lucy taps on the window and steals one more kiss. She knocks twice on the roof, grabs her guitar, and walks off toward the Leap.

WHEN KATE PULLS into the drive, Erik's truck is already there. The engine is still pinging and presses heat at her face when she walks past it. No one is in the house. She makes her way to the sliding glass door. Erik is sitting out in the yard, worshiping the sun. Chuck comes to her and licks her face.

Her breath comes shallow, her shoulders tense. It's growing humid again, the ozone thick in the air. "Hi," she says with a smile and kisses Erik's bald spot. "What'd you catch?"

"Ton of walleye. Some in the freezer."

"Have a good time?"

"Yeah, it was great. Weather was perfect."

"Brace went to work?"

"Yep. Sam's over at Jamie's."

Kate pulls a deck chair up to Erik's and clasps his hands. Their knees touch. She stares unflinchingly into his icy Larson light blues, steeling herself for the hurt and the blooming hate.

"I spent the night with Lucy."

He pulls his callused hands from hers.

She looks down for a moment. "I'm not ashamed, Erik. And I won't apologize for it. I didn't do it to hurt you."

He stares up to the sky and collapses back in his chair. "Oh. Okay. Good job. You want a gold star?"

"I needed it," she says softly. "We both did. You know that."

Erik shakes his head. "Who *are* you?"

"Your wife and I want to stay your wife."

"Where is she now?"

"Please don't."

"Don't what? Kick her ass? Come on. Give me some credit, Kate."

"At the B&B, packing."

"She coming back?"

"Next spring."

"And then what?"

Kate swallows hard. "I want her in my life somehow. You and I would have to agree on how much."

"I'm not your father. I'm not here to dole out permission." Erik remains calm. His anger of the last few weeks tamped down. "These weren't our vows, Kate. And I feel like you've been trying to warm me up to this for months, to let me down slow."

"I'm not trying to let you down. And you can't leave me for this. I know you can't. I've never seen the world clearer than I do right now. You and I are so good together. But it's not natural to pretend we don't want and need another love sometimes. It just isn't. All these ugly divorces, all these public humiliations, they're so unnecessary."

"You've been around the Funk-Abels too long."

"At least they're happy."

"Oh, are they? What a great kid they turned out." His eyes sharpen cruelly. "What if I told you I slept with Jennifer the week before you and I married."

She laughs. "No you didn't."

"Yes. I did. It was our last goodbye." Erik winces at himself. "Wasn't the best time for it and it wasn't all that great, but we did it."

She huffs once and glares at him. "Wow, you shit." She knows her anger about this will grow, but how clever of him to mention it while she's unarmed. She almost admires him for it.

"Yeah, and you know what," he asks. "It made me feel like shit. Has haunted me for years."

"But first it made you feel alive," Kate says. "Like maybe you could have any woman that wanted you because that's what you were made for. As if you were finally whole and present in this world. A sexual being. Not just a civilized animal."

"No, that's the way it makes you feel apparently. I felt like a shit. And thanked my lucky stars until now that you never found out."

"Well, if Lucy had showed up at the moment, I don't know what I would have done either. The point is, she and I would have never worked like you and I do. She *isn't* the best thing that ever happened to me." Kate sits back. "But all the same, she did happen to me. And she needs me and I want to be needed by her." Kate strikes her chest. "She's a part of this and it feels more warped to shut her out than to let her in. Life's too short."

"Why the hell can't you two be friends like I am with Jennifer?"

"We are. And maybe that's all it'll be when she gets back, maybe anything more would feel awkward and forced. Maybe we'll just hang out sometimes."

"And maybe not. Maybe you'll never be home and the kids will be like, 'hey Dad is it Mom-fucks-Lucy day?' 'Yeah, kids, you need her to pick up anything at the store when she's done sitting on Lucy's face?' Listen, I'm sorry for what the adults did to you girls. And I'm sorry I didn't listen sooner. But I don't want to hear any more maybes out of you." He waves her off with a grumble. She knows he's disgusted with the effect she has on him. His voice lowers again. "It just makes a mess, Kate. I don't think this marriage could survive something sustained like that." And he says it as if measuring Taken4Granite's competition in a global economy. "I haven't even had a chance to process the one time." He looks around. "What happened to the woman I married? Jesus, who am I going to retire with?"

"Me. Of course. If that's what you want."

He sighs long and hard. "Anyone see you go up there?"

"I dunno. I wasn't sneaking."

He looks somewhat nauseated. "Just imagine what they're all going to say."

"What they're already saying? And have all my life? I am absolutely done with the Senator Larson Family Values Circus, Erik."

"Yeah, that's right. You'll go door-to-door this fall, arguing for Mark and Ray's marriage. And what are you going to tell our neighbors about your own?"

She doesn't know what to say to this. Like his mother, he's an efficient debater and right at the most inconvenient times.

"Did you even think to ask how many partners she's had? Whether she has anything transmittable?"

Kate chews the inside of her cheek.

"Wonderful," he says and sighs through his nose, picks at his nails, lips pinched tight. Even so, the fury seems low in him, perhaps having known this could happen the moment he and the kids left for the cabin.

They sit silent for a few minutes, Chuck all flat in the grass, exhausted, soaking up the sun. A mourning dove calls to its mate from the power line, in that sad coo that's somehow nostalgic. Another monogamous species, according to Samantha, adapted to fit a short life filled with predators. Getting to fly, she'd said, must surely offset the occasional malaise.

How spoiled and reckless I have been, while there are people on this planet really struggling. And yet this only makes Kate savor it all the more, sensing she should not squander whatever sideways wisdom comes from this weekend. A better wife, mother, friend, daughter-in-law? At least one less meek. She had torn apart the family quilt and had finally grown up.

Then again, sometimes an affair is just an affair.

Kate feels Erik's eyes on her again. "Well?" He sits back, a dimple in his cheek. His tanned arms crossed and biceps bulging.

"Well, what?"

"How was it?"

"Huh?" Though she knows what he's asking.

"I want to know what it was like. That's my right."

Is that how this works?

At first she tries to hide the private joy, the sense of completion that's been bubbling under the surface since yesterday. But there's nowhere left to hide.

She has always shared her thoughts with this man. What is marriage otherwise? Only a vessel for raising kids? No. Erik is her closest friend. Her confidant. Her wingman.

"What time is it?" She asks and licks her lips. There would need to be a few adaptations, but she might be able to pull it off. She'll certainly sleep well tonight.

"I dunno, 'bout three." His stare will not let her go.

Brace would not be home from work until six and Samantha would probably hang at Jamie's until suppertime.

"Come on." She stands and runs fingers through his hair. "I'll show you."

BLOGGING MY SOJOURN

One Woman's Journey

Restart button pushed. I owe my life to Vicky's family. They did for me what my own could not.

It was touch-and-go for a bit, but I think Vicky's daughter is more anthropologist than astronomer. Kid could probably write a masters thesis already on the naked ape. Can't believe I could actually learn something from someone so young. She taught me that before I fly off to the outer reaches, I have to deal with the pack. After all, the stars have waited eons. They can wait a bit longer.

For the first time in my life I'm not so eager to buckle into an airplane seat. I'm already missing home, now that I know where home is.

Posted by Liesl ~ 6:10 PM ~ Comments closed

CHAPTER FORTY-FIVE

Kate

THE GALES OF early November have licked the trees clean. They blast Kate as she opens the sliding glass door to release Chuck to the deck. He carefully clicks his way down to the crisp grass where last week's jack-o-lanterns have been disfigured by ravenous squirrels. She shivers and takes a bitter sip of tea. Her Nordic resignation has not kicked in yet. But there's no hiding indoors on Election Day.

After that weekend on the Leap with Lucy, the kids had been distant. But on Brace's last visit home from college there were no harsh words and he actually hugged his mother tight for the first time in years. Samantha was singing in the house again and needed her mom's advice on homework and clothes and which weekends to hang out in Minneapolis with Jamie or which to meet Zev halfway to Madison. She'd even made a few new friends at WBHS.

Kate hasn't told Erik what Lucy suspected about his father and Marcus Robeson. It would just add another wall between them, something to hurt him with. And besides, it's nothing she can prove. If Bert was in a closet that he wanted to escape, Kate would be there for him, help Erik and Claudia navigate it too. But perhaps Bert has made his own sort of peace. It's his sojourn, not hers. Still, she owes the memory of Marcus Robeson something. Once the election is over, she'll invite Bert to coffee, find out what he knows.

Erik's footsteps thump down the hall, but Kate does not turn and waits instead for the mood in his voice. Autumn has seen good days, with laughter and newfound intimacy and a clear-eyed understanding of what might occur when Lucy came back to re-open the B&B. But there were also dreary days when he sat glaring at Fox News, gave ultimatums, left his wedding ring in the soap dish, and showed only his kids whatever affection he had to give.

Today, not only will he vote on his mother's career, but on the definition of marriage. And Kate's as unsure of what boxes he will check as she is unsure of what will happen to their own marriage come spring. All around town civility has gone wobbly, Facebook rants escalating, friends and family retreating to their comfortable political bubbles. Something dark and shambling is on the horizon. Heaven only knows.

Kate hears a chair slide out at the dining room table and her husband's weight creaking the wood. Is he expecting breakfast? She turns to ask what she can make him.

Erik sits, arms crossed, a manila envelope laid out before him where a bamboo place setting would normally be. He stares sternly at her and pulls out the chair next to him.

Well, this is it now, isn't it? This is how it ends. In paperwork.

She takes a deep breath, walks over, sits down, but cannot exhale completely.

Erik slides the envelope toward her. His ring is on today. Had he forgotten to take it off? Or left it on for some tortuous reason? Why was he making her purposefully read this in front of him? To sign it in front of him? Maybe he was simply being his usual egalitarian self; they would work out the details together.

"Just open it, Kate."

There is no address on the envelope, nor is it sealed. She turns it over, pinches the silver clips together to open the flap and pulls out a short stack of forms. Kate pages through them. The top of each reads:

University of Minnesota
College of Veterinary Medicine
Student Application

CM Harris is the author of novels *Enter Oblivion* and *The Children of Mother Glory*. Her short stories and essays appear in *O Magazine, Meniscus Literary Journal, Escape Artists' Pseudopod podcast, SALiT Magazine, Harrington Literary Quarterly*, the anthology *Queer Voices: Poetry, Prose, and Pride* as well as *Coppice & Brake: A Dark Fiction Anthology*. Her screenplay *The Cost of Glory* received a Gold Award for Best Concept Script and a Silver Award for Best Feature Script from the Queen Palm Film Festival.

CM Harris lives in Minneapolis with her wife and their twins. She is also the lead singer of indie rock band Hothouse Weeds. Find out more at authorcmharris.com.

CPSIA information can be obtained
at www.ICGtesting.com
Printed in the USA
LVHW091519031120
670484LV00024B/535

9 781949 290431